SHADY TRAILS
IN A LIGHT FOG

SHADY TRAILS IN A LIGHT FOG

~A COLLECTION OF SHORT STORIES~

Colin Knapp

© 2016

ISBN: 0692814825
ISBN 13: 9780692814826
Library of Congress Control Number: 2016919831
November Moon, Edwardsburg, MICHIGAN

ACKNOWLEDGEMENTS

TO MY FOLKS FOR ALWAYS standing by me. To CSA, for being an initial sounding board for a few of these stories, and for being a great mother. To Shannon Courtney, John Leonard, TTH, the late Dr. Eric Vandenberg, and the editors at Writer's Digest 2nd Draft Critique for your suggestions, encouragement and moral support. To Stephanie Ann, my first love, for helping me come full circle. To Ava & Erich, my little beacons of light, always. To my family and friends—and to the incredible people I've had the pleasure of sharing time with over the short years of our life—you know who you are. A million thanks.

~CRK~

CONTENTS

Fog
Silent Wanderer
Steady Drifter Upon
Misty Trails & Dreams
A Quiet New Day
Yearning for
Dawn

'The Webster Award'

⌒⌐

Johnny Frisina wipes the sweat off his forehead. Adjusts his ball cap. It's a sunny afternoon, perfect for a ball game. The grandstands are packed with colorful, excited fans crouching on edge because they know the end is near. Next month Johnny will be thirteen. Today he can make history.

The New Paris Yaks have never won a Major League Championship Game before let alone the Webster Award. No team has ever won the Webster Award.

This year the Yaks are close. It's the final inning. One possible pitch away from legacy and everlasting glory.

7-6, Yaks.

The catcher Ricardo Hernandez flashes two fingers between his squatting legs. He's calling for a Change. Johnny shakes it off. He's skinny but he's got a cannon for an arm and three pitches in his quiver: a Smoking-Hot Fastball; a Change-up; and a Slider, which half the time didn't slide and which most of the time his father didn't want him throwing anyway because of the twisting motion on his young arm.

His arm's already tired. Johnny's pitched the entire game, seven innings. He's feeling it, but he's also thrown twice to this big kid at the plate #9. Big 9 *loves* high heat.

One ball. Two strikes. Two outs. Ricardo flashes an index finger. Johnny nods.

He winds up and *uhn!* fires a four-seam fastball that starts chest-high and rises—too high to hit—but the kid swings anyway because it looks so fat and appetizing coming in at eye level. The ball snaps into Ricardo's glove. Big 9's aluminum whiffs the air.

"**Steee-*three!***" yells the Ump. "Ball Game!"

Big 9 chucks his bat into the chain-link fence as an explosion of cheers erupts in the stands. Fans high-five and hug. Balloons flutter into the air. Up in the booth the announcers key the mike:

*"The Yaks have defeated the Pogue Township Buccaneers, and the New Paris Yaks are **YOUR** Little League Major Division Champions! A stellar game on the mound from Johnny Frisina. Kudos to Ryan Gearhart for putting his team ahead for the win. And a HUGE round of applause for the entire Yaks community for finally securing the coveted Webster Award. Ceremonies to follow in the Field House. Ladies and gentlemen please enjoy your Saturday afternoon. Drive safely."*

The Nolan Webster Award is given to a team with an undefeated season. The winning team must have had no players ejected for unsportsman-like conduct during the course of the season. One player must hit a legitimate home run, over the fence.

Those were the criteria.

This season, Ryan Gearhart hit three homeruns. A park record. The Yaks skated the line but ended with zero players being ejected from any game. And with Johnny Frisina's last pitch they'd clinched the Major League Championship, and with it the mysterious Webster Award.

The prize for the Webster is an awe-inspiring trophy along with a beautifully-engraved marble plaque. It also includes a $10,000 stipend to be used for team uniforms and new equipment.

Nolan Webster created the award in honor of his late wife, Gloria. She'd loved baseball. Loved going to the games, watching the kids play. Before Nolan passed, he decided to add a clause stating the $10,000 stipend could be split in half. $5,000 still goes for new baseball equipment. But the second $5,000 could be split amongst the players.

If the players voted to do so.

He was dead a week later. The addendum caused instant uproar in the late '70s, much of it from community parents, but in a League Vote officials passed it 6-5.

"Difficult enough to even win the dang Webster," a few reckoned. "Might not never be an issue. Best it goes to them kids, anyhow. Park's got plenty squirreled away for stirrups and jerseys and such."

~

After the post-game prayer, the Yaks voted unanimously to split the $10,000 stipend in half amongst themselves.

~

Players, parents and fans file into the Nolan Webster Field House. The day couldn't feel more perfect. Johnny listens as someone yells: *"We got this one for Marston!"*

Marston Riley. #21. What amazing team spirit he had.

Marston had played right field. Early in the season while chasing down a fly ball his heart had burst. Marston had struggled with health issues from birth but it never stopped him from wanting to compete and to help the Yaks in any way he could. Even if only cheering from the bench. While his death obviously destroyed the Riley family, it absolutely devastated Marston's little sister Elizabeth, shocking her into muteness. This all happened three months ago. No player or parent had forgotten it.

Johnny steps into the Field House and smiles. *Feels like a different building all decked-out with streamers and balloons and popped confetti all over the floor. Like someone got married or something.* He fist-bumps a few teammates who are milling around the snack tables scarfing down hotdogs, chips and oatmeal raisin cookies. *Everyone's really happy. It's amazing. Everyone except the Buccaneers!*

"Good thing Marston ain't around," Patrick Solvas says. "That's more moolah for the rest us!" Another kid laughs. Johnny slips away.

It's true. I'm thinking about that money, too. I'd love to buy Rachel Watts that Gorgeous Turmoil *shirt. Her favorite band. I even know which one she wants: the charcoal gray electric orange long-sleeve. Yeah. I need money to do that. This award money could be sweet.*

Rachel Watts is a year older than Johnny and plays softball there at Webster Park. Over the summer they'd gotten to know each other pretty well. And it was still going well.

I'd love to surprise her with that shirt. It'd be sweeter than sweet. But something's....

Johnny's folks walk over. Dad rubs his shoulders. Mom lifts his brown ball cap and kisses his forehead.

"Why so down, bud?" asks Dad.

Johnny shrugs.

"Feel bad Marston's not here to help us celebrate. He got us excited this year."

"He was such a sweet boy," says Mom. "Very funny, too."

"They really struggled with the funeral," Dad says. He tilts his head toward the Rileys sitting alone at a table.

Johnny nods. He excuses himself to the bathroom. His stomach twists at the thought of even looking in the direction of the Riley family. Feels like he's gonna hurl. He stumbles toward a trashcan but by the time he's gotten there the nausea has passed and an idea has popped into his mind.

One by one, Johnny gathers his Yak teammates by the men's restrooms.

"I'm thinking we should donate the prize money," he says, "to Mr. and Mrs. Riley."

He watches many eyes open white.

"Jesus, Frisina, we're already donating the trophy and the plaque to the Little League field," Chip Jackson says.

"I hate to break it to you," Pete Trock says, "but Marston Riley is dead. We're alive. And my family can really use this dough, in like a big way."

"The Rileys need it the most," Johnny says. As co-captain of the team he'll stand his ground on this. "We never planned on winning the Webster anyway. What's it going to hurt? We're already getting new uniforms, and bats—"

"But we *did* win it," Chip Jackson says. He pushes forward. "That's the whole point." A few others grunt in agreement. Tension crackles.

"You didn't help much, Chip," Ryan Gearhart says. He's stocky and is hitting puberty early with a peach-fuzz moustache to prove it.

"Yeah," someone else says.

"Don't matter," Chip says. He looks ready to swing.

"Yeah it does."

"Shut up."

"Let's vote on it," Johnny says. "All those in favor?"

Eleven hands go into the air. Nine stay down. A few players groan.

"Ok," Johnny says. "Majority rules. I'll go let 'em know."

"You frickin' jerk," Pete says.

"Don't do it, Frisina," warns Chip.

Johnny approaches the Riley's table. Finished plates sit empty in front of them. Five-year old Elizabeth sits meek as a mouse between her parents.

"Mr. and Mrs. Riley?"

"Yes," they say, humble-eyed. Their simultaneous response makes him pause.

"We'd uh—"

Mrs. Riley nods her head encouragingly.

"We'd like to donate the prize money from the Webster Award to you and your family."

Mr. Riley shakes his head. He removes his glasses, rubs the bridge of his nose and then slides his glasses back on.

"Thank you, Johnny," he says, smiling. "It's very considerate of you. But you boys earned that award. It's never been done before. It should be yours to keep."

"Marston earned it, too," Johnny says. His eyes drop quickly and fill with tears. *I'm not gonna cry. Not.* "He inspired us more than anybody. Please, sir. We voted on it."

"We couldn't accept the money," Mrs. Riley says. Her lip trembles. Johnny's heart sinks to the bottom of the sea.

"We voted on it," he says again. *"Please?"*

Mrs. Riley breaks down crying burying her face in her hands. Little Elizabeth stares at the floor. Mr. Riley looks Johnny in the eye, his weathered face sensitive.

"Are you sure?" he asks. Johnny nods. A tiny tear slides out of Mr. Riley's right eye. He doesn't wipe it away. Instead he hardens his smile and says, "Well, we thank you."

"Marston was so excited to play this year," Mrs. Riley says, wiping her face with a tissue. "He wasn't the greatest player, but oh gosh, he loved you guys so much."

Mrs. Riley can't continue. Mr. Riley pulls her close and holds her. Johnny takes what he feels to be his cue to leave.

He returns to the mass majority of his teammates and their families. His own folks, he's told, are in the restroom. Word is already getting around. A few parents thank Johnny for his initiative. They commend the Yaks for their wonderful gesture. Johnny overhears a few parents grumbling. Then he listens to some of those parents come around and say they're fine with it going to the Rileys.

"You're too young to have a conscience, Frisina," Gearhart's father says. He looks like Ryan only older. Johnny turns his palms up.

"Just glad we won, sir."

"Here! Here!"

Sebastian Volnar's dad claps his hands. He fishes out his wallet and starts handing out coupons.

"Free socks! Come to Volnar's Soles! A free pair of socks with every shoe purchase!"

Johnny laughs. He retreats to the concession tables. The cancerous twisting in his stomach is fading but now it's being replaced with exhaustion. He feels *empty*. He grabs a glass of fruit punch; drains it. Coughs.

The plastic cup is knocked from his hand.

Pete Trock, Cohey Bergeron, and Chip Jackson drag Johnny off into a secluded hallway. Patrick Solvas stands watch. Pete grabs Johnny's jersey with a tight fist. The other two hold his arms. Johnny flinches.

"I oughta mash yer teeth in," Pete says. "I told you my mom and dad needed that money."

"Marston Riley wasn't out there fielding grounders," whispers Chip, knocking Johnny's earlobe back and forth. "He wasn't getting base hits. He wasn't throwing guys out at the plate, or at first base. *We* did that. We did *all* that. Not little Riley."

Pete exhales disgustedly.

"Know something? We wouldn't even *be* here right now if Riley was still on the team. Their family's retarded. His little sister can't even talk."

"We're doing the right thing," Johnny says. "That's what matters." He struggles, unable to move.

"I'm gonna do the right thing, too," Pete says. He cocks his fist and grins. Johnny tightens his jaw. Behind him he hears a smack. Somebody drops to the floor in pain. Then Pete drops from a quick shot to the ribs.

"Don't think so, amigo," Ricardo Hernandez says.

Ryan Gearhart shoves Cohey and Chip out of the way and they release their grip on Johnny's jersey.

"Butt out, rich boy," Pete says, rubbing his ribs.

"We wouldn't have won without my homeruns, punk," Ryan says. "The vote's set. Touch Frisina again and I'll hurt you."

Pete gets to his feet.

"We're only undefeated because it was a team effort. That means everybody has to agree. Nine guys didn't. It's not fair."

Pete tries to stare down Ryan Gearhart, but everyone knows Ryan would mop the floor with Pete. Ricardo laughs.

"*Ha!* Unsportsmanlike conduct! Just under the belt, *damn!*"

Johnny swallows. He smoothes out his jersey. Gives everyone a shaky smile. When he rejoins his folks they can tell he's disturbed, but Johnny knows they won't ask him what happened unless he wants them to. He kinda likes that about Mom and Dad.

Mom gathers their stuff. Dad nudges his arm.

"Tough growing up, ain't it?"

Johnny exhales.

"Proud of you, honey," Mom says. "You did a good thing today. It's only money."

Johnny does feel better. He'll hustle a few extra lawns this summer for Rachel Watts's t-shirt. It's all good there. As for his pissed-off, ticked-off teammates—well, the season was over. They'd won.

As for his mother's remark that it's only money, Johnny's listened to his folks argue about that topic more than anything else.

CLICK!

A microphone powers up. Mrs. Riley stands timidly behind the podium on stage.

"I'm sorry to keep you," she says. "Our family—excuse me," she says clearing her throat. "Our family would like to thank you for your generous donation. It will certainly be put to good use. However, we will only be accepting our share: $238.09 for our late son, Marston. Yaks, it was *your* hard work and *your* dedication that got us here. All the gifts should be equally shared. Thank you. God bless."

Coach Strindberg lines up next to the podium ready to hand out the moneyed envelopes. The kids line up for their cut. Johnny walks over and snags his glove off one of the chairs. As he's walking back, Chip Jackson stomps over.

"You're lucky, Johnny-boy," Chip says. "Me and Pete were gonna come looking for ya." He flashes the award cash, pockets it and snaps his fingers. "*Hey!* Enjoy your summer."

Chip pushes through the double glass doors of the Field House out into the beautiful summer afternoon.

A moment later, Johnny's handing his envelope to his mother. He falls in line behind his parents as they head for the far exit. He's tired. That much he knows. He realizes they're walking behind the Riley family. Elizabeth Riley looks back over her shoulder. Johnny waves. She giggles. To his surprise, Elizabeth breaks from her parents and tiptoes back to him. He stops walking.

"Dank you," she whispers. She hands Johnny a red lollipop, and then rushes back to hold her father's hand.

THE END

'DIRTY SHIRTS'

THE COUNTRY CAFÉ ON THE right would have to do. Marcus Singleton swung into the parking lot and drove his Jeep Wrangler to the rear. He backed under some low hanging branches. Grabbing his briefcase, he swallowed.

Bring the gun ... Or leave it?

He locked the door, pressing it closed with his fingertips. A low fog was rolling in. Never in his forty-seven years, *God bless it*, had he been shaken this badly, but he needed to play it cool until he knew the score. He checked the road. Nothing. Cradling his case he jogged to the front entrance.

"Welcome to *Café on the Range*," said the hostess, easing down off her stool. Her name tag read: **BRENDA**. Her smile faded.

"Quiet corner," Marcus said. "Table for one."

She took up a menu and led him into the dining area. The café was dim. Morning clouds sat full and gray outside offering little natural light through the windows. Marcus shivered as he followed the hostess through the restaurant. She delivered him to a corner booth.

"Get busy in here?" he asked.

"Not like we used to," Brenda said, handing off the menu. "But we're surviving. A waitress will be with you shortly."

Marcus adjusted his seat and looked around. The placed smelled of bacon and fried onions. Aside from nine or ten other patrons, it was empty. He wiped cold sweat from his forehead. Reaching into his sport coat, his fingers instantly felt slick. He pulled out his hand. *Blood.*

"Alrighty now, what's looking good?"

Marcus looked up. A young dark-haired waitress had appeared. She stood there with a sweetly-crooked smile with her glasses near the end of her nose ready to take his order. Marcus coughed and jerked some napkins from the dispenser.

"Ouch," she said.

"Looks worse than it is. Gimme the, uh, *Down-Home Special* and some hot coffee or tea. Something hot please."

"First aid kit to start," she said under her breath. The young waitress wasn't wearing a nametag. She slid her pad into her serving apron while Marcus kept his eyes on the windows at the front. "Sure you're okay, sir? I can at least bring you some extra napkins."

Two long black cars skidded up outside the front entrance. Shiny doors flew open.

"I'm not okay," Marcus said, grabbing her apron. "Those guys pulled in wanna kill me. We gotta get out of here. *Quick!*"

He picked up his briefcase and tugged the waitress toward the kitchen with his other hand. She went along with him and was confused, but she didn't say a word until the swinging doors were behind them. Then she screamed.

"Shut it!" Marcus said. He put up a hand to the surprised chefs and crew in the kitchen and pulled out his wallet and badge.

"Marcus Singleton, undercover," he whispered. He put away his credentials to grease sizzling in the background. The kitchen crew stared with blank faces. "Sorry to get you involved," he said. "I—"

Loud shouting rang out in the dining room. A lady shrieked. Automatic gunfire. Breaking glass. Gunshots, screams of terror.

"Brenda!"

The young waitress tried to run, but Marcus pulled her back. A heavyset cook plowed through the red and white emergency plate on the back door and an alarm started clanging. The kitchen crew stampeded out after him.

Marcus pulled the young waitress along and kept them following the train of employees out of the restaurant and down the concrete steps outside. Their feet hit the parking lot. Marcus nearly dropped his brief-case as he fumbled for his keys. They split on either side of his Jeep.

"It's open!" he yelled.

Two bullets chirped through a pistol silencer. One bullet cracked his headlight. The other thumped a hole through his bumper.

The young waitress dove into the passenger seat screaming. "I don't wanna die! I don't wanna die!"

Marcus pitched his briefcase into the Jeep. He swung the driver's door open and dropped to a kneeling position. Reaching into his sweaty armpit holster, he pulled out his semiautomatic pistol quickly chambered a round and clicked off the safety. Following a figure in a black mask coming hard down the steps he squeezed the trigger. The gun popped in his hands. Someone yelled. The figure crashed to his chest while another flipped over the top and landed with a crack across the pavement.

Marcus tossed his pistol in the back and started the Jeep.

"Let's go!" he yelled. The waitress got off the floor and buckled her-self in. "What's your name?"

"Lona."

"Hang on, *Lona!*"

Marcus gunned it. He nearly clipped a line cook in a white apron trying to flag them down, but they shot by as the Jeep whipped them out of the parking lot and onto the street.

Marcus kept heavy on the accelerator. Lona's knuckles turned white. The six-cylinder engine whined like a scared racehorse as sweat dripped from Marcus's nose onto his shirt. He checked the rearview mirror. Nothing yet. Sweat burned into his eyes.

"Were you shot?" Lona asked.

"Nicked," Marcus said. He blinked his eyes and stayed heavy on the gas. The Jeep was shaking approaching ninety miles per hour. "Grazed ten minutes before I got to your restaurant."

"Oh my God," Lona said. "Are you serious?"

"Think it's finally stopped bleeding," Marcus said. "*Damn* that hurts. Feels like a big old hunk of lead put a hole through my … m-me." He kept his eyes focused on the road. He tried to chuckle. "My wife always said I should lose a few pounds."

Lona brought a hand to her mouth. She looked pale. She unzipped the plastic window of the Jeep but at ninety-five it beat back and forth so violently she was forced to zip it closed again.

"Sorry," he said. "I'm beyond subtleties."

He dropped their speed to seventy. The road was relatively smooth and straight with no traffic, but a deer or a dog could always jump out of the mist and the road was still wet in many spots.

"You kidnapped me!" Lona screamed. She pounded the dashboard with her fist. It grew silent as Marcus slowed further.

"I was scared," he said.

"What?"

"I'm scared," he repeated, checking his rearview. "I'm not a detective or a cop or anything. I'm with Animal Cruelty."

Lona was puzzled. To her, Marcus Singleton seemed like a normal, reasonably insane man of what? Forty? Fifty? Receding hairline, normal beer gut, probably some nice lady's wedding band on his finger. What did he want with her?

"We get court orders to do these investigations when they involve the mistreatment of animals," Marcus said. "This one came around, it was legit, and it was my turn for an assignment."

Lona had found some red splotches of blood on the cuff of her white shirt and was scrubbing at them with a wet finger. She gave up a moment later. It took everything in her not to spurt into a flood of tears.

"Terrific," she said. "My only white button-down."

"I didn't mean to abduct you," Marcus said. He slowed to forty-five and wiped the fresh glisten from his brow. "I've never been shot before. Never been shot *at* before. Never had a gun pulled on me. Never even had to *pull* my gun—in fact, this is only the second time I've carried that piece. I'm surprised I remembered how to use it." He swallowed. "Sorry. I just couldn't let go of your arm."

Lona shook her head and turned away.

"People always take advantage when you're nice."

Marcus braked for a sharp curve and accelerated through the turn as Lona braced herself with one hand on the door and the other on the roof.

"So why in Hoover Dam were you ordering the *Down-Home Special?*" she asked. "Instead of, like, having me call you an ambulance or something? Or the police?"

"I don't know," Marcus said. He took his foot off the gas. His face was beaded with sweat. His eyes lifeless. Lona pointed for him to watch the road. "I shot someone back there," he said. "Heard him scream—didn't you hear him scream? I did."

Marcus pulled off the road and put the Jeep into park.

"I'm gonna be sick," he said. He opened the door. Lona opened hers as well.

He managed to keep his breakfast down. He closed his eyes long enough to center himself and regroup. *Jesus. I've got to get some help. Get this young lady to safety.*

"My cell phone fell out of my pocket," Marcus said. He still had his eyes closed. "Do you have one?"

"Back at the restaurant," said Lona.

"Can you drive?"

Lona looked down. Marcus opened his eyes and turned to her.

"Can you?" he asked.

"We called this road Backstreet Boulevard in high school," Lona said. She spoke as if she were recalling a final memory. "Someone would drive while you and your honey bunny sat in the backseat, and if things got too hot-n-heavy you could always pull off and kill the lights since there's hardly any traffic," she said. "I know, too much information."

Marcus's thoughts drifted to his daughter. It would be her sixteenth birthday in less than two weeks. Reality gave him the spins.

"Can you drive?" he asked again. "We gotta keep moving."

"I passed Driver's Ed," Lona said, pulling at her hair. "I need new glasses. Usually I ride my bike into work or I get a ride with Brenda, but I'll try. I'll try."

Marcus's side felt blowtorched. He groaned as he and Lona switched places.

"Just keep us between the lines," he said, reclining his seat. She buckled her belt. Although it was laced with pain he gave her his best smile. "You'll do ah-mazing."

She took them out slow and easy. Within a minute, Lona had them cruising down the misty highway at fifty-five miles per hour.

"You're a natural," Marcus whispered from the passenger's seat. He lay there with his eyes closed, sweating. To Lona it looked as though he were shaking off malarial fever.

"Where are we going again?" she asked.

"Just get us to Old Bridge Hospital," Marcus said. "You must know where that is."

"I don't know how to get there."

"Hold on, gettin' dizzy."

The fog was slowly diminishing. For this alone Lona was grateful. She was happy to help; she just had no idea what she was helping *with*.

His nausea soon passed. Marcus sat up. He watched Lona drive from the corner of his eye and realized she was younger than he had originally thought. Maybe only a few years older than his daughter Toni.

"Just stay straight for a while," he said. "Are you still in high school?" Before she could answer, Marcus snapped his fingers. Reaching behind the passenger's seat, he pulled out a hand-held UHF radio.

"Forgot I had this," he said. "We can call in the blue cavalry right now, *woo hoo!*"

Lona snorted in a giggle.

Marcus turned the knob. The radio crackled with static but illuminated that wonderful tiny green light that showed its battery was charged and was working. "Now let's see if I remember how to use it," he chuckled softly.

One, two, three dark cars sped silently around the corner behind them. Lona watched them pop up in her rearview mirror. She straightened up and floored it. The engine downshifted, kicked them forward. Marcus was on the vibe. He watched the cars gaining road as he keyed the radio.

"This is Marcus Singleton, ACA, being pursued by three black sedans, believed to be associated with the Bertrand, Immelman & Potter investigation. We are south on Rural Route forty-*five? Did that say?*"

A female voice responded crisp and clear: "Copy vehicle descriptions and name of firm, Mr. Singleton. Say again your location and direction, over."

"Forty-five—*fifty-five!*" Marcus shouted. "Mile marker *FIFTY-FIVE*, southbound on I-45. I'm mean Rural—"

"Read you loud but distorted, sir. Say a—"

Lona screamed.

POOM!

The dark sedan slammed into the back of the Jeep denting the car's hood and knocking the bumper clean off Jeep. It belted them forward. Marcus dropped the radio. An upcoming S-curve made Lona take her foot off the gas. The dark sedan slunk back as well.

As Marcus fumbled for the radio, another sedan crept up their side, nosed into the Jeep's quarter panel and spun them out sideways.

The Jeep's tires screeched against the asphalt. They caught and whipped them in the opposite direction and off the road as they rolled. The world went violently weightless. Smashing horizons. Pieces of vehicle. Mud. Grass. Earth. Sky.

A final jumble brought the Jeep to rest on its roof in a slow spin. Marcus and Lona dangled from their belts. Marcus sucked for air while Lona moaned next to him.

"Are you hurt?" he asked.

"I don't know," she said. "I can't feel my hand."

Marcus unsnapped his belt and fell onto his shoulder. He tried his door. It came open. He remembered to grab the keys as he crawled out careful to avoid the bent, twisted metal. He helped Lona out. Her glasses were gone. They looked around. No glasses. No cars.

There *were* skid marks by the curve. Three distinct pairs. Two of the tire tracks seemed to have made the turn, while a third set of tracks skidded into the trees. Smoke was rising from the woods. Marcus and Lona checked each other for lacerations.

"How's your hand?" he asked.

"Think it'll be okay," she said, opening and closing her fist.

A light mist chilled their faces. They perked at the sound of revving engines in the distance.

"Come on," Marcus said. "We've got a hot second to put as much distance as we can between us and them."

In front of them was a grassy hill with trees at the top. At least up there they could hide.

"Who's them?" Lona asked.

"Hit men," Marcus said. He grabbed Lona's hand and helped her climb. Every step felt like a fiery spear in his side from the bullet wound. The wound felt part of him now. Like he'd always had it. By the time they reached the top of the hill their clothes were drenched. Beyond the trees began a forest.

"Hit men?" Lona asked. "What the—?"

"Mercenaries," Marcus said. "Guys who get paid to take a bullet. Guys who think that if they get paid enough it gives them a license to kill."

Two dark sedans roared around the corner. Their squealing tires ripped up the asphalt and barreled into the grass. Marcus and Lona ducked. They caught their breath behind some bushes as car doors flew open. Six men in black masks scampered out. A husky figure carried an Uzi submachine gun. Others toted dark revolvers.

They ravaged the overturned Jeep like a pack of bloodhounds. Lona gasped. She readjusted her footing and kicked a small decayed log down the hill. One of the thugs turned on a dime and fired. The bullet whizzed through the trees.

"*Run!*" Marcus whispered.

He pulled Lona out in front of him. Another gunshot cracked behind them whizzing through the branches and leaves above. No time to lose. Running wildly, they dodged bushes and trees and bushwhacked wet brush. They moved quickly, fear and flight driving them through the forest.

Eventually, the trees began to thin. The forest opened into a large cornfield plowed up with dark earth but not yet planted for the season. The misty air and wet foliage had their clothes dripping.

"I've gotta rest," Lona said.

Marcus went straight to his back. He was seeing colors. Colors everywhere. He sucked down air and shivered. He forced himself up to check behind them through the trees. No one. Not a soul. He couldn't be sure his eyes weren't deceiving him though. Turning back, he spotted a farmhouse at the far edge of the field.

"Why are they after you?" Lona asked. "You're not a cop or a detective."

"I have evidence," Marcus said, still breathing hard. "Bertrand & Immelman Stables. We hadn't even started the case yet at Whitehall Courthouse. The thugs were already paid off. I'd barely gotten out of my Jeep and they were on me."

Marcus was feeling woozy again. He needed a few more seconds. He pulled himself through the wet underbrush to a downed tree where he rested his head. Lona sat on a tree stump nearby.

"What were they doing?" she asked.

Marcus thought back to earlier in the morning. It seemed eons ago and it all seemed like a bad dream.

"Blood doping," he said. Lona stared at him. "The Potter family owns racehorses. They stable them. They were shooting them up with growth hormones, steroids, all that."

"To win more races?"

Marcus nodded.

"Yeah," he said. "They hacked into our computer system and deleted a bunch of our files, but we still have Exhibit A, the test results that prove it. Last week, they killed all their horses and burned the carcasses so that there couldn't be an autopsy. The case is pretty open and shut regardless, but Preston Potter is pissed off, and his thugs—"

Marcus suddenly realized it. His briefcase. He didn't have his briefcase! Where was his pistol? He'd lost his evidence, and now, more importantly, he'd brought a young girl into harm's way with no way of defending her. *What kind of a man am I?*

"Hey," Lona said. She touched the wet sleeve of his sport coat. "It's all right. We're going to pull through this, okay?"

Marcus wiped his eyes. Breaking down certainly wouldn't solve anything. He refocused himself and nodded. A shadow moved through the trees.

Something else flashed.

"Oh, *shit!*"

Marcus grabbed Lona's sleeve and they slithered out into the cornfield. Once there, they broke into a dead run for the farmhouse. The scent of fresh dirt filled the air. With each step their feet sank deep into the moist earth. Marcus's legs were burning. His head was spinning. It felt like he was going down.

Lona noticed him losing ground and back-pedaled.

At the edge of the cornfield, the first of the hit men broke through the forest.

"Keep going!" he shouted. Swirling colors blurred his vision.

Crack! Another gunshot sent black dirt exploding in front of them. Marcus yelled for Lona not to look back, but that's exactly what he did. He saw the flash from the end of a revolver. A plume of wet soil went into the air to his left. More flashes. He turned back and pushed hard for the farmhouse.

Gunshots. War cries. Commotion of all kinds behind them.

Kaleidoscopes of colors assaulted Marcus's eyes. He felt like he was running through stacks and columns of rainbows. He was going under. Lona was slowing too.

In a last ditch effort, he tackled her. Lona squirmed but Marcus kept his body over hers shielding her from the hounds and the bullets on their tails. He tried to keep his head up. Ready to fight. His face, however, sank slowly into the cold, wet earth, and all of his thoughts went blank.

Two days later, Marcus returned to *Café on the Range*. He'd lain up at the hospital for a day and a half getting his bullet wound stitched and getting fluids back into his body from dehydration. Darrel, his boss at ACA, offered him a week of sick leave. Marcus said he'd be back to work by Monday.

Darrel had updated him with news from the police reports, but the rest of the story Marcus wanted to hear from Lona.

Only a portion of *Café on the Range* was open that Wednesday morning. The other part of the restaurant was being renovated and repaired with scaffolding up against one wall and a painting project started in the back.

Marcus stepped in, a wrapped package under his arm. He had a fresh shave, a clean shirt and a dry sport coat.

"Good morning," he said.

"Well, I'll be," said Brenda, sliding off her stool. "How we feeling this morning?"

"I've been better," Marcus said smiling. "I've been better."

"So happy that you're safe. Order what you want. It's on the house."

"Is Lona in today?"

"She must have gone to the little girl's room," Brenda said. She leaned forward, her eyes wide. "Gosh almighty, they spotted your Jeep in the parking lot and knew you were in here. We tried to stall them, you know, tried to say that we didn't know who owned the vehicle but they were onto us pretty quickly."

"Things could have turned out a lot differently," Marcus said.

"Amen," Brenda said. "Lona filled me in on some, and the rest I read in the *Old Bridge Gazette*. Thank you for helping those animals out there. Those poor horses."

"We tried," Marcus said. He waved his hand around the room trying to angle the conversation. "Looks like the restaurant's getting a facelift."

"Insurance is covering most of it," Brenda said. "It's nice to get a new look out of them for once."

"No one injured?" Marcus asked. Brenda shook her head, her eyes grateful.

"No," she said. They looked over at the corner table and saw Lona was back to folding napkins. "Tough little cookie. We couldn't get her to stay home today."

Marcus walked over and waited. Lona looked up. She squinted her eyes and gave him a weary smile. Marcus returned the smile.

"Back at it, huh?"

"I thought that was you," she said. "Yeah, just trying to piece my life back together. Trying to get used to these crappy contact lenses." Marcus handed her the wrapped package.

"What's this?"

"My daughter would have been fatherless without you," he said. "My wife would have lost her husband. I really can't thank you enough."

"I barely remember my father," Lona said. Marcus nodded.

"That's a shame."

"But two days ago he felt more alive than ever. I don't have many memories, you know, but I still have the feeling."

He cleared his throat.

"Next time we'll try a slightly different approach."

"Man they were right on us," Lona said. "They shot an eighty-five year old lady who'd stopped at your Jeep to help. They gunned down a police officer. Injured another. But the cops were right on them. It's like they came out of a dream or something. Do you remember?" Marcus shook his head no. "I really thought we were goners," she said.

"They traced my radio signal to the Jeep," Marcus said. "Followed those bastards through the forest and picked them off one by one. Not a second too soon, I'd say."

"There's the understatement of the year," Lona said.

"And my briefcase? Somehow wedged *under* the roof of the Jeep. Those punks never found it. They got my pistol but what the hell. Anyway, Whitehall Courthouse pushed the case until next week, and now that we've got our evidence in place and Preston Potter's behind bars, it should only be a matter of going through the steps. Someone else will be representing Animal Cruelty though. Maybe you should take a little time for yourself, too."

Lona tugged at the wrapping on the package. Marcus nodded for her to open it. Inside were three new white button-down shirts. She smiled. She held up the cuff of the shirt she was wearing to show him the faded red stains even bleach hadn't been able to get out.

"Check the pocket," Marcus said.

Lona reached in and pulled out five $100 bills.

"Hmm," she murmured.

"I have no idea how much you make in tips each day," Marcus said. "But hopefully this will help with a new pair of glasses. I know it's not all about money—"

"No, it'll help," Lona said. "Thank you, I appreciate it."

"No, Lona, thank you."

THE END

'MARGARITA'

⁓

NINE MONTHS AND TWENTY-ONE DAYS after my wife is laid to rest, I'm awakened by a presence. It's become unfamiliar. The strength of it surprises me.

It must have been early morning. Had I died? Was I being given another chance?

Michelle, my late wife, stood at the foot of our bed in soft, lavender light.

"It was a tragedy, Del, but we're fine. Don't be one yourself. Meet someone. Have fun. I'll always love you."

I knew she was gone.

I cried after breakfast. I cried again after my shower. My Michelle—the woman I had adored since high school—would never return. For nearly a year I'd been a zombie. Stumbling around my decaying apartment, losing weight, hugging myself in silent remorse. I'd given up praying for miracles.

Yet somehow Michelle's spirit allowed me to recognize my own eyes in the mirror again. This weekend had been rough. It almost got me. This would be the last time.

So when Bridgette, my older sister, called an hour ago and asked why I shouldn't take the train downtown to meet her and her friends for a late lunch, I said maybe I should. I even changed out of my coffee-stained khakis.

⁓

Bridgette and her two friends are seated at the *Café Mirá* along the river. It's a brilliant Sunday afternoon. The city is alive. Chaotic people everywhere are snapping pictures, chatting, pointing and laughing. Taxis and buses hum across the nearby steel bridge. Thankfully, the café itself is not crowded.

The ladies stand.

"Del Klein," I say, taking the hand of Daisy Salazar. I've met her once before. She's cute in her bib overalls with her Hispanic complexion, but her platinum-dyed hair seems a bit much. I also say hello to Yu Chen, a refined lady in a pin-striped jacked and skirt.

Bridgette squeezes my shoulder. She's wearing a short summer dress and, as usual, looks fantastic. She certainly got the *hot* gene in our family. I actually feel like part of the in-crowd. We're a fairly eclectic group.

Then I notice some of the outfits of the people walking in front of us on the riverwalk and I have to admit we're pretty tame. We sit.

"Great to see you, little brother," Bridgette says. She smiles. "The Lyceum said you were off yesterday. I tried to call."

"Yeah, I was kind of busy," I say. My gaze falls away. The sun sparkles like a thousand galaxies off the river. I'll never tell my sister I began the weekend convulsing with body sweats, heaving up a bottle of aspirin and two bottles of extra-strength cough syrup, out of my soul the entire next day until Michelle, or some incantation of her, intervened in the quiet hours. I had nothing to live for. Just another carnivorous cancer cell of the earth, better to be snuffed out and not to exist at all. My first silent cry for help.

In the past twenty-four hours, two words have risen to new meaning:

1. *Selfish*
2. *Grateful*

As I'm sitting here however, I'm amazed I'm not feeling worse. Probably because I'm so nervous. I haven't been around real live company since…?

"I ordered you a coffee," Bridgette says. "Black, right?"

"Thanks, sis."

Daisy Salazar drains her café latte and smacks her lips.

"Dang that's yummy! So where ya been hiding all summer, Del?"

"Hibernating," I say. I sip my brew. It's good. I realize my sister and her friends have been chugging more than cappuccinos today. And yes, Daisy is quite striking, but right now she's too in my face.

"Gawd," she snorts. "I'd be down here every single day. It is *so* beautiful. I love this city!"

Yu Chen elbows Daisy in the arm. Bridgette stays silent.

"Just haven't felt like being around anyone," I say. "Guess I'm lucky I have a job where I can shelve books all day and hide. I don't want to be responsible for anyone. Or *to* anyone. Not interested in anything new—"

I accidentally on purpose elbow my mug off the table. It hits the sidewalk and breaks into chunks. The coffee leaves a dark stain. A waitress hurries over, sweeps up the mess and brings me another cup.

"Oops," I mumble.

This is stupid. A juvenile urge that faded just as quickly as the spirit of my wife. Now I sit here betraying her? Or am I betraying myself? *Is this what you want, Michelle?*

"Sorry," I say. It feels forced.

My sister nods solemnly. My passive-aggressiveness has sent her two accomplices into nervous giggles, but you know what? I honestly don't care. I've survived thirty-five solar revolutions on this planet, and while Bridgette and her friends may have a decade on me in that regard they're only here to cat around and have fun. They've never lost true love. Death doesn't divorce it.

I shake my head. *Smile, Del. Pull yourself up. Okay?*

"Never mind *my* cynicism, ladies," I say. I tilt my pale face toward the sun. "What's burning your toast these days?"

Late lunch turns into evening. The breeze off the river has grown cooler, almost chilly. Handfuls of leaves swirl past. Yu Chen walks up the steps to the sidewalks above. She waves good-bye, late for another rendezvous. The afternoon tourists have morphed into chic dinner parties in evening attire, nightlife couples hand-in-hand, and groups of friends out for fun under the brightening city lights.

Bridgette stands. I push my chair back and get to my feet. She asks if I need a ride. Before I can answer, Daisy grabs my arm. I jerk it away before apologizing.

"Only wondering if you would like to have dinner with me at my mother's house," Daisy says. "Nothing big."

My sister's eyes are bigger than mine. Before I can answer otherwise I blurt out sure, what the heck, I'd love to. Then I laugh. I laugh at my spontaneity and I laugh at my quickening dread.

Bridgette gives me a bear hug that pops my back. She tells me she is proud that I'm her brother. I'm choked up. Only after she has turned and is walking away can I cough out: "Thanks, sis, love ya."

〰⟩

The city lights are soon behind us. With the wind in our hair, we're speeding toward the western suburbs in Daisy's sporty red Acura. Daisy *seems* nice enough. She loves to laugh, has a stunning smile. This must be a mercy date.

I won't mention that I haven't been out of my neighborhood since January.

Daisy works, I learn, in the front office at Northside Realty. She says her real ambition is to sell colorful hats and scarves on the Internet. She even has a name. *Daisy Chain.* She says being able to do something like that would make her happy. Daisy has so much life, so much *joie de vivre*, I feel like a cantankerous old Billy goat riding next to her.

And yes, Michelle, I do remember you kidding me about my secret fascination with Latino women. Teasing me that I didn't even know I had a fascination. You could poke fun because we were real. You know what? I remember a few of your secrets, too. So there.

⌒⟶

Half an hour later, we're pulling into a nicely-paved driveway. At the end of the drive is a nice-sized garage attached to a cute two-story house with burgundy shudders and a large porch. Beautiful trees give the entire neighborhood a rustic feel. Daisy tells me she helped her mother, Rosa, pick it out.

The last remnants of sun streak through the oaks and maples across the street. Daisy holds the front door. I follow her in. She takes my jacket and hangs it on a brass hook.

My senses are immediately seduced by peppers, onions and spices simmering nearby in the kitchen. Daisy's mother—who must be in her sixties yet looks not a day over forty—walks up and shakes my hand vigorously.

"Mr. Klein, Rosa Salazar, welcome to our home." She has gorgeous black hair and bright friendly eyes.

The hair on the back of my neck stiffens. *How does she know my name?* Then I remember Daisy calling her mother not twenty minutes ago from the highway.

Chill. Out. Del.

"Make yourself at home," Rosa says. She returns to the kitchen. I focus on my breathing.

Ok, wasn't so bad. I ease down onto an immaculate white sofa, careful not to disturb the pillows. I jump when a parakeet squawks from a cage behind me. Daisy grins. I feel like such an outcast. I try to sit as calmly as I can as Daisy excuses herself to the ladies' room.

The front door knob rattles. There's a key in the lock. I'm up on my feet. *Who is it? What? Who? What? WHAT?*

The door opens. A dark-haired lady walks in wearing tight blue jeans and a thin leather jacket. She closes the door. As she turns to take her jacket off, she stops. Our eyes lock. She suddenly looks a bit like Rosa, slightly younger perhaps, but who is she? A friend? A nosy neighbor? A spy? Someone selling Mary Kay? I will never understand why I ask so many rhetorical questions of myself, but what I *do* know is that this lovely Latin lady and I are staring quite intensely at one another. I'm hypnotized.

I've met her before.

Impossible.

Impossible?

She breaks our hypnosis and approaches.

"*Hola!* I am Rosa's sister—"

"Anna Marie!" Daisy runs into the living room. My hands jerk up. I trip backward over the coffee table and land with a thud on the carpet.

Anna Marie and Daisy help me up. Rosa walks in carrying a greasy spatula. The three women touch cheeks and zip back and forth in rapid-fire Spanish. I can understand maybe one word. *Sweaty. Need to run.* The ceiling's dripping? *Where am I! Hot in here ... way too hot....*

Anna Marie disengages from the conversation. She touches my arm. Sweat drips off my nose. My brain is a nuclear reactor. I gulp air and breathe and slowly the panic subsides. A moment later, I'm finally able to apologize to everyone. I turn and properly introduce myself to Daisy's favorite aunt: Anna Marie Lopez.

The ladies return me to the couch. Daisy hands me a damp washcloth. I drape it over my head. Daisy slips behind the corner bar and begins shaking white tequila margaritas. Ice clanks in her stainless steel shaker. She dances behind the bar saying a few drinks will make everyone feel better.

Anna Marie mentions something about putting Agave in the garage—whatever that means—and steps out. Meanwhile, Rosa is wagging her finger in my face, telling me I better be hungry because she is fixing a feast.

⌒

By the time the four of us sit down to dinner, I'm nipping on my third margarita and feeling quite divine. We wolf down tacos and enchiladas, burritos, tantalizing cilantro, guacamole and two kinds of salsa: red and verdé. The drinks, the gourmet food, the companionship. *Wow.* It's like an introductory course on how to feel human again.

"No work tomorrow?" Rosa asks.

"No," I say, wiping my mouth. "I'm on a Tuesday through Saturday schedule at the library. I did have this past Saturday off though."

"So you've got yourself a three-day weekend," Daisy adds.

"You could say that."

"And you walk to work?"

"I do."

"That must be nice."

"It is."

"Don't you miss having a car?"

"Sometimes."

"I don't know how I could live without mine."

"It's not so bad."

"Really?"

"Uh huh."

Rosa points to the food on her plate.

"Getting enough?" she asks. I nod. She grins and eats a piece of steak.

"It's excellent," I say. "Thank you. All of you. Your hospitality is out of this world."

We smile at one another and Anna Marie says, "You're welcome." Her smile dissolves. "Sorry for your loss. I lose my husband five years ago. I know that broken feeling, that hollow shell feeling. I do." My blood freezes. The air crackles with electricity. Daisy and Rosa set down their forks and sip their drinks.

I nod. Anna Marie is speaking from the heart and I appreciate that. My appetite, however, is gone. I'll taper back on the margaritas, too.

The alcohol is saturating my tired skinny bones. Anna Marie's condolences have grounded me though, I think. In a good way.

I offer to help clear dinner. The ladies deposit me onto the couch instead. My third margarita sits unfinished on the coffee table. A part of me is waiting for Michelle to appear—to materialize right here in the living room—to love me, hate me, or chastise me. But a larger part of me knows she won't. No matter how guilty I may feel being here.

⌒

"Oh *my! It's late!*"

I must have been dozing. My eyes snap open and I bolt upright. I blink realizing it was Daisy who had remarked on the time. The three ladies are standing in the living room, the kitchen behind them now dark. Daisy checks her smart phone against the clock on the wall.

"Should I put on a pot of coffee before I take you back?"

"Good heavens," Rosa says. "Mr. Klein is welcome to stay here. We have extra room."

"But—"

"Too late to drive," Rosa says. "I find a toothbrush."

Sitting there on the couch, I yawn and turn my hands up. I sure as hell can't drive. This night has turned incredibly surreal. I've been sucked onto a ludicrous emotional rollercoaster, fantasizing, for the love of Pete, about these three beautiful ladies taking advantage of me and breaking me out of this emotional bubble I've encased myself in.

I chuckle.

Why on earth would they do that? Rarely have I been considered attractive. Especially now after holing up for the better part of a year. I don't make much money. Not like they need it. And I don't know them well enough to be more than a friendly ear and respectful company. *And I am being respectful, aren't I? Am I an idiot? Do I think too much?*

"I will prepare the spare bedroom," Anna Marie says.

Anna Marie steps out. Daisy walks over to me. I have to admit, her platinum-blonde hair really doesn't look so bad right now. It looks kinda— She leans down. I smell the tequila on her breath. Her lime green lip gloss. It makes me want to close my eyes.

"I'm sorry," she says.

"For what?" I ask.

"I recently started seeing a guy. I just, I hope I'm not giving off the wrong vibe. I wanted to offer you the invitation to dinner this evening after what Bridgette had told us, you know, and after seeing you so down in the dumps this afternoon."

I hold up my hand.

"I've had a fabulous time," I say. "Honestly."

"Fabulous?" Daisy says. "What are you doing with a word like that?"

"Honey, I *work* with words," I say, laughing. "Only wish I knew more Spanish ones." She kisses my cheek. I blush and think what the hay. I can't remember the last time a woman turned me red.

"Irregardless," she says, "we should probably hit the sack. Some of us *do* have to work in the morning. I'll drop you off on the way into Northside, 'kay?"

⌒

By the time I crawl under the smooth cotton sheets it's 12:48 a.m. The spare bedroom is quiet. My eyelids are drooping; my head pulsing warmly. My poor body. It's been through the wringer and the meat grinder these last few days. Higher Power: thank you. You've reminded me there is light.

The house is calm. It's a sanctuary from the honking city outside my apartment window.

A knock comes at the door. I sit up, turn on the lamp. The door opens. A head peeks in. It's Anna Marie.

"All good?" she asks.

"All good," I say. I toast her with the glass of water she had waiting for me. "Gracias."

"Are you tired?"

I am absolutely exhausted.

"No," I say immediately.

Her eyebrows rise.

"More conversation?"

"I'd love some," I say.

As if penetrated by a strange bolt of energy, and true to my answer, I am suddenly not tired at all. It's exciting. Like two kids sneaking around at a slumber party after the parents go night-night. Anna Marie closes the door. She's wearing light blue pajamas with white clouds. She tiptoes to the edge of my bed and sits. She looks at me out of the corner of her eye and smiles.

We talk. We discuss family history, aspirations, what we look for when we look for love. What scares us? Frightens us? Our talk soon turns intimate.

"What makes you feel alive?" she asks.

"I don't know," I say.

She stares at me with innocent curious eyes. A smile perches on her lips. My next answer is the truth.

"Doing things with my wife, Michelle … used to make me feel, I don't know, the most engaged with life, I guess. Just knowing someone was there."

"People can help each another," Anna Marie says. "It's okay to think with your heart, Del. It's only human to feel."

Anna Marie seems to revel in lifting these heavy emotional boulders off my chest. Such a passionate listener. I agree with most everything she says. I do. But soon I'm yawning hard. The red clock digits read 2:23 a.m. I can't take much more.

"Will you mind if I lay here with you?"

My heart thrangs so loudly against my chest I'm surprised it didn't knock Anna Marie off the bed.

"I'm sorry?"

"Usually I sleep on sofa," she says, "but lately my back has been bothering me."

"Oh," I say embarrassed. "Yes, please, you should be up here; I'm the one who should be out on the couch."

"Oh no, no, no—"

"Yes, yes *please*."

Anna Marie draws back the dark brown comforter revealing my Dockers. Oh *great*. I'm not sure if I'm embarrassed I'm sleeping in my pants—which I usually don't—or if I'm embarrassed that Anna Marie now *knows* I'm sleeping in my pants, but I once again thank the Prime Mover that I'm not in my tightie whities or naked.

"Please, you are the guest."

"And you're family," I say. We're staring into each others' eyes again. One foot dangles off the bed; the other I still have plugged under the warm comforter. I've never been particularly attracted to older women. Then again I've never had the opportunity. I lean forward. Am I serious? *I'm going to* kiss *her?*

"Big enough for both of us," Anna Marie winks. She evades my un-spoken advance and motions for me to move over. I move over.

She switches off the bedside lamp. She pulls the covers up, snug-gles back into me and pulls me close. My breathing puffs like a loco-motive. I feel like I'm back on the playground in third grade, sliding down the beehive pole to the girls waiting below for a kiss on the cheek. It's exhilarating.

But I'm also fairly nervous.

Anna Marie reaches back, takes my hand and wraps it around her. *Whoa this feels way too nice.*

"Your wife must have been very special lady," she whispers.

"Yes."

"Such a gentleman."

I feel the soft rise and fall of her stomach under her pajamas. Anna Marie turns. In the soft light of the bedroom, tenderly, she kisses me. Her lips are soft. Her mouth perfectly formed. I see her smile as she pulls back. God she is an angel. She turns back around and returns my hand to her warm tummy.

Something breaks open inside of me. I'm shaking. Anna Marie seems to know what's happening before I do and she caresses my hand as I begin to weep. She turns and holds me. I don't stop. I can't. My stomach feels like it has burst open and is bleeding but it feels wonderful to let this entire thing run its course.

"Shhh," she whispers.

When I'm finally able to breathe again, she says, "My Pedro, yes, he was very special too." I feel her finger wagging back and forth under the covers. "But, he no lady, he fart too much."

It feels so nurturing holding this soul sister as she laughs in true remembrance. I laugh with her. It makes me believe Michelle is fine. And in a way I can't describe, it makes me realize how similar we really are. She doesn't have to tell me what happened to her Pedro. I won't ask. I won't tell her Michelle was killed in a crosswalk last winter three blocks from our apartment by a driver in a white panel van who failed to stop. I won't tell her about the three months of good news growing inside Michelle that was also murdered. Proud information once meant to surprise family and friends now became a dirge I would haul to my grave.

We say nothing more. I hold Anna Marie as if I hold life itself. It's good to have someone to face the night with. Even if only for a night. I never thought I would have subscribed to that notion, but I feel the truth in it now.

Anna Marie's lavender-conditioned hair gently lifts me onto a magic carpet. The carpet ascends. I drift off into a deep undisturbed sleep.

⌒

When I stir from my short slumber, Anna Marie's hair doesn't smell like lavender at all. It doesn't even feel like hair. I snuggle closer. *Fur?*

Something bounds off the bed. I jump in time to see a charcoal gray cat scamper through the doorway. I'm tired. I didn't sleep as long as I thought I did. Daisy sticks her head in.

"We're late!"

Fifteen minutes later, Daisy's honking her horn from the driveway. I'm scarfing down an egg and chorizo breakfast sandwich Rosa has fixed for me, thanking her again with my mouth full. She pats me on the back saying I'm welcome anytime as long as I am hungry. She helps me on with my jacket.

Anna Marie is still in the shower. I can't leave without telling her goodbye. I need to look into her eyes one more time. Daisy lays on the horn. We gotta go. I nod to Rosa, put my hand on the doorknob and turn it.

Just then, Anna Marie jogs in. Her hair is wet and she's tying a robe around her waist with one hand. She's holding the gray cat with the other. She hands me the cat. Reflexively I take it.

The cat watches me with blue green eyes.

"Agave," Anna Marie says. "That's his name. He likes chasing yarn." She drops her head. "Maybe I'll visit you both sometime."

Anna Marie runs from the room crying. Heart throbbing, I step toward the hallway but Rosa shoos me toward the door. "Don't worry," she says, "I will handle it. Go."

I walk out in a daze. Daisy must be in a daze, too. As I'm opening the passenger door she nails the horn and Agave claws the shit out of my arm and jumps into the front seat.

"Ow!"

"Sorry, didn't see you there," Daisy says. She drops the parking brake. "I'm late!"

Before I can completely digest everything that has just happened, we are on the highway east heading back into the city. The rising sun is just above the skyscrapers. I have scratches on my arm. A purring cat in my lap.

"I'm so tired of this drive," Daisy says.

"Get that Internet business rolling," I say. "Start knitting those hats and scarves."

Daisy looks over with half a smirk. Her smile blossoms full when she sees Agave purring.

"That was really sweet of you, Del."

"Well, I've never been much of a dog person," I say, clearing my throat. "But a cat? Well. We'll see."

"I would have taken him, but my condo doesn't allow pets. And my mother's allergic. That's why Agave slept in the garage last night."

"Why isn't Anna Marie able to—?"

"She has a medical consultation today at Prentice Clinic," Daisy says, anticipating my question. "For surgery."

Now I have another person to pray for.

"How bad is it?"

"Not *too* bad," she says slowly. "I mean, yes, they found some things they'll have to remove, but Auntie is a strong woman. She could bench press a gorilla. She probably didn't have to start giving her *cat* away and all that, but you were kind enough to take him in, so everything's good." I swallow a lump. "That's why Auntie was in from the country," Daisy says. She wipes her eyes. "My mother, Lord love her, she just mixed up the dates ... totally forgot her sister was coming in yesterday."

The sun is higher now over the skyscrapers. It looks like a fat displaced circle of fire. I take a deep breath. I'm nervous, but my exhale comes out smoothly. I'll admit it. I'm actually looking forward to going to the grocery store, maybe even the pet store, for my new roommate. Getting crazy, breaking out the yarn.

THE END

'OLD NEL'

—⁀

MOLLY SMITS FOLLOWED HER BEST friend Lemmy Brogans down the steep slope in the forest. Wisps of early morning fog drifted over the wet autumn leaves. It was chilly. The sun had yet to rise. Lemmy's orange camouflage jacket matched the color of her hair and kept her warm. Molly shivered in her jean jacket. Both girls had just started seventh grade.

Lemmy and Molly had snuck out early this Saturday morning and crossed over Alton Creek. Now they were a mile into the State's Public Hunting land. They weren't supposed to be out this far. They knew this. But when Molly stayed the night at Lemmy Brogan's house she knew anything was possible.

Actually, Molly didn't want to be out here at all. She stumbled over a tree root and brushed a wet cobweb out of her bangs.

"Let's go back."

"*What?*" cried Lemmy. "Are you scared of the deep dark woods, Mol?"

"No," Molly said. "It's just…."

Lemmy laughed and checked her pocket. Her safety whistle and first aid kit were still there. It was fall turkey season. The only thing that *maybe* concerned her a little. Being mistaken for a gobbler and getting blasted by birdshot. But still. That would never happen. Life was about having confidence. Grace under pressure. And while she may have only been a newly-crowned teen, Lemmy Brogans knew she would always survive.

At the moment, however, her t'ween mind twirled around other top-ics. Namely boys.

"Kyler Bowie is *so* hot to trot," she said. "I'd die for him. I totally would. Who are you liking these days, Mol?"

Molly placed a hand on the slick hillside behind her as they inched down the foggy slope. She shuddered at the deep valley below. A ca-nal snaked along the valley floor where a stream had once run.

"Hang on, girl," Molly said. "I ain't fixing to dive headfirst into no gully."

Lemmy balanced herself on a small rock.

"*Gully?* This is a ravine, Mol. Say it with me now: *Raaah-veeen.*"

"Why are we even out here?" Molly asked. "This is stupid. I'm starving."

"Wimp."

"Seriously, Lem. What are you trying to prove? That we can break the rules?"

Lemmy shrugged.

"My mom always gets home late from work on Friday nights," she said. "She'll still be sawing logs when we get back. But when she gets up, old Barb Brogans will fix us a big plate of bacon and a big ole stack of blueberry pancakes with real butter and real maple syrup. So chill out."

"Why don't we go back, accidentally wake her up, and have us a warm breakfast?" Molly asked. "I'm just sayin'."

"You wus."

"Come on."

"Come on *what?*"

"*You* what."

"You're just scared."

"Scared? Scared of what? You're just jealous."

"What in the world am I jealous of?" Lemmy asked. She stared at the *Psychedelic Furs* pin on Molly's jean jacket. "You're the one who still hasn't answered my question."

"Whatever," Molly said. "Like Kyler Bowie would even give you the time of day. Anyway I heard he's gay." A light breeze rustled the tops of the trees. They stopped to listen.

"He's not gay," Lemmy continued. Molly raised her eyebrows. "If he's gay, then how come he and Megan Frayer were making out at Tricky Coleman's barn party last summer? Huh? *Ha!*"

"Sometimes people can be both," Molly said.

"Well I know someone who wouldn't give *you* the time of *year.*"

"Who?"

"Ethan Torrey," Lemmy said. Molly's cheeks turned rouge. Despite the cold she felt herself go cozy. "Ha-*ha!* I *knew* you had a crush on him! You're so obvious, girl. When I see Ethan in Algebra class on Monday I'm going to tell him that you want him to feel you up."

"Feel me up?" Molly leaned against a large rock to catch her breath. "At least I have boobs."

Lemmy swallowed.

"You're just jealous," she said. "*So* so jealous."

Molly grinned. They both knew it was *Lemmy* who was jealous. Lemmy knew that Molly knew she was jealous, but she also knew Molly didn't have the nerve to go there.

"You're all green because I can have *bay-bees,*" Molly gloated. "And you still can't. All the girls in our class can have babies. And *you* still can't!"

Lemmy's face fell sour. Her best friend just totally went there.

"Well fork you," Lemmy said. Her body quivered. "Least I can beat you in every race we've ever had."

"Pppffff!" Molly's giggle made Lemmy want to slug her. "You think I care about a stupid *foot*race? I'm gonna be dating a man, soon. A real man. Why don't you join the club sometime, Skinny Hips? Oh, that's right, you can't."

"You wouldn't even know how to—"

Lemmy was shaking. She couldn't finish her sentence. So eagerly had she longed for *her* body to respond the way *other* girls' bodies in seventh grade had already responded.

Who the heck does Molly think she is? I'm the one who gets all the looks from all the guys. I'm the one. She gets all the Wing Men. The leftovers.

Lemmy scowled. Molly pulled a finger under her nose and giggled again.

"You know what you need?" she asked.

"A new BFF?"

"Your period," Molly said. "Then maybe you can chill the F-out."

Lemmy slipped and regained her footing. She marched across the wet leaves to where Molly was leaning against the large rock and dropped quickly to jerk Molly's ankles out from under her. Molly Smits wasn't expecting this. Her feet came up and her head slammed backward into the rock, knocking her out cold.

As athletic as Lemmy Brogans was, she couldn't stop herself from tumbling backward down the hill. The first aid kit flew out of her pocket. Her back hit. Her legs whipped over the top. Over and over again down the damp forest hill. It wasn't really hurting. Not yet at least.

Greater dangers awaited. Rocks and boulders dotted the hillside. Near some of these boulders lay eroded holes in the Earth's crust. Some were visible pitfalls. Others lay hidden beneath moss and leaves. Some holes dropped down into small caverns. Lemmy found one of these. For an instant she even saw it coming.

Down she fell. Fifteen feet down into a dank pit.

UGH!

Lemmy landed hard in the ancient dirt. Her tailbone fractured. Spikes of pain shot up her back and she rolled and squealed like a skewered pig.

When she finally caught her breath she lay flat on her stomach in the dirt. She tried to sit up. White hot pain shocked her lower spine and kept her down. She closed her eyes. It hurt so badly more tears streamed down her freckled cheeks. She couldn't sit. She couldn't stand. Her only options seemed to be lying on her stomach or resting on her hip.

"Mol! Help me!"

Nelly heard the thud. She knew something big had joined her down here. Something large. Something more substantial than the rats, mice and squirrels that sometimes fell down here. Nelly was hungry. She was always hungry. It was her only constant these last six months.

She could wait. Whatever was making these noises reminded her faintly of her old master, but her canine mind was clouded by ravenous primal hunger.

The possibility of a large meal made her mouth hang open and drool.

Nelly was skinny. She had little energy to subdue such a large prey. But there was time. She was patient. She could wait.

⌒

Lemmy's voice hardly penetrated the handful of irregular holes in the dirt ceiling above. *So nasty down here*, she muttered to herself. *How can I get out?*

The first rays of morning sun trickled in through the ceiling. They danced like spirit orbs off the stone walls. Lemmy's eyes adjusted. She caught faint whiffs of stagnant odor. The odor wasn't overpowering. It smelled stale, rather; like a marinating infection.

A strong sunray lit the cave. The subterranean room she'd fallen into was maybe the size of a tennis court. Forming the walls were large boulders. Like floating icebergs, the majority of their mass lay below the surface and their jutting tips above gave no indication as to how large they were below.

Lemmy cursed herself.

How could I do something so stupid?

She hoped Molly was okay. Heck, she hoped *she'd* be okay. Nothing like this had ever happened to her before.

Across the cavernous room something whined.

"H-Heeee ... Eeeeeeene! ... Hee-Heeeee-Heeeeeeeeeeen!"

Lemmy's heart smashed her throat. Something was *down* here with her? Near a rock pile in the corner something was moving. Groaning.

Moving in the darkness. Lemmy saw its shadow. Felt its presence. Blood pumping, she tried bringing her right leg underneath herself to stand, but a thousand needles dove into her tailbone and kept her trembling on her hip as she cried out.

"Molly help! Somebody help me!"

Filmy yellow orbs blinked at her from the rock pile and erected the small hairs on her neck. *It's staring at me. I'm having a nightmare. Wake up!* Dull yellow eyes continued to size her up from the darkness as Lemmy struggled to move. Pain spread like wildfire in her lower back.

"Mol!"

She stopped.

Whatever it was could certainly hear the fear in her voice.

It's injured.

Nelly slunk out from behind the rock pile. Her skinny ribs jutted out of her side like curved twigs. Her tongue dangled from her mouth. Strands of sticky saliva dripped.

For the first time Lemmy saw the dirty yellow Labrador retriever. They stared. Human being and dog. Young and one near the end of her days.

Lemmy propped herself up. She felt for the edge of pain and kept to the side of it. Adrenaline rippled through her body. She couldn't run. She could hardly move. *Fight?* She tried to swallow but her throat was parched.

"Sit!" she croaked. "Stay!"

While her hand fumbled quickly searching for a weapon, Nelly sized up her mark. Her prey was large. It would provide good nourishment. It would fill her belly and then some.

Nelly trotted forward. She made a sweeping arc toward Lemmy. Lemmy grabbed a handful of dirt and small stones and whipped it at the dog. Nelly growled and scooted away.

Hee … Heeeee … Heeeeeee!

It was working itself up.

Lemmy found a rock. Smooth but palm-sized. She was shaking. She stayed on the left side of her hip with her leg forward, balancing herself, ready to throw the rock or punch with her right hand. Her tears had stopped.

Meanwhile, Nelly's trotting arcs were getting closer. She was feeling out Lemmy's weakness. Learning her immobility.

Lemmy screamed. She threw the large rock and the effort made her wince. The rock sailed over the dog and knocked against the stone wall. The skinny yellow Lab stopped. It cocked its head. Lemmy remembered her safety whistle. She fished it out and blew. The high-pitched shriek pricked up Nelly's ears. Lemmy blew and blew the whistle until she was out of breath, but the moment she stopped, Nelly started trotting again.

Lemmy struggled to figure out a different plan. She couldn't move. She couldn't climb. The whistle dropped from her mouth into the dirt.

Trotting one way, Nelly suddenly pivoted back the other. She turned quickly. Springing, Lemmy was caught off-guard and Nelly grabbed her throat.

"Pfffrrrgh!"

Lemmy thrashed while the dog sunk its teeth in.

Killing me! Ackghhh! Kkgh—

Lemmy gurgled and clawed the air.

Nelly shook her viciously.

Blood trickled down Lemmy's throat onto her coat. She dug a hand into the dog's face trying to pry its jaws open, but the dog clamped down and shook harder. One jolt sent a spasm through Lemmy's back, and in a panicked reaction she bounced off it and spiked her thumbnail into the dog's eye.

Nelly howled and leapt off. It pawed at its damaged eyeball and socket.

Lemmy was bleeding. Feeling quickly along her neck she discovered puncture wounds but no shredded flesh. It was difficult to breathe.

Meanwhile, the sun higher in the sky was making it easier to see. Lemmy wiped her face. She searched the cave frantically where she lay. Behind her she found a broken stick about the size of her arm. She grabbed it like a spear.

She'd lost sight of the dog.

It felt like her eye was bleeding.

"Come on!" she screamed. Her neck hurt as she yelled. "Get out here! C—"

A great force knocked her from behind. The dog snapped at the back of her neck. Lemmy covered up and spun. The dog grabbed her right forearm through her jacket and Lemmy yelled in pain. She managed to pass the stick to her left hand while Nelly shook her. She stabbed the face of the dirty yellow Lab repeatedly. It wasn't her dominant hand, but with each thrust the dog whimpered. It still had her arm.

One stab went deep. It sent a shiver through Lemmy's body. Nelly howled. The dog let go and the stick was wrenched from Lemmy's grasp.

Lemmy must have blacked out. She ingested panicked air. The dog lay on top of her. She shoved it and it rolled off.

Lemmy rolled back onto her stomach.

Can't breathe! … Can't! … Ahhh! … Ahhh … ahhh….

After a while Lemmy did catch her breath. And when she finally did she felt ashamed. She had nearly given herself up for dead. She'd been ready to.

Her breathing came back with concentration and with constant checking that the dirty yellow Lab wasn't moving up to disembowel her.

Nelly's body lay still. The stick embedded in its right eye leaked a nasty cornmeal mush that dripped off the end. Lemmy gritted her teeth and got back to her hip. She found a smaller stick. With it she touched Nelly's good eyeball. No movement. None.

The dog was dead.

Lemmy dry-heaved. Plentiful sunlight was streaming through the holes in the dirt ceiling above. It was quiet. She was bruised, bloodied and dirty, but she had finally stopped shaking. She wouldn't allow herself to fathom how much worse things could have gotten. No. She already knew her future dreams would be nightmares.

Lemmy stared at the dead dog. Reaching over, she slowly spun the collar around its neck. *N E L*. That was all she could read. The rest of the name was faded.

In time, Lemmy would realize that *N E L* was probably short for *N E L L Y*. But Lemmy would never know that Nelly's old master, Jefferson Wahl, had dropped Nelly off in the forest last spring when he couldn't afford to keep her. Thirty miles from home. Lemmy would never learn that Jefferson's six-year old son, Alex, used to call her *Nelly-Bo-Belly-Pops*, and that Alex had cried for a month after they were forced to abandon his first pet. The Wahls dropped her off on an old dirt road and never came back. For nine years, Nelly had been a fine dog. A great friend. They simply couldn't afford to care for her any longer.

Stranded in the forest, Nelly had wandered for days. Searching for food. Frightened. Always on the lookout for a meal. Shelter. Like every living creature Nelly was forced to deal with scarcity, and that was the reason she'd chased a possum down the slope and fell fifteen feet into the pit Lemmy Brogans found herself in six months later.

Unconsciously digging in the dirt where she lay, Lemmy uncovered her safety whistle. Finding it opened a door back to reality. She couldn't yell. No voice. Little strength. But she could expel bursts of air, and when she brought the whistle to her dry lips every available cell in her body did this.

Her head became dizzy. The whistle dropped again into the dirt. *Lie down. Lie down, this isn't real.*

"*Hey!*"

The voice had come from above. Lemmy didn't stir. She heard it. Of course she heard it. But she must have imagined it.

"Is someone down there?"

"Yes," said Lemmy. She said it so quietly it didn't register. She looked up. At the mouth of a jagged hole were two men in camouflage caps and moustaches, leaning down looking in.

"Hang tight, l'il lady, we'll have you out in a jiff."

A makeshift basket of flexible branches and hunting cord soon came down. Lemmy stared at the rock pile in the corner. Her hand rested on Nelly's dirty yellow coat. Lemmy didn't move. Didn't speak. Not until one of the hunters hoisted her up did she scream in delayed horror and pain.

Once they were up on high ground, the skinnier of the two men asked angrily, "What in tarnation are you doing out here, little fool?" Both hunters had shotguns leaning against a nearby tree. "It's turkey season for Christ's sake! You wanna be mistaken for a Tom? Get yourself shot?"

"Dumb kid," the other hunter piped in.

Lemmy's eyes were dry and emotionless.

"Looks like you got into a scrape," the skinny hunter said. "You gotta watch your step on these slopes, I'm telling ya. Hollow spots all around."

"Oh what the hell, Bob, we're wasting daylight here. Call Clare Ambulance and find out where she lives so her mama can change her diaper. We gotta get us one!"

Barbara Brogans came out of the house in her bathrobe. The worry on her face quickly turned to displeasure.

"Mama!" Lemmy cried. She limped forward. Blood had run down her orange camouflage jacket and onto her jeans. Most of it was hers.

Barbara took her daughter by the shoulders and shook her. Lemmy cried and held her back. Her mother stopped. Tears welled in both their eyes. Barbara managed to swallow hers and stopped her hand from slapping Lemmy across the face.

"What were you thinking?"

"Wasn't Mama, I wasn't. I'm sorry."

"One of these days you'll learn, Lemmy Brogans," Barbara said. "This morning you almost bought it. I don't know what to do anymore. Daddy's gone. I gotta work. I can't do this by myself anymore. I don't know what to do."

She wiped her face. She thanked the two hunters who had returned her wayward daughter, thanked them profusely. Soon after the ambulance arrived. The hunters were replaced by three medics who wheeled out a stretcher. They asked Lemmy a few questions before strapping her in.

"We'll take her, ma'am," said one of the EMTs. He was a young man, clean shaven and wearing Gargoyles sunglasses. "The bleeding's coagulated, but she's going to need several stitches. I think her tailbone—"

"Just take her," Barbara said. "Thank you, sir."

"But Mama!"

"I need to drive Molly home," Barbara said. "Your friend, Molly? Remember? Your friend who's been icing her head for the last four hours. Your friend who had no idea what happened. And now I'll have to explain to Rita Smits why she has to watch her daughter for signs of a concussion. Thanks, Lemmy. You're such a fine, considerate daughter."

"But—"

"I'll pick you up from the hospital," Barbara said. "Right now I don't even want to look at you."

The EMTs wheeled Lemmy into the ambulance alone. As they pulled away, she watched her world getting smaller and smaller out the back window. She wasn't the sly opportunist she thought she was. But she felt thankful. Very grateful for another chance.

THE END

'SEMI-CONSCIOUS'

⌒

THE ELEVATED TRAIN CLICKS TO a stop. Silver-paneled doors open. I step onto the wooden platform and the late morning sun blinds me with warmth. *Ahhhh.* The scent of rail grease fills the air.

I'm in my powder blue bowling shirt and my white Adidas sneakers. All around me people start to scurry. An elbow presses into my lower back. Passengers apologize as they bump me aside. That's fine. I can't keep this dumb smile off my face anyway because it's me J.B.—Jimmy Babb—in the city! *Woot! Woot!*

I'm away from my small-town life. Away from all the drama. I'm excited to be somewhere new, even if it's only for a long weekend.

I spot my second-cousin, Steve. He's the one I'm coming to stay with in the city. Steve's rocking some dark blue jeans and a smooth leather jacket, leaning suavely against the wooden railing and chatting up a hot blonde. At times, Steve and I have been closer than blood brothers. That's why it's ironic we haven't seen each other in three years.

"Big Steve!"

"*J.B.!*" he yells. "There you are, man." The hot blonde walks off and we give each other a great big hug. "Excellent. So what? You're twenty-four now?"

"Twenty-four and a quarter," I say.

"Inconceivable," Steve says. "Hope the Strand ain't gonna miss ya this weekend."

"Not to my knowledge."

"Fab, then it's time to begin."

Steve grabs my duffle bag. He tilts his head in the direction of an exit. I sidestep a kissing couple in purple hip-hop gear and follow him. Steve smells like sandalwood. Maybe it's cedar. Whatever it is it's spicy.

He asks over his shoulder, "This is your first excursion to the city, correct?"

"That is correct, sir."

"Your urban extravaganza awaits my good sir."

We step down the stairs and onto the concrete sidewalks below. Steve groans and sets my bag aside with a clink. He rubs his arm. "Good *God*, man. You did bring the kitchen sink?"

"Well, I wasn't sure what I'd need," I say. "I remembered you saying there's a courtyard thingy at your apartment building. Thought you might wanna chuck some shoes."

"You brought horseshoes and stakes?"

"Well *hail* yeah!"

"Crikey."

Steve hefts my bag again and I follow him to the corner of a busy intersection. Cars whip in and out of lanes, honking and passing. People speed-walking everywhere. Nobody really looks at you or says anything. Kinda strange. Just so many people. People everywhere.

Steve waves an arm over his head. A yellow taxi pulls up. I jump into the backseat behind the driver and Steve grunts my bag into the trunk. He shuts it. The taxi wobbles. Steve slides in next to me and slams the door.

"Where we headed, gentlemen?" the driver asks. He's sporting a bushy gray moustache with a slightly askew golf cap.

"5345 Firebrand Avenue," Steve says.

The taxi driver puts on his left turn signal. A car lets him in. He guns it and I grab the door handle.

"5345 Firebrand," our driver repeats. "You got it. Your friend here must be new."

Steve nudges my arm. "He's talking to you." I reel in my peepers from the city action outside.

"Sorry," I say. "Yep, first time."

"Don't worry about it, you'll be terrific," our driver says. "Hey, did ya hear the one about the cabbie in New York whose brakes went out?"

"No," I say.

"This cabbie is taking his fare through midtown Manhattan, and as they're approaching Carnegie Hall, he pushes his brake pedal in and it goes all the way to the floor. 'I can't stop!' he yells. 'My brakes are out! I can't stop!' And the passengers in the backseat scream: *'Jesus Christ! Kill the meter!'*"

He's boisterous, but our driver seems like a genuinely nice man. For some strange reason I thought all cabbies in the city were young, wore their ball caps sideways and spouted off weird urban philosophy. I don't know. That's just what I've seen in the movies.

"Don't have *too* much fun though," our driver says. He winks at me in the rearview. "This place is a trip. Sometimes it's hard to stop."

Steve squeezes my shoulder.

"Welcome to the City of Evening Dreams."

Steve's apartment seems cozy enough. A little smaller than what he told me. I drop my stuff on the floor near a black futon with purple pillows. My eyes drift past a nude sketch on the wall.

"Henri Matisse," Steve says. "We probably won't even be in here much. You ready?"

We hail another cab to his friend Ron's place. Ron's a funny-looking guy who lives in Finite Square; an area of the city devoted to techies and self-identified geeks. Ron looks like he lives in his bathrobe and combs his hair with a tornado. He grins through grubby teeth. He shakes my hand, pulls me in for a hug and generally seems like a good guy, even though his B.O. is a little much, even for a country boy like me.

"Ron's got aces up his sleeve," Steve says.

"Aces?" I say.

"Happy-go-lucky charms," Ron says. From the pocket of his robe he produces three large pills. They're as big as horse pills. An ill feeling knocks my stomach.

"I'll pass on that."

Steve takes two of the pills and hands me one.

"Naw man, they're not *pill* pills," he says. "They're super-concentrated THC, coated with psilocybin and dusted with espresso bean powder."

"Intergalactic Acapulco *Gold*," Ron croons.

"What does it do?" I ask.

"Spiritual reconciliation," Steve says. "But then again, you've never smoked weed before have you?"

"Well, this one time Troy Hoover and I—"

"I remember that dude," Steve interjects.

"Yeah, good ole Troy Boy," I say. "Anyway, we were pretty drunk one night at his older brother's place and we found some old dried-up bud but I don't think it did anything. I only remember falling asleep."

Ron hands me a bottle of water that looks cleaner than anything else in his room. I look over at Steve. He nods. Sighing, I pop the coated THC pill and swill it down. Steve washes his down, too.

"Let's cut to the chase," he says, wiping his mouth. He sets the water bottle on the coffee table. "Cannabis is the most dangerous drug in the world."

"The *most* dangerous?" I say. Steve nods. "I thought marijuana was supposed to be pretty harmless."

"It *is* pretty harmless, that's what *makes* it so dangerous. You can have fun doing nothing."

"Sounds kind of interesting."

"Wasting time doing nothing is nothing for a person to do," Steve says. "It's that life of quiet desperation Thoreau talked about. Hey man, I think everyone should try it. Legalize it across the board—twenty-one and up. The whole paradox is to do as *little* as possible."

"But these also have psilocybin," Ron says.

"Yeah, well, there's that too," says Steve.

⟋

The massive wooden door swings open. Steve and I step into a beautiful foyer. The dark-oiled wood and the subdued lighting bathe everything in a relaxed, earthy old-school charm.

As I'm taking in this new and interesting environment, I'm thinking: *Dang these THC pills are strong! I'm walking through dream after dream after ooo!*

The brunette in the silk Kimono who opened the door smiles. She steps back. We enter. Her flowery robe is wide at the sleeves, slightly open at the neck. *She's hot as magma.* I feel my eyes bright as lanterns returning her grin.

Oh, man. I must be **REALLY** *high. Everything is f-l-o-a-t-i-n-g …
a-l-o-n-g….*

Wait. Is my memory skipping a beat? No question. Wasn't I just outside?

Wait. Am I tripping? Is this what it feels like to trip?

Oh *shit.*

I trust Steve. I know I can trust him. As connected to the pleasure underground as he may be, I know he wouldn't intentionally put us in harm's way. I *think.* I realize I'll have to take solace in it regardless.

Actually, I feel wonderful. Absolutely *wonderful.* My body's firing on all cylinders. I'm relaxed. I'm aware. I'm more at ease with myself than I've been in a long time. And in a weird way, I think this girl in the flowery Japanese Kimono can sense it, too. Like a mare in heat.

So am I the mare? Or is she?

Steve smooches her on the cheek.

"Where's Mia?" he asks.

From down the wooden hallway steps a dark-skinned goddess in a creamy white dress. This must be Mia. I'm not even sure what kind of outfit Mia is wearing. It's like a gown of the gods and it drops my jaw to the ground. This young black woman is so elegant I nearly soil myself.

"Glad you made it, Boo," Mia says pecking Steve on both cheeks. Her warm eyes put me instantly at ease. She kisses my hand with soft, warm lips. "You must be J.B. Welcome to our humble city abode."

I follow Mia and Steve down an exquisite (again, these words keep popping into my head that I never use) hallway corridor. The girl in the Kimono walks silently behind us. The corridor twists and morphs until I feel like I'm walking through a fun house. It's ... *surreal? Surrealistic?*

"This place has a monster basement," Steve says in a low voice. "Three times bigger than the main floor of the house."

"How do they pay for all this?" I ask. "I mean, how do they even keep it up?"

Steve shrugs.

"Trust funds mostly," he whispers.

The hallway slopes downward until it opens into a grand underground library. It's a large room, very old, and very well-kept. It's like something out of the 1700s or something—an ancient study with lounging chairs, shelves upon shelves of old books and two sturdy wooden tables.

"Bathroom's over there," says the girl in the Kimono. "If you'd like to freshen up."

"Thanks," I say.

"You're welcome."

"I'm Jimmy. Steve's cousin. Well, second-cousin, actually."

"I know," she says. "I'm Jana."

I shake Jana's hand because I don't have the courage to kiss both her cheeks like classy people do. Jana's left eye has a slight twitch. Nonetheless, she sports a confident, mesmerizing stare.

"I love to read when I have the time," I say. Jana smiles. I could marry this girl right now. *Take me for everything I'm worth, darlin'.* "This place is just amazing."

"We enjoy it," Jana says.

⟶

After a few puffs on an uplifting spliff that smells like orange citrus, I find myself chilling next to Jana on a chaise lounge. Steve and Mia are kitty-corner to us on a daybed. They're flipping through a book on Denali State Park. I never knew this was called a chaise lounge. It feels like it was built for the two of us. As I'm sitting here, however, I keep losing track of where my head is. It's like a Helium balloon with hair.

"It's not a bad city," Jana says. She opens an old leather-bound book and sets it in front of me. Inside is a layout of Evening Dreams. Ocean to the east; beautiful Lake Jaden and its three islands to the west; highways and surface streets running straight and true; all the farming communities to the north.

"Cool," I say.

"It was well-planned when it was built," Jana says. "Kind of pretentious though. I totally understand this is your first visit and you're having fun and everything. I just think I've been here too long."

"Everybody's been really friendly," I say.

"That we is," says Jana.

"In the Strand—that's Strandsville, my hometown in the southern part of the state—it's like every chick is either a ditz or a money-grabber, and every dude is a hillbilly redneck, drinking beer in his front yard with his shirt off working on trucks and ATVs."

"Sounds Stone Age," Jana says.

I nod thoughtfully. It makes me kinda sad to describe my hometown in this way. But in a lot of ways I'm kinda this way.

"Maybe that's all they have to believe in," Jana continues.

"They floor their gas pedals better than anyone in the county," I say. "If their vehicle beats yours off the line then it totally makes their day. Like a confidence booster."

"Chutzpah," Jana says. The word flies over my head. "Sounds like some serious Ford vs. Chevy battles."

"Tons."

"Look at how these elections are going," she says. "The talking heads on TV might not want to believe it—well, they're not *paid* to believe it—but most of this country is made up of the very people you describe. Pound for pound it's who we are. Hillbillies, rednecks, and project ghetto rats. At least we're genuine though. More genuine than the candidates themselves or their little political strategists."

Politics are the furthest thing from my mind. *Look at Jana's sarcastic smile!* So sweet. So mischievous. I'm fighting like a big-mouth bass.

"I'm from the sticks, too," Jana says. "A little Podunk town called Rugg. Someday, I may move back, who knows. But while I'm here I'll continue to milk this city for all it's worth. Carpe diem, baby."

I nod. *Carpe diem.* I could see myself never going back to the Strand. I never knew there were people like this. Or places like this. I feel plugged into another dimension. *Hello? God? It's me, Jimmy Babb. Any off-chance you might be able to make this happen?*

"What time is it?" I ask.

"6:30."

A grandfather clock along the far wall strikes a note on the half hour. It looks like something out of the Middle Ages with its rich, detailed carvings.

"Only 6:30?"

Jana nods.

"Time trudges when you're stoned," she says. "Feels nice, but also makes you kind of lazy. Come on. Come with me. We'll have us a little pick-me-up."

Jana leads me down another hallway and into a back bedroom. It might even be her bedroom. She closes the door. A California King-sized bed sits against the far wall. Through a nearby doorway I see the corner of a toilet.

From inside a dresser, Jana takes out a wooden box. She closes the drawer, sets the box on the table and opens the top. Inside is a plastic baggie filled with white powder.

"That's not crystal meth is it?" I ask. She shakes her head. "I was gonna say no thanks. We've got enough meth-heads running our factories back home."

"This is what methamphetamine was trying to replace," Jana says. "The one and only." The corners of her mouth turn upward. "We'll just do a little. But then a little gets more and more."

I feel myself swallow a dry knot. I remember Steve warning me not to try anything without him. But looking at Jana—man, there is *nothing* I wouldn't do with this woman.

Jana dumps some of the white powder onto a small plate. She pulls out a razor blade and chops at it, making it finer.

"Is this cocaine?" I ask.

Jana looks up. Her eye twitches.

"Llelo."

"*Yay-Yo?*" I repeat.

"Right as rain," she says. "Totally pure. None of that cut junk on the street."

Out of the box she pulls a straw, maybe half the size you would find in a McDonald's Coke. She plucks a tissue from a nearby Kleenex box.

"Gang way," she says, blowing her nose.

"Is this stuff safe?" I ask. I'm excited but hesitant. "I mean, cocaine's like a hard drug, right?" Jana stares at me with starry eyes.

"Relax, man," she says. She pats my hand. "Did you hear the one about the Call Girl who went to see her Psychologist?"

"No," I say.

"The Psychologist sits her down in a chair and asks her what's wrong. The Call Girl looks at him and says, 'I had this incredibly bizarre dream, Doc. I woke up in a strange bed. My own.'"

I smile. Jana scrapes the powder into four lines, each one the length of my index finger. "I do two. You do two," she says. "Then we'll talk."

Jana inserts the straw into her right nostril. She leans forward. *Vrrrpppppp!* Up goes the line. *Vrrrpppppp!* up the left. Her eyes water. She pinches her nose together, swallows and says *"Fuck."*

Jana hands me the straw. I hesitate. I see another grandfather clock against the bedroom wall, this one smaller and a little simpler. The door opens behind us. I hear footsteps.

"Whoa, hold up, hold up." It's Steve's voice. Mia is behind him. Steve walks up and plucks the straw from my fingertips. "As your counselor on urban affairs, I highly suggest you join me in the lounge, pronto."

As Steve did to me, Mia plucks the straw from his fingers, bends down and snorts up the remaining two lines. *"Ahhh,"* she says. "And leave those for me."

Steve puts his arm around my shoulder. We walk. We leave the women in the back room. Once we're a good ways down the hallway, Steve checks me from the corner of his eye.

"Dude, don't get off into that shit," he says. "It'll grab your wallet and your soul. Next thing you know, you'll be hacking Grandma Babb's checking account from prison. You wanna be a slave? You want that shit to own you? Control you?"

"I thought you said weed was the most dangerous?"

"Here's the skinny," Steve says. "Coke. The rush is invigorating. The crash and the bloody nose are worse. You get really cranky and you just want more and more because now it's in your head, eating your brain. Then you don't sleep for three days. Junk? Never tried it. But I heard it even replaces sex. All you care about is your next bag. Your next fix. Over and over again. Everything else is irrelevant."

"Geez."

"You don't get something for nothing, man. Especially with your body. Mushrooms are interesting, some of the hallucinogens and mood enhancers are a little different but they'll still wear you down. And you never know if the stuff you're taking is legit or rat poison. Keep it real.

Stick with cannabis. The most dangerous. At least then you can drift through a life of mediocrity."

"It all seems so ironic," I say.

"Drugs *are* ironic," Steve says. "Ironic how many people need drugs to get through life. More on that later. Right now, I got a song for you."

I take a seat on the sofa. My heart has calmed. I'm actually glad Steve came in. As hot as Jana is, I think I would have regretted sucking that stuff up my nose.

Steve presses a few buttons on an elaborate entertainment system. He pops a CD into the Onkyo 6-disc carousel. He skips forward to song #9 and presses **PAUSE.**

"Remember driving my old GTO down Fern Road?" Steve asks.

"Yeah, sure," I say.

"Remember the songs we jammed to?"

"Which time?"

"That one summer," Steve says. Many song titles skirt the tips of my lips but nothing specific comes to mind. "Check it out." He presses **PLAY**.

BOOM … Ba-Ba-Baaaaa … Ba DOOM … Ba-Ba-Baaaaa….

The sultry synthesizer and back beat instantly return me to the past. It's the summer after Freshman year. Steve had just graduated. It's a live version of the Eagles' *"I Can't Tell You Why"*.

"Man, we listened to *Hotel California* and *Tom Petty & the Heartbreakers* about every day that summer," Steve says. "Cruising the back roads, rolling over hills, that sweet summer breeze rushing through our hair."

"Oh man, I can totally feel it," I say.

And I can.

Steve lights up a skinny joint and passes it over.

"Train Wreck XXX," he says. "Super sativa. No couch lock in sight." The joint tastes like disco pine needles. It elevates my consciousness. Waves of sound pulse through the speakers as Timothy B. Schmit moans: *"Every time I try to walk away … Something makes me turn around and stay … And I Can't Tell You Whyyyyy…."*

"Dude, this song rules."

"I knooooow, *right?*"

"*Duuuuuuuuude.*"

"*I can't even....*"

"*Dude.*"

We finish the joint and the remainder of the *Hell Freezes Over* album. Once we're done, Steve turns off the entertainment system and slips on his jacket. I check the clock. 7:20 p.m.

"Well ladies," Steve says bowing. "Our public calls us."

I hadn't even realized that Mia and Jana had rejoined us. They look up from their conversation across the room and walk over.

"So soon?"

"Afraid so."

I float to my feet and shake Jana's hand.

"Very nice to meet you," I say. "Or to have met you, I mean."

"Likewise," Jana says. "Look me up if you're in the city again. We can hang out and party."

"Ok."

"'Cause you seem like a pretty cool guy," Jana says. She wipes her nose with a tissue. "Cool guys are a rarity these days. Know what I mean? Like we were talking about earlier. It's like *every single dude* is a cliché of a cliché anymore. It's like: *Guys! Really? Who cares if you have a barbed-wire tattoo? So what if your nose is pierced? Sheep. Sheep. Frickin' sheep. Saggy pants, backwards baseball caps, shaved heads and goatees, how original, OMG just kill me!*

It's older than dinosaur dung. But you're different, J.B. I could tell right away you're not hung up on what other people think. You're righteous, man. Or maybe I just find you so appealing I wanna gobble you up!"

"Dang," I say. I never knew I had all that going for me.

"But I understand," says Jana, calming a little. "You gotta go. Enjoy Evening Dreams."

"It still sounds so weird hearing people call it that," I think and say at the same time. Everyone knows the city's moniker. And it certainly is *dreamy.* Jana points to Steve.

"You've got a good guide here," she says. She leans forward and softly kisses me. Her lips taste like pomegranate. "Enjoy your trip, sweetie."

Mia winks. The heavy mahogany door slowly closes in my face. We're outside again. It's evening.

"Come on," says Steve. He puts an arm around my shoulder. I have to let him lead me.

"Holy moly," I mumble. "I think I'm orbiting Jupiter."

Steve's hand on my shoulder is reassuring.

"How do you feel?" he asks.

"Great," I say.

"Don't hassle it then."

Steve's right. I just need to stay on this wave and ride it in to the shore. Everything's fine. He hands me his leather jacket when he sees me shivering. It's not even cold. I slide it on. It's warm. As we walk—I don't know how else to describe it—a low-pitched purple pulse vibes out at odd angles from the city. I'm not sure how it's happening or why. I only know that it is.

"Where to now?" I ask.

"Peach's Mango Tree."

"Where?"

"The Hideout at Peach's Mango Tree," Steve says. "Peach is a real treat. You'll love her."

I must have dozed off. I hardly remember taking the cab here. Peach's Mango Tree is like something out of a trippy video game. It reminds me of that old Disney movie *Swiss Family Robinson*. The colors. The people. The exotic drinks with pineapples, cherries, and waterfalls you can slide down. *Dang. I didn't even bring my bathing suit.*

"When you're stoned you really empathize with your fellow humans."

"I don't necessarily disagree," I say, opening my eyes.

"Or you just don't care enough to argue."

"What's your name again?"

"Luke. Luke Neelese."

"Neelese?"

"I'm an old friend of your cousin Steve's. Your second-cousin, I mean."

I can hardly keep my eyes open but apparently I've been listening this entire time.

"Have you seen Steve lately?"

"Sure," Luke says. "He's right over there."

I look across the luxurious tree house we're sitting in and notice Steve talking up two young women. The one in the purple jacket and gray tie downs her martini, throws back her head and laughs. Steve looks over. He flashes the peace sign.

"Oh, okay," I say. "Neelese. It sounds familiar."

"I'm not the famous Belgian footballer," Luke says, laughing. "If that's what you're wondering."

I laugh too, although I have no idea what we're laughing about. I'm exhausted. I'm *zoned*. I start to doze as I hear Luke saying, "But to answer your initial question, I would say the only apt title is: *Marijuana: It works*."

⌣⟶

Someone or something is shaking me.

All right. All right. I'm awake.

"What is it?" I ask. I'm trying to open my eyes but they're caked shut.

"Do you wanna crash here?" It's Steve.

"Where are we?"

"Sandra, Dana and Matt's place," Steve says.

"We're not at Peach's anymore?"

"No, man, we left Peach's hours ago."

"Oh." *I sorta remember.* "Yeah."

"I've got a portable toothbrush," says Steve. "If you wanna clean your fangs."

I rub my eyes and shake my head.

"I'll let it slide," I say. "I'm good. Let's just crash."

"You're smoked-out," he says, smiling.

"Why is weed more dangerous than all the other stuff?" I mumble. My eyelids feel like anvils. "If it's that dangerous, why even do it?"

"The hard stuff will definitely mess you up," Steve says. He sits next to me on the couch. "No doubt. And that includes alcohol, tobacco and sugar. But with reefer, you can operate your entire life at 90%. That's the crash. That's the hangover. Hard to realize your true potential if you're stoned all the time. I don't know. Maybe it's not true. The heavier shit will definitely put you down. Kill you early. Turn you into damaged goods. But in the end, weed might just break your heart."

I've listened to everything my second cousin has had to say, but it really doesn't matter because I'm sleeping again and none the wiser.

⌒

"Marijuana's not a *drug*," says this girl, Barbie, sitting next to me. We've been flirting. She seems really sweet. Her eyebrow has a silver hoop through it; otherwise, she's dressed like a Catholic school girl. "It's a vitamin, man. It's like the Penicillin of the 21st Century."

"It makes you slow and dumb." A woman on the couch next to us has spoken up.

"It'll free your creative spirit," says a guy in a Rubik's cube costume. I'm thinking: *What is this? Halloween?*

"Why are you wearing that ridiculous costume, Ray?" the woman on the couch asks. At least I'm not alone in my bewilderment.

"I just got back from a '80s costume party, Meredith," Ray says. "*Uh!* You are so wrong."

"Why in holy hell did you dress as a Rubik's cube?" Meredith asks. "You should have gone as Rick Springfield."

"Because I was high," Ray says to the sudden laughter of the room. "Bringing us back to our subject at hand."

"Devil weed!"

"It makes sex better!"

A woman in a black cocktail dress starts making out with her girlfriend next to us, and I blush and try not to watch them even though I really want to.

"Think it'll ever be completely legal?" I ask.

"Nah," Meredith says. "As a country we'd have to be able to laugh at ourselves. We're not quite there yet."

"A fat joint is lovely to relax with," says a dreamy female voice behind me.

"Shouldn't end a sentence with a preposition," Barbie says.

"Oh, Barbie, you've forgotten the words of Sir Winston Leonard Spencer Churchill: *Ending a sentence with a preposition is something up with which I will not put.*"

"I've never met Mr. Churchill," Barbie says. She winks. "Well J.B.— have you been enjoying your estrangement from rural life?"

"I have," I say. "It's been a lot of fun. But I have one more question. Why is it called the City of Evening Dreams?"

"Because, man, this city comes *alive* in the evening," Barbie says.

"Don't most cities come alive in the evening?"

"Not like Evening Dreams. Every person, every project, every *thing* is driven during the daylight hours to produce the magic that happens at night. It's by design. You bust your butt during the day, hope and dream, and by nightfall your dreams start coming true."

"Sounds like a Disney card," I say. In a weird kinda way it makes sense.

"It's stoner advertising," says a guy from across the room. "*Caveat emptor.* There isn't anything special about this city."

Suddenly I'm confused.

"Wait, what day is it?" I ask.

"Sunday," Barbie says. "Sunday night. Why?"

"Whew. I've gotta catch my train in the morning."

"I've got my alarm set," Steve says. "We've got your bags packed, we're ready to roll. Everything is in good order, brother."

Steve's been sitting next to me the entire time. My reality seems to have drifted. Or shifted. Or something.

"It's time, my man."

Steve's voice again.

I roust myself up. I say good-bye to a bunch of people I barely remember who are also up and having coffee. Last night seemed so magical. Now, in the morning light, we all seem awkward and ordinary.

Steve and I take a cab to the train station. Up on the wooden platform, he gives me a big old hug. I hug him back. He's my second-cousin. My soul brother.

"I had a great time," I say groggily. My eyes are bloodshot and I'm still waking up. Steve hands me a traveler's cup of coffee. He also slips me a bottle of eye drops.

"Naphcon A?"

"The best," Steve says. "How long's your train ride?"

"Three and a half hours."

"How's your stomach?"

"Meh."

"Well, have a safe journey, my brother," Steve says. "Always a pleasure."

"You too," I say. We keep a hand on each others' shoulders. "Don't be a stranger to the Strand."

"I'll be back for Christmas," he says. "Maybe Thanksgiving."

"This weekend really flew by."

"Now you know. And knowing…."

"Is half the battle?"

Steve winks.

As I'm lugging my bag through the open doors of the silver-paneled train, I hear commotion starting behind me on the platform. I turn to watch. A fiery redhead runs directly up to Steve. His face crinkles in fear. He has nowhere to run.

"Jill?"

"Ah *ha!*" the redhead says, sticking a finger in Steve's face. "Found you, you bastard."

I inch onto the train unable to take my eyes from the spectacle on the platform. Other passengers are watching, too. A few step back for safety.

"What do you mean?" I hear Steve ask.

The redhead slaps Steve across the face. Hard. I recoil from the smack. I wonder if I should go out there to help, but it doesn't seem to be any of my business and I really don't want to get in the middle of it. Onlookers are stupefied. The fiery redhead cracks Steve in the face again.

"I'm knocked up, you jerk!"

The train toots its whistle. The pre-recorded voice announces: *Doors closing! Doors closing!* The train gives a jolt and starts to move. I fall back into a seat. Pulling my bag between my feet, I hear the horseshoes and stakes clink. I can still see Steve and the redhead arguing as we leave the station. A group of people are gathered near. I hope my second-cousin is all right, and by the sound of it I may soon have another distant relative, but in any event I'm glad to be leaving Evening Dreams. I'm done with all this stuff for a while.

THE END

'Heart in a Cold Night'

Her headlights jittered off the stop sign through flurries of snow. Julie Wadleigh down-shifted her forest green hatchback. She wasn't a tall woman. The pillow she was sitting on forced her to use her entire leg to get the clutch in. She checked the clock on the dash. Three minutes to midnight.

"*Tonight,*" she said. "*Tonight is all about patience.*"

She clutched again and tapped her brakes. Her tires skidded over black ice. Julie screamed, dropped the cell phone she'd been holding to her ear and stood on the brake pedal. Her hatchback started to spin. She turned a complete circle, sliding past the stop sign in the night before finally coming to rest in the middle of the intersection. Her car sputtered and died.

Julie tried to catch her breath.

Monstrous headlights suddenly roared over the hill. Her heart spasmed. She cried out, cranked the stalled engine and threw it in reverse—and was nearly mowed down by a massive semi laden with timber. Its air horn bombed her car as it blew past in a hurricane of snow.

Back at the stop sign, Julie set the parking brake and rested her head against the steering wheel. The cell phone barked at her feet.

"Jules? *Julie!*"

She reached down and grabbed her phone.

"It's okay, Magda," she said. "I'm here."

"I'm going to *kill* you if I keep calling," Magda Pryce said on the other end. She was Julie's friend. Her confidante. So much more. "We have our entire lives in front of us, baby bear," Magda said. "Just take it one step at a time, okay? I'll pick you up at 2:00. My lights will be off. Love you."

Julie closed her phone. She hooked it to the car charger. She felt alone. Scared. Listening to her car choking against the subzero Minnesota winds, with only Magda who had an inkling of where she was going and what she was doing.

Julie let go a few tears. She wiped her eyes and felt behind her seat. Her white backpack was still there. She popped an 800 mg. Ibuprofen and washed it down with hot chocolate. Opening her window, she tossed out the paper cup. She hated littering. But tonight there would be no evidence of her in the car.

Julie turned right onto Interstate 2. As she was picking up speed, her cell phone lit up beeping its tune.

"Hello?"

"Where you at?" It was Craig. Her future ex-husband. "Karate practice" must have gotten out early tonight. "Hey! You there?"

"Yeah, I'm here," Julie said. "The roads are slippery. I'm trying to concentrate and not end up in a ditch."

"Well concentrate and drive faster, ho," Craig said. "Doug's closing the Dojo early and if you haven't guessed you're my only ride."

"I'll be there in fifteen minutes."

"*Christ.*" Click.

Julie calmly set her phone down. Self-absorbed prick. That was how he ended every conversation with her anymore. Never a proper goodbye. Never even a proper hello. Not that she wanted any of that from him anymore.

She clicked on her high beams. Swaths of light sliced deep into the cold night. It felt like she was sending out an S.O.S. Legally married or not, she was no longer Julie Wadleigh. *I'm Foster, damn it. Julie Foster.* Reclaiming her name felt empowering.

Headlights approached from the other direction. She cut her brights.

Ironic how wonderfully their relationship had begun. Craig Wadleigh was a Division II Champ at Grand Valley State. Offensive Lineman. He'd been a tough player but that was over ten years ago, and as the years went on it was the only memory he ever talked about. The only ring he ever wore. At 4′11″ Julie stood close to two feet shorter than Craig. For a while they were labeled the "Cute Couple".

For a while.

Life, however, moved on.

Craig Wadleigh had only slid backward.

He'd begun riding Julie like some beast. Blaming her for things she'd never done. Insinuating other things. Earlier in the month, he'd nearly suffocated her, laying a pillow across her face and himself across the pillow, pinching her and laughing as she screamed for air.

She blacked out.

When she finally came to, shaking, realizing her tiny flame had almost been extinguished, Craig's indifference was terrifying.

Alpha male insecurities. Morbid jealousy. All the while, *he* was the one with a guilty conscience.

Then he lost his driver's license.

Then he got mean.

Then he got evil.

Julie slowed, passing between two open cornfields. Blowing drifts temporarily blinded her vision. The **LOW FUEL** warning light beeped on the dash. The snow died. Visibility cleared. She sped up. She checked the odometer and made a mental note. Glancing at her eyes in the rearview mirror, Julie nodded. Everything was on schedule.

Out on the dark horizon, the town lights of Crane Mills moaned like a dull yellow beacon.

The town of Crane Mills lay sleeping. Somber streetlights, empty pale sidewalks. Julie rolled up to the first light. The only other vehicle at the intersection was a tan pickup truck waiting on the other side. From the pickup's tailpipe puffed little white clouds.

She snapped her fingers. One last thing. To the left of the steering column was a fuse box. Julie pulled off the plastic cover. Running her finger down the row of fuses within, she counted to the seventh fuse and plucked it out with her fingernails. The dashboard lights went dark. She blinked. Her homework had paid off. In her pocket was the blown 15 amp fuse she had brought from work. She pulled it out, clicked it into the empty fuse slot and returned the cover.

The tan pickup drove slowly past her window. Julie sat upright. The stoplight had turned green. She waited until the truck passed before opening her window and dropping the good 15 amp fuse outside.

She got moving again. Her tires creaked over the packed snow as she watched the taillights of the pickup fading in the rearview mirror. Her own smiled faded as well. Around the next corner was the Dojo.

The Dojo was owned by "Disco" Doug Proctor. Disco had won a scratch-off lottery ticket that paid out $2,500 a week for life. Over the next several years he built the Dojo in Crane Mills. The Dojo was indeed a small karate classroom and Asian grocery store up top; but down below it was a speakeasy bar and brothel with an extensive wing of underground beds, occupants and other happenings on the down low.

Craig had been intimate with this place. Many nights she found the evidence. Washed it from his underwear. Smelled it on him. Tasted it.

Julie cut her lights as she parked. She slipped on the pair of red-rimmed glasses she'd brought along. She spotted Craig at the front window. He was drinking a tall can of malt liquor, his hairy gut sticking out of his karate gi and bulging over his red Speedos.

Disco stood at the front entrance. He was gnawing watermelon off the rind. He flashed a shady smile. Julie dropped her head and pretended to be messing with the radio. Nonetheless, she could see Disco do a double-take. This was good. She didn't wear glasses. She'd never worn a white snow suit. She rarely wore lipstick, but tonight her lips were fire-engine red. Her hair was tucked up into a new white hat. The pillow she was sitting on made her noticeably taller in the driver's seat.

Julie Wadleigh looked like a different woman.

Craig paused in the doorway. He and Disco grinned and shared a soul-brother handshake. Disco held the door as Craig tucked a paper sack under his arm and tiptoed out into the snow in his Oriental slippers.

Julie unlocked the doors, locked them, and then unlocked them again. Craig climbed in. Nasty steam rose off his ratty hair.

"Bring my boots?" he asked. His foul breath was stale.

"You stepped in doggy doo, Hun," she said. "I didn't have time to clean them off."

Craig pulled a six-pack of *Pale Jethro* beer out of his paper sack.

"Guess I'll be pounding these to keep warm," he said. Julie put the car in reverse. Craig cracked his first beer and toasted her. "Drive good now. I can't be losing my chauffeur on no open alcohol violations."

They rolled quietly through the lifeless town. The Dojo was the only place that got any late-night action, and while it brought in customers from all around it closed early tonight for the approaching snow storm.

Craig backhanded Julie's arm. She kept her eyes on the road. He pointed to the dark dashboard.

"What'd you do now?"

She shrugged.

"I don't know. They went out just as I was coming to get you."

"Jesus, now the *gas* gauge don't even work?" Craig said, adjusting himself. "Foreign piece of junk. And you know what? I'm about done fussin' with your little Shih-Tzu. Little bastard crapped in my slipper again."

Julie forced down the corners of her mouth. Craig stared at her.

"What are you wearing?" he asked.

"Snow suit," she said. "Supposed to be the coldest night of the year."

"Where'd you get it?"

"Good Will."

"When did you go to the Good Will?" he asked. "And why are you wearing glasses? You don't wear glasses."

"You never noticed," she said.

Craig paused, a hand on his chin.

"They look familiar," he said.

"I only wear them at night," said Julie. "When I drive."

Craig shrugged. He gulped down his beer and cracked another. Julie watched the final stoplight of Crane Mills fading in the rearview mirror.

Stand your ground, Foster. Stand it now, or die in this hell.

Night slithered in around them. They stayed silent for the first part of the drive. Outside, the darkness was cut by the occasional streetlight, or even rarer headlights from the other direction. Not many were foolish enough to be out tonight.

Snow was falling. Thick flakes streaked across her headlights. Meteorologists predicted the snow would turn extremely heavy, giving way to record low temperatures in the early morning hours and then more snow for Monday and Tuesday. It was the best weather Julie could have hoped for.

Meanwhile, Craig was downing his *Pale Jethro* beer like a thirsty camel.

"Losing my buzz," he muttered. "Fucking working tomorrow." His *one* day of work compared with her five or six.

But Craig was wrong. He *wasn't* working tomorrow. He was getting drunk. He was getting his days mixed up. Julie would let him go on believing it.

As she drove, she watched him out of the corner of her eye pointing and jiving some imaginary fool in front of him while trying not to spill his beer. His weight and his hygiene had become atrocious. He'd go weeks without showering. Told her he was cultivating that funk.

But it wasn't how big he'd become. Or his lack of bathing. It was the choking. The punching. The emotional abuse. Those were the catalysts.

Julie fingered the bruise around her left eye socket, a memento from Wednesday night's backhand. Her ribs still ached. The Ibuprofen was helping. Craig said he'd kill her if she said anything. He'd cut her into little pieces. Take her out with the trash. Yes, she believed he'd do it. No, Craig Wadleigh was not the man she had married. She didn't have a husband anymore.

"You missed it!" he yelled, spilling his beer.

"What?"

"You missed our turn!"

"No, I—I was going to surprise you," she stuttered. "Tower Lane is supposed to be beautiful this time of year. Thought we'd take that route. Might be romantic."

Craig gagged on a mouthful of suds.

"What the hell are you talking about *romantic*?" he said. "Tower Lane is an avalanche of snow right now. Nobody lives out there. It never gets plowed. And it's after midnight for Chrissakes, what the hell are we going to see?" He slapped her upside the head. "Why so ignorant?"

Julie's eyes welled with tears. She punched the steering wheel, honking the horn.

"You'd better *never*—"

She trailed off, unable to finish. This was the last time Craig Wadleigh would ever touch her. *Ever.* Craig wasn't listening anyway. He was shuffling through the front console, the glove box, and then around the floor at his feet. He looked exhausted. He turned, belched and blew it in her face.

"You forgot my cell phone, too, didn't you?" he said. "God you're worthless." He shivered. Sliding one of his slippered feet into the paper sack the beer had come in, he reclined his seat and crossed his arms. "I better have a warm bathroom when I wake up. Or I'll use you."

Julie blinked. Her gloved hands held tight to the steering wheel.

Within a few minutes Craig was snoring. Whatever woman, or women, he'd been with this evening had sucked him dry.

Perfect.

Julie unzipped the breast pocket of her snow suit and pulled out a small bottle of Gorilla glue.

Thirteen minutes later, Tower Lane appeared exactly how Craig had described it: unplowed with lots of snow. Julie's hatchback didn't have the greatest clearance, but it was all-wheel drive and the snow tires she'd saved for helped immensely with the traction. She figured if she could keep moving, keep forward momentum going, then she should be able to make it to her destination. Her goal was the most secluded area in Pine County. She only needed a few more miles.

The road sign for Tower Lane was difficult to see in the daytime. Even more obscure in the wintry night.

In her excitement, Julie was going too fast and turned too late. Her hatchback hydroplaned across the snow. Sweat popped on her forehead. Julie spun the wheel in the opposite direction. The car shook. She downshifted. Gave it gas. The car swung back in the other direction as the engine leapt to life. She countered that swing, straightened it out and shifted. Brought up speed. A moment later, her little green machine was burrowing through the snow at thirty-five miles per hour.

Craig stirred in the seat next to her. He sat up and rubbed his eyes.

"Sweet move, Colombo," he said. "So we really did travel fifteen miles out of the way to prove I was right. How romantic." He shivered. Staring at the climate control he asked, "Why the hell is the A/C on?"

"Oh, is it?"

The car suddenly jerked and died. Julie's heart crashed into her teeth. They rolled quickly to a stop in the deep snow. Cold January night waited outside their windows. Craig chuckled.

"You *dumb, skanky, worthless....*"

Julie tuned out the remaining insults and cranked the stalled engine.

"You forgot to get gas, didn't you?" he asked.

"It was full," she squeaked. She pumped the gas pedal. *Just a little further. So close.*

"You ran out of gas last month too!"

"Exactly, Craig, don't you think I learned my lesson?"

The engine vibrated to life. Julie swallowed a jagged hunk of fear.

"See? See, everything's fine."

She put the car into first gear and floored it. Oceans of white snow crashed over their windshield.

"What the hell are you doing?" he yelled. "Get us out of here!"

"The pedal's stuck!" Julie lied.

The car fishtailed again and spun sideways. The tires caught and launched them forward—they were thrown into the air momentarily their seatbelts restraining them, but not before Craig nailed his head on the car's ceiling as they jolted to a sudden stop. The front end was buried. She'd hit a drift.

Craig rubbed his head and then slammed his fist into the dashboard almost knocking the cover off the airbag. He ripped Julie's phone from its cable.

"Who are you calling?" she asked. She knew there was no signal out here, but she did *not* need Craig going through her phone.

"Doug," he said.

Julie grabbed her charging cable and slid it into her pocket. She turned the ignition. The engine coughed and hacked. The tank was bone dry. With Craig's attention diverted, Julie dropped the back window halfway behind her seat. She continued to crank the engine. She cranked and cranked until the battery clicked dead. The muted headlights faded pulling them into darkness.

"Gonna tell Disco to bring his tow truck, his derringer and a shovel," Craig said. The cell phone at his ear lit the interior in an eerie glow. "Cuz my wife is a dumb-ass, ignorant … God *damn* it's cold in here!"

Julie worked her door open. With the battery dead the dome light couldn't come on to give her away, but the snow outside the car was deep. She struggled quietly. She almost had it open enough to slither out.

"What the hell is this?" Craig asked. "These messages from Magda. I thought you didn't talk to her anymore."

No! Her text messages! She had forgotten to delete them. Her connection at Bell Cellular would permanently delete all the messages between her and Magda later this week, but that wouldn't help her at all tonight.

Craig's face stared into the blue screen of her phone.

"Grab all the pens so he can't leave any notes."

Julie reached for her phone. Craig palmed her face knocking her glasses off and continued scrolling through Magda's texts messages.

"Pour water on him - make it colder, Jules," he read. "She calls you Jules? What in tarnation are you bitches babbling about?"

Julie ducked away out of Craig's grasp. She unzipped her other breast pocket.

"It's hilarious," she said. "Look, I'll show you."

Craig finally pulled his attention away from Magda's texts. He closed Julie's phone. The second he turned, Julie pepper-sprayed him in the face. She coated his eyes, gritting her teeth. Craig dropped her cell phone and lashed out. His fist knocked her hard in the chest.

Choking through fog, Julie grabbed her phone. Craig screamed.

"AHHHHH! Aghhh, you—fukgahaaaaaaaakkk kkgh kk ... ahhhhhgggh!"

Julie wiggled out into the snow. Frigid wind lashed her face. Her heart thumped madly, her chest was sore but time itself slowed.

Command each moment. Make it count.

Inside the car, Craig continued to scream. He was still a few moves behind as Julie kicked the driver's door closed. She tried to lock the doors with the key fob but the battery was dead and the locks wouldn't respond. She reached through the back window.

Craig must have sensed what she was doing. He flailed wildly with one hand trying to grab her.

Julie ripped her white pack through the half-open window and put it over her shoulders. She'd chosen white for tonight in the hopes that it would camouflage her movements against the snow making it more difficult for Craig to follow her. If it came to that.

A few miles out on the horizon, the silhouette of Walnut Hill beckoned. Julie took off running toward the rendezvous point.

Craig realized something had frozen the latch mechanism on his seatbelt. Some kind of goo had seeped in and sealed it. The release button wouldn't budge. He wiped the remains of the pepper spray from his eyes and sneezed.

"That *frick*ing little…."

He was too large to wiggle out. He grabbed an empty beer can off the floor and smashed it repeatedly into the latch button. After several whacks the belt popped free and retracted.

Craig dove for the driver's door. He pushed out into the snow.

"I'm a coming, girl!" he howled. "You don't *never* ditch me!"

Now that Julie was out in it, things looked and felt a lot different than she had imagined. Dark eerie solitude. Snow clouds. No moon. The wintry night was emitting a strange glow, however, giving her just enough light to see by. She knew what she was doing. She knew where she was going. She just had to get there.

Nonetheless, she could easily be the one left for dead tonight.

Behind her, alcohol surged through Craig Wadleigh's veins, temporarily boosting his short-term endurance. He grunted after her. He could see her up ahead trying to run.

"Gonna git girl!"

He was chasing her down in a chaotic fury. Julie's boots handled the snow better than Craig's Oriental slippers, but each step he took was twice hers. He was close. His huffing was right behind her.

"Gon git! Gon Git! **GIT!**"

In another second she would feel Craig's hands around her neck. There would be no playing this time. He would kill her. A small part of her wanted to give up right there, get the whole thing over, just lie down and die, and cry....

No.

Julie planted her foot and dove off to the left. Cold white blinded her eyes as she hit the snow. Craig hurtled over the top of her, slobbering and ending a shadowy poof a few yards away.

Julie scrambled to her feet. Feeling for the Velcro cord on the side of her pack, she ripped free an industrial can of dog spray repellent. She'd planned non-lethal force tonight so there would be no signs of a struggle. The cold air was lethal enough.

Julie stepped forward. She pointed the nozzle at Craig's shadow in the snow. Squeezing the trigger, she enveloped her ex-husband in a fog of untraceable pain. Julie sprayed and sprayed until the can was empty.

She reattached the empty canister. She felt numb. She never heard Craig's moans. Never heard his defeated screams as he thrashed in pain in the snow. Never heard herself repeating: *"You'll never ever touch me again."*

Dark snow clouds churned in the sky.

Thick white flakes cascaded down.

Julie set off at a brisk pace toward the shadowy mound called Walnut Hill. Her legs felt weary. But somehow with each step she was gaining strength. Blood pumped through her body like never before. The cold air tasted like freedom. She felt invigorated. Alive.

⌣⟶

Julie stumbled around the side of Walnut Hill. She checked her watch. 2:11 a.m. She spotted the silhouette of Magda's Nissan pickup truck parked along the side of the logging trail. Julie gave a cry of joy. She ran toward the truck.

The door opened. Magda jumped out. The two women met in an embrace.

"You made it, girl," Magda said. She had tears in her eyes. Julie looked back once more. No one was coming. No one was behind her.

She *had* made it. *Almost.* As long as Tower Lane didn't get any traffic for the next couple days she was good.

"I know we won't see each other for a while after this," Magda said.

"We'll have time," Julie said. "Come on, let's leave this night behind us."

It was early Tuesday morning when a knock came at Julie's apartment door. Carlos, her little Shih-Tzu, barked furiously. As predicted, the falling snow had continued. All schools and businesses—including Zimmy's Auto Warehouse where Julie worked—had been closed the last two days. She was glad to have a little more time to get her story straight. She felt confident in her alibi.

Still, when Julie peered through the peephole her heart jumped. A man in a smoky bear hat and police uniform stood on her front porch.

She opened the door. It was Sheriff Barnhart. The Sheriff of Pine County. He removed his hat and smiled.

"Morning, Mrs. Wadleigh," he said. "Mind if I come in?"

Sheriff Barnhart sat at the kitchen table while Julie placed a steaming cup of coffee in front of him. The Sheriff nodded and took a sip.

"Much obliged," he said. "Well, we might as well get right into it. We found Craig."

Julie perked up.

"Oh, thank *God*," she declared.

"Found him out on Tower Lane."

"Oh, my. What was he doing out there? Where is he?"

Sheriff Barnhart dropped his head.

"He's okay, isn't he?" Julie asked. Barnhart shook his head. Julie pulled a hand to her chest.

"No, Julie, he isn't."

She allowed her lip to tremble. Her eyes filled with crocodile tears.

"Your husband froze to death," Barnhart continued. "We don't know exactly *what* happened or why he was out there. Looks like he'd gotten in a wreck. We're working out a few theories. I'd like to ask you some questions. But before that, let me be the first to say I am very, very sorry for your loss."

Julie let herself go. For her answered prayers she bawled tears of joy. Sheriff Barnhart patted her shaking hands and allowed her to finish. She jerked a few tissues from the Kleenex box on the table and padded her face.

"He must have taken my car Sunday night," she said. "I hadn't seen him since that afternoon I visited Ms. Shaw. I—I usually walk to her place to save gas, you know, and then I'll often stay the night with her."

"You're an angel to look after the widow Shaw," Barnhart said. "She sleeps so much anymore it's probably the most boring job in the world, isn't it? Yes, I agree. Craig must have taken your hatchback. I know his license is revoked, and the last thing I want to do is speak poorly of the dead. Anyway, we found him, Julie."

On Friday afternoon, a day after the small funeral for Craig Wadleigh, Sheriff Barnhart again knocked on her door. Julie scooted Carlos out of the way and opened it.

"May I come in?"

"Of course, Sheriff," she said. "I have a pot of fresh coffee."

After getting them both a cup, they sat at the kitchen table. Barnhart seemed more business today than he did earlier in the week.

"We found some things," he said. Julie nodded and sipped her coffee. Barnhart eyed her intently. "Listen, I know that you and Craig were high school sweethearts and that you loved each other very much."

"Yes," she said.

"I also know," Barnhart continued, "that Craig used to frequent the Dojo in Crane Mills. Have you ever heard of it?"

"He was taking karate lessons there," Julie said. "I'd picked him up once or twice. But he hadn't been there in a while."

"Do you know any other rumors about that place?"

Julie masked her face in simple innocence. Eyes wide, she shook her head no.

"Well," Sheriff Barnhart said, "we also know that he was having an affair with Magdalena Pryce. Do you know the woman?"

"Mag-Da-Lena?" Julie said, as if sounding it out for the first time. "It sounds familiar. Maybe I met her once?"

"We recovered her red-rimmed glasses and her pillow from your car."

"From *my* car?"

"Yes," Barnhart said. "It looks as though they were together that night. We couldn't locate any other tire tracks in the area with all the snow that had fallen. But all signs point to them being together."

"On Tower Lane?" she asked. Barnhart nodded. "Sheriff, this is too much. I don't know how—"

"Don't you worry, Julie," Sheriff Barnhart said. "We've got Ms. Pryce down at the station. She's not saying anything. But she will. She's an adulteress. She's cuckolded men before and gotten away with it, used every excuse in the book to make herself look clean. She's a home wrecker. My gut tells me it's her. And I ain't never wrong. With the evidence we've got this case is a slam dunk."

Julie brought a hand to her mouth.

"Don't you worry, Julie," Barnhart said again. "Look at me. Justice will be served."

Julie Foster's face showed surprise like never before. Now she would give her greatest performance.

THE END

'Three-Flat Storm'

Sam Watters tossed his backpack into a corner—a corner only big enough for a backpack. Last week he'd turned thirty-four. He was tired. Tired of working as a server. Tired of chasing around incompetent managers and waiting on customers with zero manners. This week had really kicked his butt. He needed a new job.

Dang it's humid.

"Why are all the windows closed?"

"Storm's coming in," said Linda. His girlfriend had her back to him at the kitchen counter. She was still in her fuzzy pink bathrobe and slippers.

"There *is* such a thing as heat exhaustion," Sam said. Linda didn't reply. He needed air. "I'm opening a window."

Linda was pounding garlic with a small hammer and peeling off the skins.

"Don't," she said. "It's raining."

"It *was* raining. And then it stopped."

"I don't want it coming in."

"It probably won't even rain again."

"Wanna bet five bucks?"

"I don't have five bucks," Sam said.

He opened the kitchen window. A healthy breeze swept in. Sam closed his eyes as his thirsty pores gorged themselves upon the cool air. He indulged a minute longer and then plopped down on the couch. The couch took up half the living room. Half the living room was in the kitchen. *Garden Apartment. Ha! What a shameless marketing tool.*

"Sam come *on*," Linda said. "I don't want our stuff getting wet."

"How will our stuff get wet if it's not raining, Linda?"

Sam kicked off his work shoes and stretched out his legs. *So so nice.* Aside from getting naked with Linda if he didn't move for the rest of the evening he'd be a fully content man.

"I checked the Doppler on my Android," Linda said. "Looks pretty bad."

"That smart phone is smarter than you are."

"Har *har.*"

A knock came at the front door. Sam and Linda looked at each other. Strange, even for a Friday afternoon. They'd become fairly reclusive people in their mid-thirties and the few friends they did have always called before stopping by.

Linda lingered just long enough for Sam to hoist himself off the couch with a groan. He shuffled across the floor to the front door. Actually, it was a side door—a side door that opened into the basement, or Garden Apartment, of the vintage three-flat building they rented. The only other door was along the back wall in the kitchen that connected to the laundry area used by all three floors of tenants. Sam opened the door.

"*Allô!*"

A smiling woman with long, carefree hair stood outside. Her orange summer dress swayed in the growing breeze. She looked familiar.

"Uh, hi."

"We live zee Penthouse," the woman said, "and were wondering if, ahhh...."

Penthouse? Sam wondered.

A man came down the stone steps behind the woman and put his arm around her waist. He was a good-looking guy in a white button-down shirt and a purple paisley tie. He also seemed vaguely familiar.

"We live upstairs, on the third floor," the man said. He offered his hand. "Hi, I'm George Patrick."

"Sam Watters."

"I am Ambrosia," the lady in the orange dress said, extending her hand. "Eetz very nice to meet you."

"Ambrosia?" Sam repeated.

She nodded, sweet as the sun. *"Oui, c'est moi!"*

"We were wondering," said George, "if the storm gets bad enough if y'all don't mind us shacking up down here till it passes?"

"Yeah, no problem," Sam said. "Just knock on the back door. If we're dead, break it down."

"Cool, thanks."

"Wonderful to meet you," Ambrosia said. "Hope *not* to see you later, only in meaning—"

"Likewise," Sam winked.

He closed the door, paused, and then ambled back into the living room/kitchen. Linda looked up from her stove.

"Who was that?" she asked.

"Upstairs neighbors," Sam said. "Guess you're not the only one who thinks we've got a whopper coming."

"Airheads."

"They wanna hole up down here if the storm gets too bad."

"You offered our place?"

"Yeah, what's the big deal?"

"I'm not a big fan of them. You know that."

"Why? What have they ever done to you?"

Linda shot him the stink eye.

"Those two idiot children that live right above us? Really?"

"No," Sam said. "In zee *Penthouse*." It made him grin to say it. Although Sam had never seen the top floor of their three-flat, it was surely nice. George and Ambrosia paid $2,200 a month to rent it. That much he did know. The second floor rented for $1,600 a month. And their little Garden Apartment went for 800 American dollars each and every month. It was the cheapest place they could find in this slightly upscale neighborhood of Lakeview.

He slid his arms around Linda. He nibbled her neck, allowing himself a moment in her Victoria's Secret *Rapture* perfume. Linda shuddered. She twisted clear.

"Stop it," she said. She was stirring in her saucepan, trying not to smile. "I need to get dinner done."

"Zee *Pent*house, baby."

"What the hell are you even talking about?"

"The people on the top floor," Sam said. He bent and stretched his tight hamstrings. "George and Ambrosia. *Zee leetle French maid.*"

"You're so gay."

"Hey, you're not supposed to say that anymore. It's offensive to some people."

"Oh shut up," Linda said. "I thought you were talking about the couple right above us. The second floor."

"Oh *hell* no," Sam said.

He came up behind her again. He set his chin on her shoulder and watched her stir the simmering garlic, mushrooms and olive oil. Fascinating, delectable art. He loved watching his girl cook.

The lights went out.

The refrigerator's compressor hummed down to a stop.

In an instant, their apartment was thrust into dusk. The only light was the blue flames dancing under the skillet. Sam went to the window and closed it. Dark skies swirled outside. Drops of rain began pelting the windows like birdshot. There was still enough light in their apartment for Sam to smirk at Linda as if to say: *All right, I owe you five bucks.*

"I'll light some candles," he said. He shuffled into their bedroom. *It might add to the atmosphere. Lordy be, it's been a helluva week.* If Linda could finish cooking, then eating a great meal, getting comfortable and listening to the storm rage safely outside actually didn't sound too bad.

From their bedroom, Sam grabbed the large vanilla candle with three wicks. He lit all three and set it on the kitchen table. The only other candle he could find was a half-used tea light. He placed that one on the floor speaker by their TV. Neither candle gave much light.

"Are these all we have?" he asked. Regardless of how Linda answered he was sitting his butt down on the couch and that was that.

Linda didn't answer. She killed the stove and pulled two new candles out from the bottom cupboard.

A knock came at the back door in the kitchen. Linda was closest, but she busied herself trying to get the other two candles lit. Sam moaned as he pulled himself off the couch, shuffled to the back door and retracted the dead bolt.

"Bonjour Sam."

It was Ambrosia. Behind her, George stood tall and smiling although his face showed worry.

"Come on in," Sam said. He opened the door, allowing their guests access to their tiny kitchen.

"Hope your offer still stands," George said. Sam nodded. "One of our windows got blown out up there."

"Jesus, yes of course," said Sam. "Watch your head." George was close to their 6'6" ceiling. He'd be all right as long as he didn't jump or stand on his tiptoes. "Are you guys all right?"

"Yes, fine," George said quickly. "Felt like the proper time to come down."

"Ooo lá *lá*," Ambrosia said. "Zomething smells good." Linda and Ambrosia touched cheeks. Sam knew Linda was probably feeling embarrassed for being caught in her bathrobe and slippers.

"Nice to see you again," Linda said. "Make yourselves at home. I'm going to change into something more appropriate." *Yep, she's embarrassed.*

"Can I get either of you a glass of red wine?" Sam asked. Their guests said thank you. Hopefully this storm would soon pass. He didn't mind helping his neighbors, but more than anything tonight he wanted peace and quiet with Linda. "What do you do, George?"

"I'm a Legal Associate at *Harris, Bell and Lloyd*," George said.

"Is that on LaSalle?"

"It is."

"I might have bartended there once at an after-hours party," Sam said.

"You know what?" George said. "I think I remember seeing you."

Another knock came at the back door. Sam unlocked it again.

Standing outside in the laundry area was the second floor couple. The *annoying* couple. The couple that lived right above them. The guy and the gal stood with agitated expressions on their faces. They were entitled Millenials in their mid-twenties—privileged above their means—or at least that's how Sam and Linda imagined them. To be fair, he didn't really know them. Only what he could glean through the un-insulated floorboards, which, in retrospect, was quite a bit.

"Good evening," Sam said.

"Hullo," said the guy. He was wearing a pink Izod shirt with the collar turned up. "I'm Gary. We live on the main floor. Mind if we stay down here in the laundry room until this thing is over?"

"Knock yourself out," Sam said. "Let us know if you need anything."

He started to close the door, but Linda elbowed him out of the way.

"Good grief, Sam, let them in," she said. "You guys don't have to wait out here."

"Yeah, that's what I meant," said Sam. *Jesus, Linda,* you're *the one who said how much they irritated you!*

Gary moped in. His blonde girlfriend scuttled in behind him. She kept her eyes on the floor as if she were afraid someone might see her down here.

"We have a lantern," the girl mumbled. She was wearing hot pants and a neon green Zumba shirt. Sam grinned. He couldn't help it. She had one of those bodies that would never be fit, no matter how many *Buns of Steel* classes she took, no matter how athletic she tried to dress. She was a woman who would always have fat ankles.

"Thanks," Sam said. He took the lantern and set it on the kitchen table. "That'll help."

"I'm Rebecca," the girl said.

"Sam."

"Linda."

"George."

"Ambrosia."

Bunched together in the tiny kitchen, everyone's sweaty faces glanced awkwardly. It was close quarters. The Garden Apartment was getting humid again. They couldn't open any of the windows due to the rain, and they couldn't turn on their fans because they had no power.

"Relax and get comfortable," Sam said. He marched over and took the best seat on the couch. The three women stayed at the table. George joined Sam on the couch, while Gary sat in the broken beige recliner, the only other available seat.

"Glass of wine?" Sam asked. Gary shrugged.

"Sure."

"You don't have to."

"I'll pass then," Gary said. "I'm not a big wine guy."

"What's your poison, then?" George asked.

"Belvedere rocks," Gary said.

"Well, I don't have *Belvedere*," Sam said. "Only Smirnoff."

"*Smirnoff?*"

"It was good enough for James Bond, wasn't it?"

"I thought Bond drank Stolichnaya," George said.

"Whatever it was he drank it shaken, not stirred," Sam said.

"It's stupid to stir a Vodka Martini," said Gary. "You only stir Gin Martinis. It bruises the Gin if you shake it."

"A Kiddie Cocktail, then?" Sam asked.

Gary shook his head.

"Green River? Shirley Temple?"

At the kitchen table the conversation wasn't much better. The candles and the lantern dressed the ladies' faces in an unfriendly glow.

"Sorry I'm not dressed," Linda said. She had changed from her robe into her pajamas. A slight improvement. "Had a long shift at the Pub last night. They offered me the cut today so I took it."

"May I ask where you work?" said Ambrosia.

"Mickey Finn's Irish Pub."

"Oh, I've been there before," Rebecca said. She sipped the wine Linda had poured for her and scrunched her face. "I found a hair in my food. Had to send it back."

"Really?" asked Linda.

"Yes, it was disgusting."

"Our chefs are usually super conscious."

"Sorry," Rebecca said. "It was disgusting."

BOOM! A mega clap of thunder made everyone jump.

"Whoa," Sam said. "That sounded pretty close."

"I don't like this," whined Rebecca. Gary got up, walked to the table and draped his arm around his girlfriend. He whispered in her ear. "I don't care," she said. "I don't like this at all."

"Everything all right?" Linda asked.

"No," Rebecca said, standing up. "I don't want to be down here anymore."

Sam turned his palms up and grinned. *Don't let the door hit ya in the ass on the way out!* The phrase nearly jumped out of his mouth.

"This is probably the safest place," he said instead.

"It's too muggy," Rebecca said. "This basement is making me claustrophobic."

"You certainly don't have to stay down here," said Linda. "The storm will probably pass soon anyway."

"This place is so tiny," Rebecca whined. She looked like she was ready to have a seizure. "How do you even *live* down here? And by the way, you all play your music too loud. Way too loud."

"I'm sorry?"

"It's really annoying."

"We'll try to keep it down from now on," Linda said. She glanced at Sam. "Thanks for letting us know."

"Please do."

Sam couldn't take it any longer.

"We hear a lot of what goes on upstairs, too," he said. "We hear a *lot of it* down here."

"It would have been nice if Rudy Crider had installed floor insulation," George said. Rudy was their landlord.

"Well, he didn't," Gary said.

"Too bad," said Sam. "It's hard to mute your five-minute sex-capades."

Another big flash out the window. Sonic **BOOM!**

"*Jesus,*" Linda breathed. "That sounded *really* close."

George laughed. "Five minutes, huh?"

"Sometimes six and a half," Sam replied.

"Fuck you," said Gary.

"Would we have any time to enjoy it?"

A large rumble of thunder shook the building. The storm seemed right on top of them.

"Come on, babe," Rebecca said. "We don't have to stay down here with these lowlife Gen X'ers. You're a bunch of sick degenerates."

"I'm considered Generation X?" George said. He smiled at Ambrosia. "Sweet!"

Rebecca took the lantern off the kitchen table. She opened the back door and she and Gary walked out.

"Enjoy the rest of your night," Sam called behind them. He got up, walked to the back door and started to pull it closed.

POOM!

"*Aaaggghhh!*"

Sam went down. He heard himself scream. At the same time he heard glass shatter up the concrete stairwell.

"Help!"

It was Gary's voice.

Linda helped Sam up. He sprinted up the stairs. Ambrosia and George were close behind. But Sam got there first. And what he saw made some of his hair turn white.

Rebecca, the young Millennial who lived upstairs, stood stiff as a board. She turned. Sam felt himself shrink as she stared him down. Rebecca looked crazed, haunted. The window behind her was shattered. Rain was streaming in.

Rebecca turned to Gary and then back to Sam.

"Souls," she hissed. *"I want your souls you horrid sinners! Back off! Get back! Want them now! Get back!"*

Gary shrunk back into himself the way Sam had moments before. Rebecca drew her hands to her face. She began to cry. Gary paused. He inched forward and took her in his arms.

Behind them, George said:

"Ambulance is on the way."

Sam turned and watched George slide his cell phone back into his pants pocket. Linda grabbed him by the shoulders.

"Are you okay?" she asked.

"I'm not sure," Sam said. "I need to sit down. I'm not sure."

"She *spoke* to you?" Linda asked. The large vanilla candle flickered next to her. Sam sipped his warm beer.

"Yeah, it was creepy," he said. He still wasn't sure what had happened. He had a small streak of white hair on the right side of his head. They wouldn't discover it until tomorrow morning. His heart was finally calming. "You didn't hear her? It was like supernatural possession or something."

"All I heard was that Rebecca girl crying," said Linda. "All I saw was the broken window behind her. I never heard her say a word."

Sam took a long slug of beer and shook his head. He heard the ambulance outside. He listened to its siren getting quieter and quieter until it was gone.

"Ridiculous," he said.

The thunder and lighting had stopped. The rain continued to fall in a steady shower. It sounded soothing outside their windows.

Just then the fluorescent ceiling lights flickered on. The refrigerator's compressor kicked on and began to hum. Power had returned.

"I guess things aren't so bad," he said.

Linda dropped her head a little and looked at him. Her eyes looked like little elf eyes when she did that. So cute.

"Be thankful," she said. "We got the world right here, baby."

Sam was grateful. He was. Absolutely. Grateful, ready and willing to work for more, but at the moment ready to enjoy some rest and relaxation.

"We did our good deed for the year," he said.

"Wanna go lay down?" Linda asked.

Sam set his beer bottle on the end table.

"Uhh, *yeah!*"

They kissed. After blowing out the candles, Sam tiptoed after her toward the bedroom. He could relax afterward.

Just before he turned out the lights in the living room, the power died again. He slammed his big toe into the bookcase. Stubbed it badly. Sam yelled and hopped around in the darkness, trying not to bump into anything else. Linda challenged herself not to laugh and lost.

THE END

'Humble Surprises'

⌒

T<small>HIS AFTERNOON WE'RE ENTERTAINING SOME</small> old friends with a late lunch and then tea. Our guests seem intrigued when, at their request, I say I *will* recount the events of our infamous afternoon at the G-Force Amusement Park. Some people have heard bits and pieces. Tiffany and I haven't spoken about it since counseling.

Franklin, Gertie and Liz lean forward on the couch. With a glance at Tiff who nods, I close my eyes and begin to rehash the events of that fateful vacation day.

"Okay, here goes."

⌒

I felt like puking. My stomach was over the side. It was a warm sunny day, and of course the Ferris wheel has to stop with our passenger car at the top. My girl and me. Tiffany and Terry. Fiancés Extraordinaire.

As you know, we're not the flashiest of couples. I'll admit, we might seem a little mismatched at first glance: me, shorter and fiery with black hair; and Tiff with her fairer complexion and reflection. She's always been the golden apple of my eye. But when we argue people realize a bomb has been lit. The smart ones duck.

That day we were really broken. My heart lay in Death Valley.

"You bold-faced lied," I croaked.

Tiffany looked away. She was wearing the teal sun dress spotted with seashells I had bought for her thirty-fourth birthday.

"Look baby," she said, holding my hand. I *let* her hold it. I made sure to slide my promise band into her warm fingers. I really wanted to slap her though. Or at least flick the end of her nose. "Can we *please* just let this go, whatever it is?" she asks. "You're not totally innocent either."

"Chris told me about Frank Ackerman," I said. My throat was so parched it hurt to swallow. I had to take a moment as we were hanging there in the air. "The night we proposed to each other you went down on that jerk? You went *down* on him? Don't look at me!"

"I made a mistake."

I took my hand back, managing to swallow a little saliva.

"Got one in before the bell," I said. "Classy. Real nice. What'd he do? Loosen up those long legs of yours with his hand-crafted moon-shine and his Turkish cigarettes? His greasy chest hair?"

I felt awful. Tiff was ready to uncork a tsunami of tears. I love her, damn it, and I hated seeing her like this, but I hated *feeling* like this even more. And I wouldn't any longer.

Meanwhile in the distance, a sparkling red rollercoaster plunged down a monstrous hill. Peoples' hands in the air. Screams of joy. We loved amusement parks. Especially Ferris wheels. This should have been such an epic day. *Had I always been this naïve?*

I took some air into my lungs and let it out in a shaky rasp. For a while now I kinda suspected you know? But, hell, I'd take Tiff's word over any hearsay, any rumor at all.

Maybe we shouldn't have been intimate. Tiff swore it would only make us stronger. It only made my heart more vulnerable.

Our car jolted. I'd forgotten we were suspended in the air. We grabbed onto the chrome safety bar as the Ferris wheel jerked to life and slowly began to descend.

"Sweetkins," Tiff said, wiping her eyes. "We had such a wonderful time last night. We have two more days of vacation—can we *please* try to enjoy them? Wasn't last night a beautiful experience?"

As we approached the bottom my emotions were really rocking and rolling. The old man in the brown vest who'd helped us onto the Ferris wheel put a hand out to steady our car. He unlatched our safety bar with a smile.

"Please don't hate me," Tiff said.

"I hate that you ate me out."

The old man appeared shocked, but, like I said, when Tiff and I get into it back the hell out.

"H-hope you had a pleasant ride, ladies," he said, offering his hand. I was closest and I took it. He helped me off the Ferris wheel. Tiffany helped herself off. She stormed down the wooden ramp, arms tight across her chest, her blonde hair and teal dress flowing behind her. She stopped halfway to wait for me. I shook my head. *Oh girl, I have not yet begun to fight.*

"What are you doing later?" I asked the old man in the brown vest. His face showed surprise. Then his brow crinkled. "Wanna have some fun? We could sneak off into the bushes right now."

"Sorry, Miss," he said. "I'm probably twice your—"

I slapped him. Hard. Wide-eyed and in shock, the old man brought a dark-veined hand to his pink cheek. I could tell he wouldn't retaliate. I didn't really *mean* to hit him, I just....

"Bravo!" I said. What a world-class jerk I was. I hated Tiffany. I hated myself. I hated the world and everyone in it.

Halfway down the ramp, Tiff closed her eyes. I could see her shoulders quivering.

"That's assault," said a nearby man who had noticed our little scene. The man was balding and wearing a Bermuda-style golf shirt with a nametag that read: **William Watkins** ~ *Fun Zone* ~ *Manager*.

"Whatever," I said.

"I'm serious as a heart attack, Miss," Watkins said. "Assault and battery. Stay right here." Watkins turned to the old man. "Mr. Parker?" he asked. "Would you like to file charges against this young woman?"

Mr. Parker slowly shook his head. His look of surprise had morphed into a twinkle of amusement. He looked like such a sweet old man. Nicely-trimmed beard. Like my Grandpa. I was really hoping he wouldn't do anything.

I spotted the blue-pressed uniforms and the shiny handguns before I even turned my head. A policeman and a policewoman with fixed, determined stares were clacking up the ramp straight for me. Tiff stood at the bottom. Waiting patiently nearby were three men in beige suits and silver badges. My heart froze. I was petrified. *What in Mother Earth is the matter with me?*

"Good day, gentlemen," Watkins said. He stepped down with a smug grin to greet the forces of authority. I wanted so badly to close my eyes. I knew I was being arrested.

The cops stepped past Watkins. He looked astonished. They walked past me and stopped in front of the old man in the brown vest.

"Mr. Parker?" said the Policewoman.

"Yes?"

"No relation to a—"

The old man twitched. He eyed the two officers with growing anxiety.

"Buzz Getty?"

It was the male officer who finished his partner's question.

The old man suddenly made a slow run for it. The cops apprehended him easily. Old man Getty snarled as they marched him back toward Watkins, the Fun Manager. But before they could handcuff him, Getty slipped a hand inside his vest pocket and clicked out a switchblade.

"I'll gut your ass, motherfucka! I'll gut your ass!"

The policewoman sidestepped Getty's attack and secured his wrist. The male cop grabbed his other wrist, put a hand to Getty's shoulder and cranked him down to the platform until he gave up the blade. They jerked him up and slapped the cuffs on him.

Meanwhile, the plainclothes men in badges ran up and flipped out their credentials. One agent in a crew cut stepped up.

"Buzz Getty. This is the F.B.I. You're under arrest for the drowning deaths of Kenneth Martin and Mrs. Louise Rasmussen, in addition to multitudes of other charges of which I'm sure you're aware. You know the drill. You have the right to remain silent. Anything you do or say can and *will* be used against you in a court of law."

Getty issued an evil grin. He looked nothing like the sweet old man moments before. As the entourage guided him down the wooden ramp, I heard him cackling.

"I'll take the fifth boys, get my lawyer on the phone and tell him to break out the Johnny Walker Blue. *Heh heh.* A special occasion. Grand times … Grand old times…."

The agents stepped Getty past Tiffany who was bent over the railing backward in horror. A crowd of people had also gathered. A young Asian man snapped a few pictures with his smart phone. Behind us, a lady screamed to be let off. There were still passengers stuck on the Ferris wheel.

I couldn't say a thing. The manager, William Watkins, also stood silent. Then, as if he finally accepted the situation, he straightened up, trudged over and took up the controls to the wheel. Reluctantly he turned to me.

"I still want you both out of here."

"Deal," I croaked. My throat was drier than a desert bone.

I quickly joined Tiff at the bottom. She was red-eyed and shaking. I felt pretty terrified, too. I hooked my arm in hers. We walked silently through the G-Force Amusement Park toward our hotel, The Sands, hardly conscious of the commotion, the laughter, and the shrieks of delight.

"I'm sorry," Tiffany finally said.

"Me too, baby."

⟨⟩

Our three guests sit back and take a quick look at each other. They return their surprised faces to me.

"Wow, Terry," says Franklin.

"Geez," says Liz.

"Quite a tale," Gertie says, sipping her chamomile tea.

Tiff's dimples sparkle.

I clear my throat and say, "So, after we get back to our hotel room, I find out Tiffany was only testing me. She was trying to get *me* to confess to something. She'd put Chris up to it. She gave him a line to feed me about her and Frank to see if I would take the bait or come clean. She never did anything."

I swallow thinking back to Buzz Getty—the old Dutch-Shultz mobster with a sincere desire to go straight—and how differently things could have ended that day at the G-Force Amusement Park. Counseling has stilled some demons. I can already tell that talking about it this afternoon has helped too.

"Tiff never did anything," I repeat. "Neither have I. And you saw the thing on the news with Getty. In the end, I guess it was a seminal step in learning to control my anger."

"It was a good lesson for both of us," Tiff says.

Our guests exhale collectively.

"So anyway," I say. "You know we got hitched last month."

"Here! Here!" says Gertie, toasting us.

"Thank you," I say. "Thank you, and thank you to our state for coming around on marriage equality. It's been a very humbling experience."

THE END

'A Slight Misunderstanding'

⟶

THE MISSION END OF THE shotgun quivered. Lisa May Hudson held tight to the 12 gauge as she stared down with rage at her enemy. Sweat glistened on her sleeveless forearms. Crickets chirped nearby in the night.

"You son of a bitch," she snarled. "Now you get what you gave my husband." The man on the ground, Cullen Morgenstern, stared up at her with a bloody nose. A car passed over the bridge they were under. "How *dare* you, sir."

"Mrs. Hudson, you've got it all wrong," Cullen said. He wiped his nose on the sleeve of his green dress shirt. It smeared a dark stain. "Benny was my friend, my *compadre*; I was only trying to help you guys."

"Do you smoke?" she asked.

Cullen swallowed hard, sweat running down his face as he stared into the gun barrel.

"Whenever I'm stressed out," he said. "Sure."

"This is your last chance," Lisa May said. She tossed her pack of Newports at him. The cigarette pack hit Cullen in the chest and fell to the ground. He didn't even notice it. "My husband completed that entire job for you," she said. "He did it well. Maybe it wasn't the most pleasant work in the world, but maybe that's why you weren't man enough to do it."

"No, *no*," Cullen pleaded. After Lisa May had bashed him in the nose with the butt of the gun, Cullen thought she might leave it at that. Now it felt like she might actually pull the trigger. "I loved Benny! I paid him well *very* well!"

Lisa May pulled the checkered forearm of the shotgun back just enough to ensure a round of magnum buckshot was chambered.

"Mrs. Hudson, you're absolutely right," Cullen said. "I paid your husband for work I couldn't do myself. But that doesn't mean I thought any *less* of him. Benny started hanging out with some shady contractors. He was getting into some bad stuff. I also heard he was going behind your back, and I just—"

"Good-night," she said.

Cullen glared at her. Their eyes locked. Tears slid out of Lisa May's swollen red sockets as she clicked off the safety.

"And after you're gone...." More tears slid down her cheeks. "'Cause there's no meaning here without my love."

"It wasn't me!"

Lisa May covered Cullen's face with the bead sight at the end of the barrel.

"*No!*"

She squeezed the trigger. The shotgun blasted backward, startling her with its kick and astonishing her with the bloody explosion it caused. Cullen Morgenstern's headless body flopped to the ground. Blood squirted from his ragged stump of neck. He was dead. She had killed him. She had killed a worthless back-stabber who loved rubbing your shoulders, pilfering your pockets, and selling you out to ... whomever.

There was no time for happiness or regret. Only an instantaneous sense of justice for her late husband, Benny Hudson.

Cullen's head was all over the ground. He was a dead man. He realized he was dead. Nevertheless, what he couldn't understand was how he was able to continue to glare back up into the eyes of Lisa May Hudson. How was he able to *think? And how could Lisa May think I would have wanted to hurt them?*

Lisa May pulled the pump back and ejected the spent shell. She pushed it forward, chambering a fresh round.

"God, I know you're up there," she said. "Please forgive me."

She placed the butt of the shotgun on the crumbled asphalt with the barrel pointing up. She opened her mouth and slid it over the end. Reaching down, she put her finger against the trigger. Her final memory was not of Benny, of his quietly withdrawn face and beautiful pouty lips, but of that bastard Cullen Morgenstern reflecting her own hatred with his defiant eyes.

The buckshot blew her head apart. Her lifeless body slapped to the asphalt. The shotgun skidded off into the night.

Lisa May Hudson was dead. She *knew* she was dead. Nonetheless, if she and Cullen were both really dead, then how could they continue to defy each other? *How* were they still staring at one another after what just happened?

Because they were.

It made no sense.

Cullen's face moved. His eyes blinked. He smelled burnt gunpowder. He heard crickets chirping in the night.

Lisa May's face relaxed. She inhaled the night air. She listened to the crickets and the frogs calling to one another, heard the cars passing over the bridge. No longer did she feel anger or rage.

Was Cullen smiling at her? For some reason she felt like a teenager again. She felt giddy like she'd just gotten her driver's license. *How on Earth is this possible?* This man—this odious man she had just murdered—was now beginning to attract her? It was an idea she could have *never* entertained. But here it was. Cullen Morgenstern: her soul mate.

"I told you I was sorry," Cullen finally said. He floated off the ground and onto his feet, head attached as if nothing had happened. Lisa May was also standing. She felt detached from her feet and outside her body. She found herself smiling.

From beyond drifted a most wondrous scent: an indescribable aroma that elevated their awareness and lifted them. Cullen understood. He realized how Lisa May had come to believe that he'd ripped them off and *not* paid Benny for the beautiful work he'd done in Cullen's bathroom: the two oval sinks, the soapstone bathtub, the light fixtures, the linoleum flooring. No. Benny Hudson's money had gone elsewhere. Lisa May understood that now, too.

But who cared for those cheap earthly frills?

Lisa May had ended their mundane lives. She'd freed them from bondage! They had vision, they had focus, they had energy beyond anything on earth. In a flash, they knew it all. It was all divine. Her torn blue jeans and ripped sleeveless shirt was replaced by pure light. Every particle of her gleamed.

They didn't need voices or words. It was clear communication transferring directly.

Cullen: You're everything to me, Lisa May. Know this now; we will always be together.

Lisa May: Of course we will, silly man!

Cullen: Benny Hudson was unfaithful to you. As Cullen Morgenstern, yes, I participated in unpleasant dealings in my former life, things I am not proud of, but never once did I harm you or your late husband.

They were letting themselves go completely. They didn't laugh. They didn't smile. They were above any sensory reactions.

Lisa May: I know, my love. I was no angel either. But isn't this just an irrelevant memory? We must be in *heaven*.

Come. Don't look back, Cullen. Fly with me!

Off they soared through the stratosphere.

⌣⟶

Things happened in the smallest flicker. Lisa May wanted to experience a full family. She and Benny never had any children. In this afterlife, she bonded to Cullen and they had progeny surpassing any Happy Family label from their previous lives. It was beyond fulfilling. It was joy absolute.

Cullen wanted to indulge in the cosmos. They sailed through space and time more beautiful than a million earthly dreams of paradise. He understood the universe. How it came to be. He comprehended most everything.

The colors! Different shades of harmony!

Listen! Chords of creation! Timeless composition!

Let's go back to our old life. We need to experience it one last time together.

They returned to Earth and lived a thousand lifetimes together. Everything lasted so long and seemed to take so little *time.* Eternity was at their fingertips. Perpetual rapture.

"Forever as one."

DING!

It sounded and felt like a distant chime. It echoed down through their minds and into their bodies. It seemed to have come from somewhere higher.

"I'm not exactly happy," Lisa May finally said.

Cullen Morgenstern pursed his lips.

"I know," he said. His eyes dropped. He noticed the crumbled asphalt at his feet. It felt as if they were both awaking from the same dream.

"We've done some terrible things," she said.

"I remember them, too."

Cullen watched the beams of light fade back into his black wing-tip shoes. Lisa May regarded her sweat-glistened forearms with disgust. She laughed. She was trying to minimize the seriousness of the situation, but she felt revolted by herself. Sickened even.

"We all make mistakes, Lisa May."

The voice echoed down. The voice was knowledge.

Their newfound knowledge was regret.

It trickled into their bodies. Tragedy bloomed as if someone had played an unfortunate message on an answering machine from long ago.

They knew their sins. Felt the constraints of their flesh. Clothing peeled away from their bodies. Cullen's cheeks sank in and turned gray. Lisa May's skin withered. The scent of fresh earth filled the air.

It was real.

They were back under the bridge where their dirty deal had gone down. Cullen watched a toad hop past his feet. He shivered in the night air. He listened to a semi truck barreling across the overpass.

"Baby?" said Lisa May. Cullen couldn't answer. He was shrinking. Lisa May spotted her parents and called out to them: "Mom! Dad! Over here!" Horrified, she drew back. They were not her parents. Only two toads hopping by in the night.

She began to lose form, to shrivel. Her back cracked and broke in indescribable pain, but she no longer had a voice to cry out with. Everything was incinerating inside her. Painful ash, caving in.

Tall blades of grass swayed darkly in the breeze. With silent screams they were on their bellies. One long belly, in fact.

Nightcrawlers.

Long, fat earthworms and they needed moisture. Their lives depended on it. With all their might, they inched toward the wetness of a nearby puddle. *Desperate.*

The two toads sat hungry. They were very hungry. They were patient. Few flies and mosquitoes were buzzing around this evening as the breeze was keeping them away. Basic stimulus churned the toads' stomachs. It fed their minds the notion that they'd eat anything tonight, whether flying or slithering across the ground.

THE END

'ALWAYS NEVER'

I'M TWELVE GOING ON EIGHTEEN. But tonight, I'm acting the nerd sixth-grader playing this murder mystery game on the computer called *Misty Creek Affair*.

It's Friday night. School's done for the week. I'm staying at my good buddy Nick Hammond's house, and wouldn't you know his folks are out of town for the evening. Imagine that.

This fall we'll be teenagers. My grades may have slipped a bit this year, but you know what? I'm tired of studying. I'm ready to have some fun. Summer vacation is literally around the corner.

Besides, it's a perfect night. This computer game is awesome. I've never played something so interactive before. It's like we're taking part in our own play. I've never had a computer. Or a ColecoVision. *Or* an Intellivision. *Or* a Nintendo. *Or* a Sega. Only an Atari 2600. And it's always been good enough for me.

Also here tonight is Nick's older sister, Kelly, and Kelly's friend Gabby Faustmann. Gabby's wearing a black turtleneck and Kelly's rocking out her faded jeans with rips in the knees. Nick's in his Ron Jon surf shirt with his usual hairstyle: spiked in the front, permed in the back. And I'm jamming in my *Bo Knows Diddley* tank top with my favorite blue Spandex shorts.

We're cool. We know it.

So anyway, *Misty Creek Affair*. I'm operating the joystick, moving our character Lillian Brooks around the screen while Kelly types the commands. She tells Lillian what to do—*Pick up the shovel; Look at the*

candelabra; Talk to Rogers, the Butler—and the game shows us and tells us what Lillian sees and hears.

Aside from *Misty Creek*, Nick and I are still in disbelief. Turns out Gabby Faustmann has the hots for Nick. *What?* And Nick's sister—the one and only Kelly Hammond—thinks *I'm* cute? *What-the-Whaaaaat?* She's like three grades in front of me! Insane. Completely insane. But it's also bad to the bone.

We're playing the game on Kelly's computer in her room. I glance at her Michael Damian calendar. It's May 5th, 1989.

"1990 next year," I say.

"Unbelievable," Kelly says.

"So why computers?"

"They're the future," she says. "We'll be in virtual reality in ten years. You'll actually live your life inside a game. You'll date people, work, marry, travel the world, live, die, everything."

"I wouldn't bet against it," Gabby says. Personally, I've always thought Gabby Faustmann was hotter than Arizona asphalt. And Kelly is white hot. Needless to say Nick Hammond and I are two pre-teens who've hit the hormonal jackpot.

When the girls aren't looking we make funny faces at each other.

"It's got a 16 MHz processor," Kelly says, pointing to the CPU under the monitor. "Screaming fast. And it has two disk drives: a 5 ¼" floppy and the new 3 ½" drive."

"Is it better than the Commodore 64 in the Junior High library?" I ask. Kelly laughs.

"That thing's a dinosaur," she says. "Remember *The Print Shop*? You could print banners for your classroom? And the little jokes and puns: *Who's buried in Grant's Tomb?* Come on. That's kids' stuff."

"It was kind of boring," I admit.

"I saved for this Dell for almost two years," Kelly says. She works at Godfather's Pizza near the mall. I remember seeing her there recently, but I didn't say anything because I was with my parents. I don't think she saw me anyway.

Nick and Gabby aren't saying much. They're tickling each other, trying to keep their squirms and their giggles to themselves. It's difficult to see them. The only light in the room is coming from Kelly's monitor.

"What are you doing over there?" I ask.

"Mind your own beeswax," Nick says.

"Yeah, yeah, yeah."

"It's got a 256-color VGA monitor," Kelly continues.

"VGA?"

"Video Graphics Adapter," she says. "*Misty Creek* only uses 16-color Enhanced Graphics, but my monitor will support up to 256 colors. Pretty gnarly, huh?"

"Radical," I say. "How did you learn all this stuff?"

"Computer magazines," Kelly says. "Believe me I take plenty of flak from my friends. Especially Jamie Miller: *"Oh SPARE me Kelly that is SO boring! What are you even THINKING reading that dorky stuff? Did you land a cameo in Revenge of the Nerds or something?"*

Kelly drops her head as if collecting and choosing her thoughts.

"I'm looking out for my future," she says. "Computers are the future. They've got these crazy chat rooms where you can meet people online. Bulletin Board services. You can call Spain, Germany, the Philippines. Pretty soon they'll be connected to everything. I want a good skill so I never have to waitress again."

As impressed as I am with Kelly's good looks and computer smarts, I'm just as impressed with her as a person. She's different. Thoughtful. I may only be on the doorstep to thirteen but I'm learning how to listen to people. I can feel who's genuine. Who's sincere. Maybe I'm an old soul, but—well, I've always liked older girls that's for sure.

"I catch my share of grief, too," I say. "None of my football buddies knows I love to play *In the Labyrinth* and *Talisman* except Nick."

"You are who you are," Kelly says. "Good for you."

"Besides, I heard girls like it if you're a little different."

"Perhaps," Kelly says.

"Are you guys gonna yap or play?" Gabby asks.

Kelly belts out a sharp laugh and says, "Oh *gag* me, Faustmann. You've been trying to get my little brother's shirt off since you got here. So I don't wanna hear it."

"Your little brother can handle himself," Nick says. "Why don't you mind *your* beeswax and throw us that blanket, sis. *S'il vous plait?*"

"You don't even know what that means."

"It means please in French."

"Only because I told you," says Kelly.

I know precisely what Nick is trying to do. I'll do my best to support him. Casually I reach over, snag the checkered afghan off the back of the chair and hand it to Kelly. She smirks and tosses it over.

"Danke schön!" says Nick.

Kelly reaches past me, grabs another blanket and drapes it over our legs. *Sweet Mother of Judas Priest ... I'm under a blanket with Kelly Hammond!*

"Are we doing the Butler's cellar?"

"Oh, yeah, sorry." I'm slacking on my job. I move Lillian Brooks down the stairs and into the Butler's sleeping quarters.

"Think he's out," Kelly says. We're both staring at Rogers the Butler on the screen who appears to be dozing in his bed, but it's hard to tell. The graphics are awesome. But they're still not that great.

As we're deciding what to do, Kelly lets her hand slide off the keyboard onto my knee. *Oh. My. Dear. Lord. I can't hide much in these Spandex shorts.* The joystick controller trembles in my hands. *How does this work? Do I put my hand on her leg, too? How will I be able to move the joystick? What if she bumps my other joystick?*

"Hmm," Kelly murmurs. "Let's take the bouquet of roses."

"Ok," I say.

I walk Lillian Brooks over to the end table. Kelly types *'get roses'* with one finger. Lillian picks up the bouquet.

"Hey, Gab?" Kelly says. She turns around and shouts: "Hey, hand check!"

Gabby and Nick slowly lift their hands from underneath the blanket. Nick twinkles his fingers.

"Hand check yourself, girlfriend," Gabby replies. Nick whispers something in her ear. Gabby grins. "You guys are too loud. Nick's gonna show me the Ball Python in his terrarium."

I want to cheer: *Go Nick Go! Go Nick Go!* They mosey out of the room. Sly move you sly dog. Say anything to get more privacy. Pull something out of thin air. When you're young you've gotta strike when the iron's hot, warm, or even lukewarm.

"Whatever," Kelly says. She squeezes my knee, disrupting my thoughts. "Looks like we'll have to solve this mystery ourselves."

I guide Lillian Brooks around the old plantation on the screen. My mind—my entire *being*, however, is focused on this fifteen-year old young woman sitting next to me. Kelly. Hammond. Can't believe it. I'm totally thrilled and totally intimidated.

"Get in there," she says. I walk Lillian through the doorway of the old chapel. Kelly pauses, takes her hand off my leg and rubs the bridge of her nose. "Hang on a sec. Need to give my eyes a rest."

"I love the music in *Misty Creek*," I say.

"I know, right?" Kelly blinks her eyes back to life. She points to a little black box on the side of the computer. "I picked up a Roland MT-32 synthesizer with stereo symphony. Totally cutting edge. So much better than the *Beep! Bop! Boop!* from the internal speaker."

"Sweet."

"They used an actual orchestra to make the music for this game."

"It sounds pretty magical," I say. I'm losing confidence. I have no idea what to say. Not say. Do, not do.

"I plan on studying Computer Science at State," Kelly says. "What do you want to major in?" I turn my palms up. She smiles. "You've got time. Keep getting good grades." She returns her hand to my knee. *Yes!*

I check the clock. 9:49 p.m. *May the Force be with me.*

"So whaddya wanna do?" Kelly asks. "Should we start prying up floorboards with the crowbar and looking for the Secret Diary of 1864? Or go back to the cemetery and read the epitaphs?"

"Let's do the cemetery," I say, yawning.

Maybe it was something in my voice. Maybe it was my yawn. Kelly yawns, too. She saves our game and powers down the computer. The monitor goes dark. The yellow streetlights outside outline her silhouette as she turns toward me.

"We'll play more later," Kelly says. She pats my knee and stands. "Wanna come over here for a minute?"

"Yeah," I say. I'm not sure where she's referring to, but I'm ready to say yes to anything. It's up to me now. I'm the only one who can ruin this night.

Kelly takes my hand. I ease off the fold-out chair and shuffle over to her bed. I stand there. She gets in and motions for me to join her. Her sheets feel nice, smooth; her pillows smell strawberry delicious.

Kelly pulls me under the covers. I see her white teeth as she smiles.

"You know I think you're cute," she says.

"Really?"

Kelly laughs. "Oh *what*ever." She leans forward. I feel myself leaning too. Our lips meet in the middle. I'm petrified. I kiss her. I kiss her as well as I can, but it can't be very good.

"Relax," she says, brushing the hair out of my face. "It's not a competition."

We start kissing again. She wraps her arms around my back and starts to pull me on top of her. I go with it. I feel her chest. *Holy Moses! I'm lying on top of Kelly Hammond's boobs!*

I kiss Kelly's neck. She moans softly. I keep kissing her and she keeps moaning and moving underneath me and spreading her legs and pulling me in between. *Holy—*

BBBbbbrrring! BBBbbbrrring!

"Crap," she says. "The phone."

"Can Nick get it?" I ask.

"Nick! Get the phone!"

Halfway through the next ring it sounds like Nick has answered it. Kelly brings my hand to her mouth, kisses it and places it on her warm chest. Beneath her bra I feel her nipple rising. Muscles jerk instinctively in my pelvis.

"Now," she says. "Where were we?"

I lean forward and we start kissing again. May this night last forever. My dreams are slashed by Nick knocking on our door.

"Positively bogus," Kelly says, rolling out from under me. For a moment I'm terrified it's Kelly's old boyfriend Rick Spear on the phone. Or maybe she's got a new boyfriend she didn't mention.

"Hey Bobby," Nick says through the closed door. "It's your mom."

"We got it, Nick, thanks." Kelly points to her phone on the nightstand. "You can get it here. I'm going to powder my nose."

Kelly heads for the bathroom and shuts the door. *Why is Mom calling? Uh oh.*

I pick up the receiver.

"Hello?"

"Bobby Newberry Jr.," says my Mom's voice. "Get your *ass* home this instant!"

"But Mom, why? What's the big—?"

"Your father and I got your progress report in the mail," Mom says. My stomach shrinks. "4 D's and 2 C's? Yep. You've got some explaining to do. Get your butt home right now. We're dealing with this tonight."

"But Mom, you dropped me off. I don't have a ride."

"Mrs. Hammond can give you a ride. It's late, but that was our agreement."

"She's busy," I say.

"Whatever," Mom says. "I'm coming to get you, and believe me I am not happy. Be ready to go." *Click.*

Oh, *man.*

I hear the toilet flush in Kelly's bathroom. She opens the door and turns out the light to find my sorry shape sitting on her bed.

"What's up?" she asks.

"I'm in trouble."

"Aw, that sucks," Kelly says. "Bummer." She turns on the light, sits at her vanity mirror and sighs. She begins brushing out her sandy brown hair very softly. I watch for a moment, defeated. "You can't always get what you want."

I gather my stuff. I say good-bye to Nick, Gabby and Kelly. Moments later, my mother is knocking sternly on the Hammond's front door. She's made it here in record time.

I open the door. Mom grabs my *Bo Knows* tank top and jerks me toward the Honda Accord. She doesn't let go.

I'm six years old again.

My stomach quivers. My lip trembles. I shake a few times just enough to make me feel like a little twerp.

"Interesting," Mom says. I sniffle and wipe my eyes. "I don't see the Hammond's car. There's two lies you'll atone for tonight. At this rate, Dad and I have your entire summer. The back fence *definitely* needs scraped, primed and painted. New fire pit needs to be dug. Wood split. Lots of weeding. Yes sir."

This night's going to last forever.

As angry as I am at Mom and Dad, I slowly realize my frustration will amount to very little. My own plan put me where I am. I won't admit it to myself. Not yet at least.

THE END

'Ground Halcyon'

⌒⁀

THE UPPITY GIRL IN THE skinny black pants joined Beth and Ritalia at the bar. Her name was Jade. She slung her purse over the tall bar chair.

Alan Delaney, forty and single, waited in his usual black pants, black shirt and black tie. His hair was graying on the sides. It was probably one of the reasons he kept it short these days. Smooth jazz drizzled through the ceiling speakers. He slid a black cocktail napkin in front of Jade. In the corner of the napkin was fine gold script: *Halcyon.*

"What's it tonight?" he asked.

Jade fluttered her eyelashes. She tapped her trademark green-star fingernails on top of the bar. Alan stood there amazed. *Why me? Why not sit at the other end and let Cheryl-Lynn wait on you? Why do you always come to me?*

"Melon martini, Allie," Jade said. "Thank you please."

Alan plunged his cocktail shaker into the ice and scanned the shelves for the emerald bottle of Midori liqueur. The crowd was starting to pick up this Thursday evening. No matter which side of the bar he worked, Jade, Beth, and Ritalia always found three open chairs together in his section. It felt like cruel and unusual fate.

"Put it on the tab, Jade?" Alan asked. He placed the green cocktail in front of her.

"That'll be fine."

Alan walked to the Micros touch-screen computer to update the girls' bill. A shady reflection stared back in the computer screen. Cold sweat dripped off the end of his nose. It splashed the cash register. He felt his world spinning out of control, teetering on the edge, going over....

Help!

"Allie, are you okay?" Ritalia asked. "Oh my God, you guys, he's having a panic attack."

Alan held up a shaky finger. His face was sweaty and pale. The three girls were calling his name but he couldn't hear them. Could only see their mouths moving. He focused everything he had on not going down behind the bar onto the sticky floor.

Breathe, man ... breathe....

The bar back—a dapper kid from Mexico named David Rivera—tapped him on the shoulder.

"Mr. Alan? Are you all right?"

Alan exhaled hard. He sucked down a large breath. Another. Blood circulated at a normal rate again through his system. Color returned to his cheeks. The weight of the world lifted. He opened his eyes.

"Thanks, D-River. I'm good, brother, I'm good."

David grabbed his empty ice pail and strode off. Alan found a clean bar rag. He patted his forehead.

"I thought he was tripping," Jade said.

Alan returned the bottle of Midori to the shelf. He tried to reassure himself that he could still serve alcohol responsibly to Halcyon's customers, and his eyes stared back in the bar mirror worried, frustrated, but ready to do their duty. He adjusted his clip-on tie.

"*Gawd*, Allie," Ritalia said. "You are *sooo* Metro." She was wearing a crimson top that pushed her girls up into everyone's face.

"Excuse me?"

"Metro sexual, Alan," Jade said. "It means up on city trends and dressing in such a style. Or it could mean you're a touch effeminate. Perhaps that's merely an opinion."

"Don't you even know who you are?" Ritalia asked. "You're so Metro and you don't even know it."

"Maybe that's what you were panicking about," Beth said. She was probably the nicest of the three, yet her IQ level was her pant's size.

"I am *not* Metro," Alan said.

"You are too, Allie."

"No, I'm not."

"You're really not yourself tonight," Ritalia said.

Alan stared at her as if she'd announced she was running for president.

"If I'm not myself, then who am I?"

"You're just not you."

Alan thought back to Mixology 101. The instructor, Karl "So Co" Jones, made it a point to stress that you had two ears and one mouth and that should remind you to listen twice as much as you speak. You never discussed politics or religion. And the only color you responded to was green. He wished Karl had given a third lecture on dealing with three bimbettes who got off giving you grief.

"What kind of a name is Ritalia anyway?" Alan asked.

"It's like Rita with a Talia on the end," she said. "*Ree-TAL-ee-ahh.*"

"*Uh!*" Beth exclaimed. "That is so cool!"

If the evening continued like this Alan knew he'd be standing around blowing his brains out. It wasn't the girls' usual mindless banter that had caused his panic earlier. He'd been at Halcyon for eight years now. Hired in at thirty-two. He'd originally come to the city to paint skyscraper canvasses, and in order to make ends meet he'd picked up a job slinging drinks. When he was behind the bar he had millions of great ideas and visions. But by the time he got home he felt drained and reluctant to paint.

Time kept ticking.

So, here it was: eight years and three dozen city paintings later. Respectable work. Nothing that would fetch an independent living or garnish any adoring criticism. Nobody was itching to buy it. Now he felt stuck in the great deadener. Habitual routine.

Alan poured two glasses of Cabernet Sauvignon for an older couple who were dressed to the nines and having fun. He sighed. His eyes drifted to the front windows. Colorful autumn leaves floated past.

If there's an invisible machine, I'm an insignificant screw.

Where were the friends who'd once inspired him? Where was the great music that once stirred his soul? Everyone seemed in such a rush to sprint to the middle. Maybe he should have, too. Instead, he'd chosen to chase this silly artistic dream. *We are the choices.*

"'Nother Melon Martini, Allie," Jade said. She slid her empty cocktail glass at him.

Alan snapped his lament and went to work fixing another. At least the three girls tipped him well. Unless they were completely bombed.

"What *is* wrong with you tonight, Allie?" Ritalia asked. "No jokes, no goofy smiles, nothing."

Alan slid Jade a full green martini. He turned to Ritalia.

"Please stop calling me Allie," he said. "My name is Alan."

"Sorry, Allie."

"Where are peoples' manners these days?" he asked. "I tried to help this older lady across Sampson Boulevard yesterday? By Trader Joe's? She slaps my hand away and says: *Do I LOOK like I need your help?*"

Beth smiled blankly. Jade and Ritalia merely stared.

"Doesn't anybody read anymore? Damn, all I get behind the bar are Horny Housewife quotes and the same old tired Hip-Hop swagger. I read this short story the other day by Melville. *Bartleby the Scrivener?*"

"I prefer not to waste my time reading," Jade said.

"I read *Cosmo* and *People*," said Beth. "Those articles are pretty interesting."

"Why don't you sneak a quick drink, Allie?" Ritalia said. "Come on, we'll cover for you. Chrissi Mangold won't say anything."

"Your boss is cool like dat," smiled Beth.

Alan wasn't sure if they were messing with him or what. Beth and Jade slid off into a barstool confessional, while Ritalia slowly spun her glass of Pinot Grigio in front of her eyes and hypnotized herself. Alan's eyes moved again to the windows at the front. Across the street something was happening.

"What are you looking at?" Ritalia asked.

Alan kept his attention out the windows. In the dim alley on the other side of the street, something was twitching. Some*one* was twitching.

A leg. A foot. A foot with no shoe. No sock. He could see toes wiggling in the pale yellow light. The foot belonged to a body leaning against the building on the left, just out of view. Was it a homeless person? A shoeless person? Obviously. But something else was—

"*Alll-eeeee*," Ritalia droned.

At the other end of the bar, a guy in a gray suit was calling for a Ketel One and tonic. It diverted Alan's attention just enough to see the other bartender Cheryl-Lynn pick up the order.

Alan returned his attention across the street. The sidewalks on the far side of Ramsey Street were empty. But the twitching foot in the alley wasn't the only thing moving.

A man and a woman hustled down the alley toward the street. They stopped at the front of the alleyway and looked around. The man slipped back. The woman lit a cigarette and put a hand on her hip. Alan's view was partially blocked, but he could see the man take something out of his jacket. Something shiny. The man plunged the shiny object into the person lying against the building. The twitching foot went crazy. The toes spread. They shook. Alan's eyes grew wide.

"*Ahhhhh!*"

Jade and Beth glanced up.

"What? What is it?" they asked. A few other patrons heard his yell and paid a moment's notice before resuming their drinking.

"Something just happened across the street," he said.

"Where?"

Ritalia turned on her barstool and stared out the front windows. The man had already joined the woman at the front of the alley and the two of them were strolling casually down the sidewalk. Alan watched the twitching foot shrink out of sight like a curling piece of bacon.

"Right there!"

"Allie, honey, take a chill pill," Jade said.

"Like, I think you're overworked or something," Ritalia said in a motherly voice. "You're imagining things."

Am I? Alan tried to suppress his intuition but it wouldn't.

"I think I just saw something terrible happen," he said.

Jade looked up, slightly annoyed.

"Who are you trying to be?" she asked. "Michael Harvey? Agatha Christie? Do you think there's some mystery to solve here?"

"You're totally paranoid," said Ritalia.

A group of four guys bellied-up down the bar. David Rivera told Alan that Cheryl-Lynn was in the kitchen getting fresh olives.

"Excuse me," Alan said.

Ritalia tried to respond, but Alan was already picking up the guys' orders. They needed three Dos Equis and one Pete's Wicked Ale. With his heart racing, Alan snapped out four beers and printed their tab. The guys fumbled for their wallets. Alan called to Jack Guida, the old security guard. Jack ambled over. Alan pointed.

"What the hell happened over there?"

"Where?" Jack asked. He looked around as if it could be anywhere.

"Across Ramsey," Alan said. While Jack stood there with a perplexed look, Alan slid the guys their change. "Right across the street."

"Where?"

"The alley over there."

"Which one?"

"Right across from Halcyon, Jack."

"Right over there?" Jack asked, pointing.

"Yeah," Alan said. "It looked like someone got stabbed."

"Stabbed?"

"Could you send one of your doormen over to check? We may have a homicide to report."

"Stabbed, like with a sword?"

"No, a knife. A big-ass shiny knife."

"A big-ass knife is basically a sword."

"What difference does it make, man? Somebody could be laying over there dying!"

"Take it easy, Alan," Jack said. "Sure, we'll check it out. Might-a just been a prank."

"Jack—"

"You've got customers," he said.

As Jack Guida ambled back to his post, Alan realized the customers he was referring to were Jade, Beth and Ritalia.

"Allie, *baby*," Ritalia cooed. She tapped the lip of her empty wine glass. Alan grabbed the bottle of Pinot Grigio from the cooler and filled her up. "You're hallucinating."

"What?"

"You dropped acid?" Jade asked.

"Coolio," said Beth.

"What in God's name are you talking about?" Alan asked.

"LSD, Alan," Jade said. "Lysergic acid."

"I know what it is, Jade. I don't do that shit. I don't do anything."

"Maybe somebody slipped you some bad X."

"You're *rolling*, Allie?" Ritalia asked, an eyebrow in the air.

"Cool beans!" said Beth.

"I'm telling you, somebody got stabbed in the alley across the god-dam street," Alan said. "Someone with no shoes on. Why aren't you guys listening to me?"

"We're not *guys*, Allie," Ritalia said. "We're *gals*."

"Get real," Jade said. "That kind of shit does *not* happen in this area of the city. You know this."

"Why don't you walk across Ramsey then and check it out?" Alan asked. "You're so sure. Go check it out."

Jade stared at him like he'd asked her to go out in public without green eyeliner.

"Are you crazy? This is my night to drink. Why don't you go?"

"Every night's your night to drink," Alan said. "I can't leave the bar, you jackass."

"Then there's nothing to be done," said Jade. She pointed her finger at him. "Don't call me a jackass."

"How will you feel if someone was killed over there tonight?"

"Allie, honey, people sacrifice all the time," she said. "One day you and I won't be here. It's the way of the world. Grow up. Be a good sport."

Alan seethed.

"What are you even good for, Jade?"

"What am *I* good for?" she asked. "Honey, I know you're trying to change the world with your art and everything, but *I* deal in reality. I deal with wants and needs. I mean seriously, what is a painting, or a book, or some stupid-ass pop-song compared with giving and receiving multiple orgasms? That's what *I* do, Chicken Little. People pay me for the ultimate physical experience. I have orgasms, Allie. Lots of them. I'm very good at that. I give people what they need. People don't need that stupid art shit. I mean, you wanna call a diamond a diamond?"

Alan paced behind the bar. His patience was eroding. *Need to do something. Need to run. Scream. Pull someone's hair. Something.*

"Just *chill*," said Beth.

"Take a *drink*," said Ritalia.

"Allie, you're a good man," said Jade. "Good man's hard to find."

"Don't you mean a hard man is *good* to find?" Ritalia asked.

"No, you're thinking of the porno flick," Jade said. "Actually, it was *A Hard Man in My Mouth is Good to Find.*"

Alan backed against the coolers. He was getting dumber. He actually felt himself getting dumber being around these late-twenties bimbos.

Just then, Chrissi Mangold appeared all spiky hair and dimples. She smiled.

"Getting what you need, ladies?" she asked. They nodded. "Peachy keen." She turned to Alan. "How we doing on liquor? Aside from the Dewar's, I know, I've ordered—"

"*Out!*" Alan screamed.

"Excuse me?" Chrissi said, taking a step back. Everyone stopped talking. Even the smooth jazz from the speakers seemed temporarily muted.

"I said I quit," Alan said. He unclipped his black tie and tossed it into the ice bin. "I hate this stinking place. This freaking city. And you three," he said, pointing at the girls, "are the biggest waste of below average, nothing to the imagination, money-pimped baggage handlers I've ever ... I hope your toes get run over by a steamroller!"

"Gee, thanks Alan," Jade said quickly. But Alan was already out the front entrance. Jack Guida called out: "*Wait buddy!*" But Alan was already high-stepping it down the sidewalk through crowds of people in the city night. Cool autumn breeze chilled his skin. *I can't believe I did it. Fuck yeah! Watch out. Coming through! You'll move. You* better *move.*
Crack!

Alan slammed into a young couple walking down the sidewalk and sent them sprawling backward into a group of older people waiting for a taxi.

"Watch it, jerk!" said the young man. He shoved Alan backward and he fell to the sidewalk. Feet pattered all around him. Alan lay there for a moment. He got up. His moment of liberation was dissolving. *What in the hell am I doing?*

He had very little money saved. He had bills coming due. Bills were always coming due. His paintings? Damn it!—Now he couldn't use Halcyon for a reference. And he wouldn't be eligible for unemployment since he was the one who'd walked out.

"Arrraaaagghhh!" he yelled. Some people standing in line for Cilantro's Mexican restaurant nearby backed away. "I'll die for my art! Kafka was willing to! Hemingway! Vincent Van Gogh! Virginia motherfucking *Woooolf!*" He pointed to an older gentleman waiting in line. "*I'll cut your ear off!*"

"Back off," said the man.

"He ain't gonna do nothing," said another man slightly younger.

Alan stopped at the corner crosswalk. He jumped up and down. People gave him room. The crossing light switched to **WALK**. He stood there. People started walking. He couldn't move. He jumped as high as he could and flapped his arms quickly and almost hit someone but only landed with a thud where the sidewalk met the street.

"Alan! *Alan Delaney!*"

A strong breeze drifted through the city. Alan smelled the subway. Chrissi Mangold was dodging people on the sidewalks running toward him. She caught up to him out of breath, her short hair spiky and stiff.

"Come back, Alan," she said. "You're a good bartender. Can't lose you. You're like family."

Alan's mind flashed white. Everything went blank. *Yes. Can't lose me. They need me. It's good to be needed. Servin' drinks for all time, baby.*

Chrissi took Alan's arm. She led him back toward Halcyon, negotiating the growing nightlife crowds as everyone strove to get to where they were going. She patted his back.

Alan walked in a daze, his eyes glazed over. They approached the *Halcyon* sign. It was a sign with double daggers over running water.

"You had the hiccups tonight," Chrissi told him. "You've still got a job. Come on. We'll finish out your shift. Then you can go straight home to your apartment, lie in bed, pull the covers up and get a great night's sleep."

"Still got my job," Alan said quietly to himself. *"Have a job? Oh, I got a job. Need a job? Yes I do, do, do...."*

Across Ramsey Street, red and blue strobes twirled from a second police car arriving on scene. A cop stood over a dead body in the middle of the alley. Light glinted off an object sticking out of the corpse. The second cop got out of his cruiser.

"Homicide?" he yelled.

The cop in the alley nodded his head.

"Any witnesses?"

The cop in the alley said nothing.

At Halcyon, Jack Guida held the front door open and didn't say anything either. Chrissi still had Alan's arm. She led him back to his station behind the bar. She buttoned Alan's top button, pulled his black tie out of her shirt pocket and clipped it to his collar.

Alan turned.

"What can I get you, Madam?" he asked.

"Oh, Allie," said Jade. "After *that* escapade, I think I'm going to need another Melon Martini." She looked drunk. Her skin was flushed pink. She looked like she'd been laughing.

"Melon Martini," Alan said. "You got it."

He turned and scanned the bottles row by row until his eyes zeroed in on the wavy green bottle of Midori. He started to laugh. *It's a riot!* He laughed and laughed until his sides hurt. Then he went to work.

"Aw, you guys look," Beth said. "Allie's back."

THE END

'THE OLD GOAT MEETS LOU MCGEE'

~Homage to a Classic Tale~

⌒

TWO DICE SAILED THROUGH THE air, bounced off the pit wall and rolled onto the green craps felt a six and a one.

"Consarn it!" yelled Lou.

"Seven! Seven out! Line away!" said the stickman. "Collect the Pass Line and pay the Don'ts."

The man on Lou's right grunted: "It's gettin' cold, buddy. You ever play the back line?"

"Cold nothing," Lou growled. "It never rolls my way. These dern dice are rigged. And I'm tired of it. All of it!"

He'd be damned if he let this Elk River Casino play him for a chump any longer. He'd burn the place down, piss on the ashes and take all the money himself. The pit boss ambled over. He touched Lou's arm.

"Please manage to keep your voice down, sir."

Lou drained his whiskey sour.

"Manage this!" He dropped his glass into the craps pit scattering chips and ice. The shooters groaned as Lou shoved off through the meandering tourists and the blinking casino lights.

Up ahead in the waterfall atrium stood his friends Burt Coolidge and Arnie Stephens. Perfect timing. It was still early afternoon and Lou wanted to pitch some horseshoes.

A warm hand slowly closed around Lou McGee's wrist.

It stopped him.

The casino lights kept flashing, people all around him kept gambling, but the noise faded off as if he'd been pulled into a padded sound booth. Lou stood facing dapper gentleman with slick black hair. The man wore a dark suit. He sat casually in front of a slot machine smoking a long cigarette out of a knobby wooden holder. The man blew out a cool stream of smoke. His fingers plucked a silver coin out of the air. He handed the coin to Lou.

"Try this one, low boy," he said.

Lou followed the man's pointing finger to a slot machine. The machine was covered with black storm clouds and white lightning bolts: **CLOUD NINE ~ WINS *ALL* THE TIME**

Lou slid the coin in. The Cloud Nine machine perked up. He grabbed the handle and pulled.

The reels spun insanely fast. Lights exploded. The slot machine trembled as three dark clouds appeared one right after the other on the winner's line, but no money came out. Only a distant rumble of thunder.

"It's R-R-R-R-Raining Money!"

The dark-haired gentleman grinned. Lazy smoke twirled off the end of his long cigarette. Lou shivered. The man demanded from him a certain earthy respect that Lou rarely gave anyone. A few tourists stopped to watch. But still no money came out.

"Patience," the man said.

A ticket printed. Lou snatched it. An older couple in matching Hawaiian shirts patted Lou on the back as a shift manager in a red power tie walked over. The manager glanced at Lou's ticket. He put a checkmark on it in invisible ink.

"You may get this cashed, sir," the manager said. "Then I will kindly ask you to leave."

Lou looked again at the dapper gentleman who'd slipped him the winning silver. The man looked to be around Lou's own age. Yet the man was so suave, so impeccably dressed, that for the first time in Lou

McGee's life he felt embarrassed for not being more up on the ways of etiquette. The man turned up his palms.

"No return on my investment?"

Lou returned the slick man's smile with a cockier one and marched to the cashier's cage. A window opened.

"Cash it," Lou commanded.

"Yes sir, gimme one sec," said the girl behind the window. *Girl,* Lou thought. They were all girls anymore.

"All-righty," the cashier said returning. "That is $1,194.00. You just made the threshold, sir. Six more dollars and it would have been 1099G Form at tax time."

Lou grinned.

"Hurry it up," he said. "I'm being asked to leave."

Silver prongs spun backward through the air, glinting in the afternoon sunlight. The horseshoe sailed over the pit. It landed and rolled down the hill in Lou's backyard. He got there just in time to watch it disappear into the forest below. His three buddies pointed and laughed.

"Fetch it, Lou-baby!"

"That's *your* partner throwing that trash!"

"Just like you throwing them bones today at Elk River!"

His friends hollered they were going for more beer. Lou flipped them off. The late Sunday sun rested just above the treetops. He figured he had a few more hours and a few more beers before he'd have to call it a night. That's all it was anymore. A work week here. A few yuks there. A few more beers. The same bonehead friends. Maybe Lou wasn't the sharpest macheté in the tool shed, but *damn it* he'd had dreams once, too.

The extra cash from the Cloud Nine machine had been a nice little bonus. His thoughts drifted back to the strange man. A flash of insight bolted Lou's mind. He *did* know him. Grandpa Leonard always said they had royalty in their blood somewhere's down the line. That guy must be it.

Lou started down the hill after the horseshoe when he tripped.

"Wh-whh-whaaaaa!"

He fell in slow motion. Like some sort of time warp. His arms were beating like mad, but when he looked out at them they were slow like cold molasses. Lou was floating down the hill. The woods at the bottom crept nearer. His body was horizontal now. He flapped his arms. He was trying to balance himself. But he kept tipping forward, and time was catching up now, faster and faster and—

"Oomph!"

Lou's head slammed into the ground. He plowed into the grass and dirt, his body trenching a tunnel out into the forest. He couldn't see. He couldn't breathe. He felt no pain. Only a powerful ache—an incredible pulling sensation at the core of his being—dragging him through the ground.

The summoning began to wane. He was out among the trees, the leaves, the roots, the songs of the birds. His head crashed into something so hard and unforgiving that the soles of his feet went numb.

Lou pulled himself out of the ground. He rubbed the dirt from his face and blew his nose farmer-style. His brain was ringing. *Did I head-butt a glacier?*

"Dear me, oh my," came a timid voice.

A stubbly old man in an orange cap stepped out from behind a tree. The man wore a checkered flannel shirt, blue jeans and a vest. He muttered as he helped Lou to his feet.

"Apologies, mister. We didn't even see you there. Mighty terrible you'd a gotten hurt."

Lou spat out a leaf.

"Why you on my property, old man?"

The old man rubbed the gray stubble on his chin.

"Oh, this is *your* property?" he asked. "I always wondered."

The old stick was probably ninety years old. He was so scrawny he looked like he might crack in two and blow away. Lou had a working-man's beer gut and clogged arteries but he still had jackhammer hands and he'd always get rowdy to protect his turf. He'd thrash this guy.

So why was he hesitating?

Lou regained his composure and lowered his brow. The elderly tres-passer stuttered.

"As I was saying, my faithful hunting companion led me out here, and now I can't seem to find—"

"Ain't seen him, Chief," Lou said. "Now git 'fore I call the cops. I own these here three point five acres and they're mine. Savvy?"

The old man dropped his head. He stared down at his brown hiking boots. A sudden breeze rustled the leaves.

"I understand," he said, looking up. "If you happen to stumble across Morningstar, my little Chihuahua, tell her Daddy—"

Lou roared with laughter.

"You take a Chimichanga out hunting? *Bwa-ha! Ha! HA!*"

The old man joined in the laughter. When the amusement was over, he plucked the orange stocking cap off of his head. A silver bushel of curly locks bounced down around his shoulders.

"Like my new hairdo? Louis *Rainier* McGee."

"Your pumpkin's got seeds, old timer," Lou stammered. "Wait. How did you know my name?"

"You told me."

"Like hell I did."

"You called me earlier," the old man said. "Remember?" Lou shook his head.

The old man grinned like a fiend. He dropped his pants, unbut-toned his vest and stepped out in a British Royal Navy Officer's uni-form. War medals clinked upon his chest. The birds of the forest fell silent. The old man looked much younger and in much better shape. He tipped his officer's cover. Lou stumbled backward over a log and landed on his arse.

"Man overboard, Cap'n McGee!" the officer said.

Lou got up, brushed himself off, and put his hands on his hips. His heart was racing like crazy. Some of his hair was even frightened stiff. But he still wasn't buying into any of this B.S.

"What are you, an Englishman or something?"

"Negative, sir."

"Or a British-man. Whatever you Bulls call yourselves—"

The man's arm shot up.

"Look!"

Lou snapped his attention to where the man was pointing. Thirty feet away, a young deer hopped out of some low brush. A doe. Her ears perked up as she spotted the two men. She turned and her white tail bounded back into the greenery. From out of the bushes where the deer had disappeared stepped a beautiful young woman. She was fair, bare at her chest, with a green loin cloth dangling off her hips. She mouthed the words: *I Want You.*

Lou couldn't help it. Dirty ideas multiplied. He licked his lips.

"*She* can stay," he said.

The young woman leapt back into the brush the way the doe had moments before. Lou turned back. His knees buckled and he fell.

"What boy?"

The old man's skin was black as pitch. He was an African spear-chucker, some sort of tribesman. Lou pulled himself to his feet. He slapped himself. He was losing it.

"No, no, *no*," the old man said. He was back to his original, feeble self. "*You're* doing that, Lou. You're looking at things with the wrong set of eyes." The old man sat next to him on a large fallen log. "Rest easy, son. You took a real bump. Let's just shoot the breeze for a spell."

They made small talk for several minutes. The old man began with vague questions that quickly turned pointed and personal, and Lou, for some reason, kept giving him honest and truthful answers. He gave more than he was asked to provide. By the end of their little conversation, he had given the old man everything.

Lou felt himself growing angry. He struggled to remove the old hick's arm from around his shoulders. It felt like he had to peel the old bastard off.

"Don't be trying to be some math-magician here," Lou said, getting to his feet. The old man struggled to his own.

"What about your head, Lou-baby?"

"My head's fine, Jack."

"Hey, whaddya know, that's my name."

"I thought I told you to get gone."

"What'cha gonna do, Lou? Get out your 10 gauge?"

"Hells bells."

"Shooting not double-ought, but *triple*-ought buckshot, no doubt."

Lou smirked. The old man brought a wilted finger to his mouth. His smile drew back in a dog-like grin.

"Bet you're the kind of guy who's got one of them old Coach Guns. Short double barrel, side by side. And I'll bet you were talking all tough to your wife, Amy, when you bought it: *'Old West, darlin'! I'll blow them claim-jumpers clean off our site! Whoopty-hoo! Riding shotgun, baby!'*

Lou turned white.

"Sound familiar?"

The old bastard had quoted him verbatim. He remembered saying it to Amy that afternoon at the Irving Gun Show. Along with:

"Two big's all you need. Two barrels of heavy metal will de-bone any spine."

It was the old man who spoke again, finishing Lou McGee's memories aloud. Volcanic fire sliced Lou's heart. It burned his sunken soul. The old man swatted his knee.

"Sam Hill, you trying to be a poet?"

Lou stepped back. The forest had grown darker. He didn't recognize any of the trees. They stood under an especially old gnarly tree now, and the old man stretched himself and seemed to grow taller. He kicked a brown boot onto a log and hiked up the cuff of his jeans.

"We got a lot in common, Lou." From out of the old man's woolen sock came a sleek revolver. Darker than midnight. "Looking down on others. Knowing they should be serving us. Having the power to own it *all*."

The old man straightened up. He aimed the revolver at a branch above Lou's head as if he were sighting it in. He let the barrel slowly descend. Lou ducked.

"We prey," the old man said.

Lou spun away with his hands in the air.

"*Watch it!* You crazy ole sumbitch!"

"Me? The Old Goat? I like more than six shots."

Lou dropped to a crouch ready to run. The old man scampered up onto a high tree stump. His agility was uncanny.

"Don't run, Lou," he said. "I'll have to shoot you in the back."

Lou eased up and raised his hands.

"Look, Mister. I just come down here to get my horseshoe. Which rolled down here. On *my* property."

"I'd rather give it to you straight in the mug for always spouting your ignorant, arrogant malarkey," the old man interjected, then corrected himself. "No, I concede, the heart. Putting a bullet through any man's heart is the ultimate satisfaction. Or any woman, for that matter."

Lou's eyes turned gray. He was certain his ticket was being punched. The old man towered above him and laughed—a cruel, throaty hack— and then tossed the gun at Lou who barely had time to catch it before it hit him in the face.

"I'm only pulling your choke-chain, McGee. You'll learn to begrudge me that. Now listen. About this little offer I'm proposing. Unless … you're *chicken?*"

The cold steel of the revolver tickled Lou's palm. Invisible tentacles slithered up his arm. Lou was curious about a lot of things, but he was still forced to ask the most pressing question.

"Who are you?"

The old man sat down on the log and twiddled his thumbs.

"Oh, *Lou.* If I say my name it's like finding out there's no Santa Claus, right? I mean, what's in a name anyway? I'm telling you, brother-man, this is a sweet deal. All those years of manual labor. All the back-sass from dumbass bosses. All that wasted *time*. Just sign it, man! We will begin the greatest period of your life."

Lou suddenly came to. Why the old jackass had thrown him the gun he had no clue, but the spell, the Voodoo, or the hypnosis had vanished. He stepped back and pulled the revolver's hammer.

"Big mistake, old boy!" Lou shouted. He aimed the revolver at the old man's chest. "Straight to hell."

Lou couldn't pull the trigger. He kept the gun on the old man who clambered to his feet, applauding.

"You beautiful redneck hick! *Bravo!* I love it!"

"I'll plant your skinny bones," Lou growled. "I done it before. Some young teenage punk out here one morning lighting off fire crackers. I put him ten feet under by them scrub oaks."

The old man said that he knew.

Lou shoved him against the gnarled tree and searched him for more weapons. He found nothing. The old man giggled. Lou pushed him to the ground and made him interlace his fingers behind his head. The old man turned his face up. An eyebrow rose.

"If I was any younger, Lou-baby, I'd knock your teeth out," he said. "This is no way to treat an elder."

Lou laughed.

"So you're a killer?" asked the old man.

"I'll kill your ass."

"Wait a minute. You said this was *your* property?"

"I told you it was."

"Astonishing," said the old man. "I never knew you owned all of *this*."

Lou spat on the ground. When he glanced over his shoulder, his jaw dropped. Mountain. Huge. A huge mountain had appeared, dominating the sky behind them. It looked like something out of a storybook. White clouds drifted past its snow-covered peaks.

Lou turned back. The forest was gone. He stood alone in a field of thigh-high golden wheat that swayed in the breeze for miles. The forest, the trees, the trail that led back to his double-wide trailer, *everything* was gone. He stared off into the vast landscape. An arm crept around his shoulder. Lou jumped. Suddenly they were back in the forest and the old goat had the gun.

"Caught ya napping!" he howled. "Dang it, Lou. You're a good'un. Almost as defiant as I am. But then again, we know close only counts in nukes and horseshoes."

The old man plucked six rounds of ammunition out of his vest pocket, each cartridge a different color of the rainbow. He swung the revolver's cylinder out, loaded it to full capacity, and then pressed the gun into Lou's palm.

"I've had pretty good luck with this heater," the old man said. "I go out to the range, shoot it all day, and still come home to six beauties in the cylinder. I don't know; maybe it's me. Check it out. A different turn of the cylinder, a different outcome. It's slightly more special than your average .38."

With a swipe of his arm, the old man wiped the landscape clean. He pointed to a single solitary tree—a huge oak—fifty yards out. The only thing visible for miles. The forest had been completely replaced with a lush green prairie. Beautiful sun danced in the sky. Billowy clouds. Lou felt like he was drowning in déjà vu.

"Give her a tug, *low boy*," the old goat cooed in his ear. "This is the power shot."

Lou raised the revolver. He pointed it at the oak fifty yards away.

Pop.

The report was like popcorn. The gun hardly kicked at all. But the oak tree in the field exploded as if a cannonball had just blown through it.

"Holy *Jesus!*" Lou yelled.

The tree gave way and came down with a distant roar. Lou was forced to drop the gun and cover his ears. The old man shrieked.

"Watch Yer **CUSSING***!"*

He paced back and forth, smoke rising from his nose, ears and eye sockets. Lou turned white, horrified. The old man was pure evil. Just as quickly he seemed to calm. With a quick puff of smoke he bent down, retrieved the revolver and handed it back to Lou.

"Well, hell," the old man said. "That's some mighty fine shooting, Lou. What say we seal this deal right now and get you living the good life?"

"This can't be factory ammunition," Lou stammered. "Did you get this at Wal-Mart?" The old goat smiled. From the sleeve of his flannel shirt came a scroll of legal parchment. He tapped Lou's chest with it.

"Superiority," he said. "Unlimited firepower. Teleportation. Invisibility. All the best inventions you meddling humans will have perfected in nearly 1,000 years—all wrapped up in a snub-nosed .38. *This* is my gift *to you*. Oh, I almost forgot. How's about a little traveling change?"

The old man emptied two handfuls of Hessian gold coins into Lou's jacket pockets.

"What's the catch?" Lou asked. He fingered the coins with feverish delight.

"No catch," said the old man. "Quick as a handshake and a signature. Wanna know what you get? Not *seven*. Not *fourteen*. But **Twenty-One YEARS** of the best life that money can buy. I've got wicked connections, Brother Louie. You'll see. You don't want to be bothered with sissy fine print, do you? *Sissy fine print?*"

"What do you need from me?"

"A little mercenary assistance in the future," the old man said. "Got a large order to fill. Are you my man? Or are you still Chicken Little Breast?"

Lou cocked his head. He shook the old man's hand. Something sharp stung his palm and Lou jerked his arm back. The old man smiled. They held up their hands and Lou saw a thorn embedded in each of their palms. They pulled their thorns and shook.

"You're not afraid of a little blood are you?" the old man asked. Lou shook his head. "Brother?"

"Suppose I die before my twenty-one years are up," Lou said. "What then? Do I get a rebate or a refund?"

A jet black crow's feather drifted down from the sky. The old man plucked it out of the air. He smeared the quill into Lou's palm and then his own.

"Won't happen," the old man said. "You're my boy."

Lou batted his eyelashes.

"All right, Old Timer, where do I scratch my Johnny Hancock?"

With their crimson ink Lou signed the agreement. He handed the feather back to the old man. Immediately Lou had the sensation of falling again. It was a feeling before it was real. The old man towered over him, looking younger still and more powerful, and for some reason Lou couldn't speak.

The old man saluted. Lou was gone.

He floated up over the mountains, past their snow-drenched peaks, miles up over the prairies, the fields, the forests, leaning back now, coming down through the pink and purple skies of the late-summer sun back into the town of Johann and into his trailer park.

⸎

Lou awoke fighting for air. It felt like he'd been tear-gassed and knocked in the head with a Billy club. When he finally came to, he was lying on his back at the bottom of the hill. He sat up. The dark revolver fell into the grass next to him. Coins jingled in his pocket.

His friends stood at the top of the hill with fresh beers.

"What the *hail?*" Arnie Stephens yelled. "Ya looking for that horseshoe down there, or are ya playin' with yourself?"

⸎

Lou laughed with the boys a while longer that evening. He fingered the evil piece in his pocket. Six unprecedented capabilities. Two pockets of gold. He'd stashed the coins in the wood shed, but not before tossing his three compadres one coin each calling it an early Christmas present. His friends couldn't believe it. It was the first real gold they'd ever owned.

He liked his friends. But already he was buying favors. All those times they'd laughed behind his back. Made passes at his wife. Jerked him around. Mmm hmm.

⟳

That night, after his buddies had gone, he and Amy got familiar. They got familiar three times that night. Lou teased her with coins from the stash. Rolled them across her body. She didn't even ask where he'd gotten them.

Afterward, he stroked her red hair. Lou couldn't remember a time when they'd shared such a fine night. It made his heart heavy. He knew it would be their last time. *Amy*. With him from the beginning and she'd never strayed. He'd miss her.

Tomorrow he was a new man. It pulsed in his bones. He'd know many women. Many *younger* women. He would have anyone and anything he wanted.

⟳

That night, the old man's voice came to him in the dark. Lou sat up in bed. He slipped on his robe and crept into the living room.

At the corner window, the old man stuck his head in. He spoke quietly and succinctly. In the darkness of the trailer, he told Lou to buy a lottery ticket tomorrow. Quick pick. 1:14 p.m. Levisky's Corner Drugstore.

"Fat of the land, Lou-baby," the old goat whispered. "Get 'er done."

⟳

The following evening, Lou watched the winning lottery numbers float across the TV screen like destiny on a golden platter. It was unbelievable.

For the first time he considered the contract he'd signed with the old man and what it might entail. In his arrogance he had failed to even *look* at it.

Whatever it was, he'd find a way out.

Lou re-checked his lottery ticket and pumped his fist in the air. He hugged Amy. She checked his numbers, fell against the wall and swooshed to a sitting position. Her lips started to tremble.

Lou McGee wasted no time. Endless parties. Manic celebrations. Land grabs amidst orchestrated construction projects. At the base of the Appalachian foothills, he purchased a large tract of land within the town limits of Johann and erected a fortress. Most of his original neighbors sold and moved out. Lou gobbled up their property, too.

He reveled in the fear being heaped upon his name. He put on airs when he could remember. He threw wild gambling parties and other gatherings of debauchery, all with plenty of security backup, technology and armory. At his parties, his guests became more notorious. Ravenous women played games at all hours of the night across the fortress lawns.

Embarrassing amounts of money tumbled in. Murder after assassination. Death after kill. Louis Rainier McGee had become the dark horse thinning humanity. He staked ownership over the thousand residents of Johann and renamed it McGeeville. The residents who remained understood that living a quiet, unassuming life was their safest bet. Their only bet.

Strange gifts also arrived at Lou's palace. Technology light years ahead of what humanity was producing. An eerie orb, for example, that when thrown to the floor slowed time so that Lou had fifteen minutes to do what he needed while everyone else rippled unknowingly in the current. Compared with any mortal, Lou was unstoppable.

Lou took Venus Blaque, a lithe exotic dancer, as his new wife. He'd moved Amy out and set her up on her own. They'd parted on amicable terms. At least it seemed to Lou. But this new black-haired vixen loved taking the reins.

As the years went on, Venus toyed with Lou. Learned all his secret spots. Knew him well. Stuffed him so full of gourmet food that he couldn't move. Lou knew from the beginning that this one was trouble. But in the danger Lou also found excitement in the extreme.

No person, place, or animal was safe from McGee. If he'd been paid then he would collect. He harvested hundreds of souls for the Old Goat. Souls down since conception. Souls caught in limbo. Souls who only wanted to descend. The wise stayed to the backside of his dark scythe.

On the eve of their twenty-first as blood brothers, the old man returned. Lou was hosting a full moon party. The full Buck moon. He'd forgotten what day it was. He heard a quiet rapping on the front door, a knocking no one else seemed to hear.

"Consarn it, Dorian," Lou said walking past his Butler. "Ya gonna answer the door?"

Dorian turned his palms up and resumed his position against the wall.

"I am sorry sir," he said in a heavy voice. "It will not happen again."

Lou opened the door to find the old man leaning in the jamb. In one of his trembling hands was a cane. In the other something the size of a shoebox wrapped in newspaper.

"You're a real angel, boss," Lou said. "You shouldn't have."

The old man smiled.

"I never show up to a celebration without a gift, Lou-baby. Hey, where'd you find that graybeard?"

The old man was older and slower, too. He must have been well over 110. As Lou led him down the halls and through rooms of bubble-headed guests, pop music and balloons, through other rooms of more distinguished guests mingling to swing music, he thought of how little he had actually seen the old man over the years. Once they'd had their covenant in the forest and Lou had signed the agreement, it's like the old man had disappeared. In his arrogance, Lou nearly assumed *he'd* given himself these powers and special gifts.

They arrived at Lou's recreation room. Lou ushered the old man inside, closed the door and locked it. He went to his fake bookcase and broke out a compartmental box disguised as an encyclopedia that was full of Dominican and Cuban cigars. He got a Dominican going.

"Nice wrap job," Lou said, nodding at the newspaper.

The old man kept his smile and set his gift on the end table. He eased onto a red leather sofa. As he struggled to cross a leg over his knee he nodded admiringly at the exotic trophy heads adorning the walls.

"Come to give your number one provider a bonus?" Lou asked. He handed the old man the Dominican. "I've sent you tons of sinners, loads of them, right on the gravy train." Lou got a Cuban going for himself. "And don't forget, I've always done it with a smile. But, you're right, I couldn't have done it without you, boss."

The old man raised his eyebrows. He plucked the cigar from his mouth and ran his tongue across his lips.

"Nice taste," he said.

"The wizardry you've given me…." Lou said, trailing off and sitting down. "It's almost been too easy. I've wiped out the best. The savages. The greedy. The crooked. The wasted and the wasteful. Man, I would have sliced and diced Napoleon, blitzkrieg'd Hitler, learned Sun Tzu a thing or two."

Lou's head dipped. The cigar smoked silently between his fingers. Sweat beaded on his pale brow.

"I've been put down so much in my life," he continued, "all I ever used to think about was putting it back on others."

The old man climbed to his feet.

"They say a miser is just a terrified man hiding behind a fortress of money," he said. "But that ain't you, Lou." The old man started to say something else, but then seemed to change his mind. Instead he asked: "Where's your lovely wife, Amy? I always wanted to meet her again."

Lou felt like he was swallowing a saber. Out of everything in his life, Amy was the only thing he really loved and missed. The only one. She'd once cleared the overgrown path to his heart. She knew him when he still had a sliver of soul. He remembered the hunger they once shared so many nights ago when they had nothing but they had each other and it was something. These days even his friends were dead. The last, Arnie Stephens, was on the run. Lou prayed he'd stay gone. He didn't want to rub him out either.

Sweet Amy.

"I kicked her to the wolves years ago," Lou muttered. "Anyway, you've met Venus Blaque? She does the trick."

The old man nodded and said he knew her.

"No heirs, Lou?"

"You know something," Lou said. "I *did* have a kid. Eighteen years ago after a one-night love affair. Crazy bastard up and joined the church. Can you believe it?"

"*Crazy,*" said the old man.

In an uncharacteristic move, Lou brought out a small bottle of liquid. His hand trembled as he held it up to the light.

"What's that?" the old man asked, perking up.

"Holy Water," said Lou.

The old man grinned.

"Holy water is just water, Lou."

"Holy water is blessed by a priest."

"But it tastes just the same."

Lou swallowed. He placed the small bottle on the fireplace mantle.

"Well, Big Lou, this feels like the celebration to end all celebrations," said the old man. He ambled over to the sofa where Lou was sitting and handed him the wrapped package. "It's time, old boy."

"Time for gifts?" Lou set his cigar in the ashtray on the end table and rubbed his hands. "Roger wilco."

Outside the room, music and laughter raged in a muffled roar. Lou ripped it open. Inside was a wooden box. He opened it.

"It's empty," he said.

The old man looked amused.

"Put it on the floor," he said. "Leave the top off."

"Will it slither out and bite me?" Lou asked. The old man cackled.

Lou placed the box on the hardwood floor and tossed away the lid. He stepped back and waited. Nothing. He glanced at the old man. The old man nodded, a smug smile across his face. Cigar smoke twirled.

"Patience," he said.

From somewhere inside the box a red light began to glow. Lou backed up. The box collapsed, unfolding itself to lie flat on the floor. Suddenly it sprung up and revealed itself as a door. Lou felt his eyeballs tremble.

The door swung open. Thick white smoke poured out. Through the open doorway stepped a shiny pair of black stiletto heels. Attached to the stilettos were long legs, a red skirt and jacket, and then up top an unbelievably beautiful dark-haired woman with a white fox fur wrapped around her neck. She looked like a celebrity from the Roaring 20s. The lady adjusted a black satchel on her shoulder.

The old man was next. He snapped his fingers and stepped through the doorway with a cocky smile. The old man came though the other side morphing into a dashing young gentleman with dark, slicked-back hair. His crisp tuxedo and red silk bowtie complemented the lady's attire next to him. She looked so familiar.

"Amy!"

Lou finally recognized her. She stood there like the spitfire viper he'd met forty years ago. Amy met Lou's gaze with fiery eyes. Behind them, the door sank into the oak floor. The dashing young man stepped forward. He scooped up Amy's arm.

"Smashing party, McGee," he said. He waved his arm at the trophy heads on the wall. "A most splendid room. Amy, my dear, I believe you bear the gifts for our host?"

Lou stared unable to move. Amy unzipped her black satchel, pulled out a small brown Chihuahua and handed it to the man.

"Miss Morningstar!" the man said theatrically. He lifted the pooch into the air. Morningstar yipped. "I thought I'd never find you girl." Amy giggled. Lou found himself laughing, too. His sanity was somewhere over the rainbow.

"That bad man frightened my Morningstar once," the man said, pointing at Lou. His tone had turned grave. "Ran into her in the forest and never apologized. How crass. And why, *Dahling*, do you insist upon hiding her in your handbag?"

"She likes it," Amy said. She reached into her satchel and pulled out a small Tommy gun. She cocked the metal bolt and raised the gun at Lou. "Besides, she keeps my Chicago typewriter warm. Any last birthday requests, Mister?"

"It's not my birthday, Amy," Lou said. "Please ... *remember me.*"

"Hold it!" the man barked. He pulled a silencer out of his tux pocket and screwed it onto the end of her barrel. "We can't be disturbing the guests."

Lou's eyes were glazed over. They'd been fixated on his former spouse, but now they saw nothing. Lou felt nothing. In a monotone voice he said:

"You finally dyed your hair. Hells bells."

Amy laughed.

"Did he say *dyed*?" She squeezed the trigger. The Tommy gun tatted a three-round burst into Lou's left knee, destroying it. He crashed into the floor face first. His two front teeth scattered across the floor.

"Oh peanuts," Amy said. "Not where I wanted. Well, time is money." She aimed again, but the dapper gentleman turned down her barrel. He handed Miss Morningstar to Amy. Lou pulled himself up and hopped around on his good leg. He was a red frothy mess.

The man smoothed back his hair.

"Allow me, Dahling," he said, reaching into his tux. He came out with a sleek semiautomatic pistol. The pistol blended right into the man's hand. "There's an old joke between me and Mr. McGee here. I'm sure he's anxious to catch the punchline."

The clock on the wall struck midnight.

The man fired. The hollow-point bullet hit Lou in the chest and expanded, peeling back and snagging his heart to spray it against the back wall. Lou's body crashed into the end table, spilling his martini and sending his cigar flying onto the white polar bear rug.

Louis Rainier McGee was a dead man.

But he hadn't quite caught on yet.

His brain held the juice for one last call.

As he lay on his back, Lou looked up with fading eyes at the dark man standing over him. The man slid the pistol back into his tux. He leaned down and whispered: "Always loved that about you, Lou. For a small fish that could never see the forest for the trees, you were always willing to take one for the team. I will enjoy having you close, low boy. Much to discover."

He stood and rejoined Amy in her elegant red outfit. They looked quite the stunning pair. The man brought her hand to his mouth and kissed it.

"Simply ravishing," he said. He tapped his forehead. "Please forgive me; I had completely forgotten to introduce you. Amelia—that was Lou McGee. Please extend him your fondest farewell."

"Bye, Lou," she said.

The dark man opened the door. Amy kissed him on the cheek. He took her arm and led her out, whistling as they left the room.

Seven minutes later, a man in a tux said he smelled smoke. Dorian the Butler said he did as well. A lady ran down the hallway screaming that the west wing was ablaze.

The staff, the servants, the guests and all the pets made it out of the McGee palace safely. Aside from Lou, no life or limb was lost. And although the Fire Department arrived in record time it wasn't quickly enough, and the entire McGee estate was reduced to a vast pile of glowing orange cinders.

None of the fire made it into the Appalachian Mountains. No other homes were destroyed. No other lives seemed to have been touched by the blaze.

The Rumor Mill had it that Lou McGee had burned himself alive. Some kids joked that he spontaneously combusted. Everyone agreed he'd been the angriest, greediest hot-head they'd ever known. Only one man said he was there. He'd seen it all go down. He watched Lou's ex-wife leaving the rumpus room with a tall dark drink of water on her arm, and the man was clomping down the hallway in a strange pair of platform shoes. Like clogs. He couldn't forget those shoes.

No one listened to the man. He was one of McGeeville's biggest drunks.

Although most were glad Lou was gone, not many spoke of it. Year after year and the days since, the small town grew brighter. Townsfolk opened up. Neighbors said hello to each other. They smiled. They grew more grateful because they realized a dark shadow had passed. The residents reclaimed the town of Johann.

Hardly a scratch had been heard about Amy McGee. The Bellevue Sisters said they'd seen her in Paris a year ago, but nothing could be confirmed. Later the ladies reneged on their statement anyway. It was impossible, they said, completely preposterous it could have been trailer trash Amy McGee looking so chic and stylish; acting like she'd stumbled upon the fountain of youth.

THE END

'A Bathroom
Patriotic'

～

Hot unfiltered sun scorched the Valley. It baked the rocky hillsides. The dense dry chaparral. Stucco terracotta housetops. Gray asphalt. It even steamed sprinkler water unlucky enough to land on the sidewalks.

A sleek Tesla electric pulled into the driveway of a beautiful hillside home. Fifty-eight year old Ehren Hensley—one job, one wife to his name—got out. He was in his usual light gray business suit. The suit wasn't bad. It shed the heat and the sun well. Today it would be tested.

It was already a hot one.

Ehren had driven all the way down to San Fernando Boulevard this morning only to turn around and drive all the way back up again. He'd remembered to sign the contract agreement. He'd remembered his briefcase. He'd forgotten to put the contract agreement *inside* his briefcase.

He had time. The company reps from Norville would be there all day. If worse came to worse he could always overnight it to them.

Scorching summer, he thought jogging toward the front entrance. Ehren prided himself on getting as much work done as early in the day as possible. Jan used to love it about him. Now, well—just this morning his wife blew a gasket when he put his peanut butter knife on the counter instead of in the sink. So he washed it himself and she got even more pissed. Not that she ever did the dishes.

Do I honestly need this in my life? Jan had been with him for ten years. Ehren felt like he'd done fifteen hard labor with her. *It wasn't even fun. Am I happier ... alone?*

Jan was out running errands anyway. Eating her Kefir. Getting her Mani and her Pedi.

Ehren paused. The front door wasn't locked. It wasn't even latched. Open just a crack. He pressed it with his fingertips and the door swung easily on its well-oiled hinges.

"Jan?"

He stepped through the doorway. Their part-time maid Ora Salazar looked up. She was on her knees dusting the base of a standing lamp. He'd been in such a rush he hadn't even noticed her car in the driveway.

"Buenos días," said Ehren. He felt confident he could still handle himself in a number of situations, but when you expect your front door to be locked and it isn't the finger of apprehension gooses you. With this pleasant surprise, however, it dawned on him just how long it'd been since he'd been home in the morning during a weekday.

Ora cleaned for the Hensleys on Tuesdays, Wednesdays, and Thursdays. She'd been cleaning for them for almost five years. Ehren hadn't seen her in at least a year.

"How's your morning, Mr. Hensley?" Ora asked, standing. A bottle of Amish Dutch Glow hung from one hand, a dust rag in the other. A smile drew across her face.

Ehren found himself entranced at her smile and her perfect brown nose. He had a bit of an eagle beak himself. Physical imperfections never bothered him. He wasn't that superficial. But Ora, she was really something.

"Are you all right?" she asked.

"Yes fine," Ehren said, shaking himself. "I remembered my briefcase but I forgot to put anything in it." Ora's smile glittered. Ehren laughed. It was spontaneous. It felt good. Ever since her first interview, Ora Salazar had always intrigued him.

"I'm glad I didn't move those papers," Ora said. She pointed to the table where the Partnership Contract Agreement and its amplifying information were neatly stacked.

"You're perfect," Ehren said. "You make coming home to this house a joy."

"I do?"

"Absolutely."

"It's still only a house," Ora said, dropping her eyes. "It takes a lot of loving between you and Mrs. Hensley to make it a home."

Ehren paused.

"I'll have to remember that," he said.

"So, how is life?"

Her directness caught him off guard.

"Changing," he said. "Slow changes finally coming to fruition."

"At work?" Ora asked. He nodded. "I read articles in magazines where they say a person is an overnight success, and that woman says, no, I've been working at this for many, many years!"

"Unless you've had an ethical bypass or you're an outright genius, most overnight successes I've known are twenty years in the making."

"Sí."

"And sometimes what you think you're doing is not really what you're doing."

They chatted away catching each others' eyes like playful butterflies flitting to the same flower. They danced away. A playful tango in bloom—full colors on display. Ehren realized two things. One, he felt no guilt. And secondly, in a moment like this, many things in his personal life were painfully obvious. Ora pulled off her vinyl gloves.

"Pour you a coffee?" she asked.

"Have one with me? Otherwise, I haven't the time."

"Well, I—"

"You talked me into it," Ehren said. *I feel your rumblings, Higher Power. Or is this Satan? Satan, you devil! Five minutes ago I was ready to be done with all this melodrama.*

Ora headed into the kitchen. Ehren sat at the breakfast credenza. He listened as she opened a cupboard, took down the coffee grinder, opened another cupboard, took out a bag of coffee beans and then two distinct clinks as she set one mug and then another on the granite countertop. He listened to her fill the coffee pot with water. Listened to her grind the coffee beans. The coffee percolating.

Soon, aromatic brew drifted out into the dining room filling his imagination with wildfire. *What am I? A teenager with a crush? Please. But who knows, maybe this is real.*

"You were born in Indiana?" Ora asked from the kitchen.

"Southern Indiana, yes," Ehren said. "What about you? I thought I remember you saying that you grew up here in the Valley?"

"Sunnyvale," Ora said. "A little north." The Hensley house was large, but the acoustics were phenomenal. You could hold entire conversations across entire rooms in a normal tone of voice. It was ironic. He and Jan spoke less and less and yelled more and more.

"Very nice," Ehren said.

"I lived in San José a few years," said Ora.

BANG! The floor rattled.

"Everything all right?"

"That was me," she said. "Sorry, dropped a skillet."

Ehren heard her groan to pick it up. Housework got to a person. He'd trudged through his share of menial labor when he was younger. He washed, cleaned, ironed, folded, scrubbed. Plus all the other "man" stuff. He felt fortunate during this second phase of his life to have developed another skill set that was more in line with who he was. Or who he felt he was.

"I started my Associate's degree at San José State," Ora said. "Then a few years in Phoenix. And then here in the San Fernando Valley."

The German cuckoo clock on the wall chirped. 11:30 a.m. Ehren's mind was adrift imagining younger Ora. It wasn't difficult. Although only a few years younger than himself, Ora's innocent face and unique beauty gave her a classic, timeless look.

"But yes," she said, "I lived most of my life here and in Sunnyvale."

She walked out of the kitchen carrying two large mugs. She set one in front of Ehren. His mouth watered. He took the handle, blew across the dark liquid and toasted her.

"Cheers."

"Cheers," she replied.

Ehren brought the mug to his lips. He missed. He tried again and missed again, this time spilling a run of coffee onto his suit jacket and pants. What the fudge, he muttered. He mopped it up with his napkin. At least it hadn't burned him. Ora slid another napkin his way. Ehren tried for a third sip, but it was difficult to hold the mug steady. His hands were shaking. They were really shaking badly.

The floor was shaking.

The walls were shaking.

Even the ceiling fan was wobbling erratically.

The rim of the mug never touched his lips. He and Ora stared. Their mouths couldn't move, but their eyes said it all. *Earthquake.*

Ehren dropped the mug of coffee in his lap.

"Ahhh!"

That spill got him. He jumped up and yelled as the mug broke apart all over the floor. Ora got to her feet.

"You okay?" she asked.

"Yeah," he said. He grabbed her hand. Coffee dripped from his suit jacket and pants. "Let's go!"

Go? Go where? He couldn't think. The house was shaking so violently he couldn't' remember what to do. *A million different safety drills at a million different companies and I'm drawing a blank? How long have I lived in LA County?*

Ora tugged at his arm.

"We gotta get outside and lie in a ditch!" he said. Ora stared at him with terror-stricken eyes. "No! No, that's not it—"

The cuckoo clock fell from the wall and smashed. It sounded like a freight train outside. Glass splintered in the windows. Dishes shattered in the kitchen. The ceiling fan threatened to fly off and decapitate them.

"Mr. Hensley!"

Small light bulbs popped next to them raining down from the chandelier. Pictures on the walls splintered and fell. Artwork crashed. Lights exploded.

"Under a table!" he shouted. "No, a doorjamb! *We gotta get under a doorjamb!*"

Ehren pulled Ora under the threshold in the hallway. They squared themselves underneath it. He nearly fell but Ora kept him on his feet.

"Arms in," she said.

The house groaned. Loud pounding and knocking. It felt as though they were sliding right down the side of the Verdugo Mountains. Ehren put his hands over Ora's head.

"I'm sorry," he said.

She looked up with worried eyes. Their world was breaking loose. "What?"

"I'm sorry," he repeated.

Ora shrugged her shoulders.

"I'm sorry too," she said, her voice vibrating.

There was a loud sawing sound, as if the house were skidding across rumble strips. Was the entire mountain collapsing?

Ehren tilted Ora's chin upward. For a millisecond he gazed into her frightened eyes, and then he kissed her. He pulled back. He kissed her again. She kissed him back, sort of. The house jolted. They screamed. Both of their arms shot out to counter the sudden shift as dust and plaster floated down.

Ora covered her ears and looked up at him for some sort of answer.

"I've wanted to do that since forever," he said, his voice jittering.

"Was nice," she replied.

Ora closed her eyes and wrapped her arms around Ehren. He held her tight against the roar of the quake. He was ready. No kids. No wife who loved him. He felt more at peace and ready to accept his fate with this sweet, honest lady in his arms than at any other time in his life. Ora figured if the Lord was calling her then she would go. She'd rather the quake took all of her. What scared her most was being maimed. She had enough pain already.

The rumblings were becoming more distant. A huge, unearthly jolt made them scream again and hang on. Dust-caked tears streamed down Ora's cheeks. The house groaned and creaked. Car sirens blared and beeped outside the shattered windows.

Once again, the commotion began to fade. Like a monstrous freight train that had finally passed, the rumblings slowly sank back into the earth.

Ehren and Ora released their grip on each other. Both had their eyes closed. They pulled apart and brushed the dust from their faces. Ehren thought for sure he'd see his house balancing on a single spire of mountain, tilting back and forth, ready to plunge into the abyss.

Ora tapped his arm. Ehren cracked his eyes. Dust was settling. Picture frames, lights, glass, lamps, drywall and other piles of junk lay scattered and broken. His teak bookcase had collapsed and spilled his novels, manuals and study guides all over the living room floor. Sun streamed in through jagged holes and splits in the roof.

"Oh *my*," Ora said. She coughed.

"We made it," Ehren croaked. They kissed a dusty kiss. When they pulled away, Ehren laughed. He was approaching sixty and this was a brand new lease on life. "Ora, we're alive!"

Ora lifted her eyes. "Gracias, Señor," she said.

They crept into the living room. Ehren was in his house. This was still his house. All of his and Jan's things had been tossed about and smashed into haphazard piles of debris. And that's all it looked like anymore. Junk. Debris. Ehren shook his head. It had so little value.

Down the far hallway he could see natural light streaming in. At a certain angle he could see clear outside. He decided against investigating that portion of the house.

Beep, beep, beep, beep! His smart phone. For some reason he was shocked it was still working. He reached into his suit and checked the number. It was his colleague, Brad Cerdan.

"Bradley!"

Ora checked her bag. Her cell phone was right on top. She sighed in relief.

"Yes," Ehren said. "We're all right. Totaled. Huh?" He stepped over to a window that was no longer a window. The driveway had been torn in two. His new Tesla Model 3 was gone. "It's looking pretty horrific," he continued, the phone to his ear. "You're kidding me. Oh man, yes—great, great, we'll see you soon. You're the best, partner."

He slid his phone back into his suit. Ora touched his arm.

"My car," she said. "I don't see it out there."

"We'll worry about it later," he said. "Right now, grab whatever stuff you can. We've got a ride coming."

"I only have my personal bag," she said. "Should we bring any food?"

Ehren put his dusty fingers to his chin. What to do? What to get? He felt more anxious now than when the earth was cracking. He figured it best to gather what he could and then get out in case the house decided to move.

"We shouldn't need to bring any food," he said.

He walked toward the bathroom. Of all the things he owned, his grandfather's Navy ring was the one heirloom that couldn't be replaced. The rest was filler. Filler for a home that never existed.

Ora came in behind him. Surprisingly the bathroom didn't look too bad. The mirror was cracked. The shower curtain and curtain rod had come down. The Irish Spring body wash and the Herbal Essence shampoo and conditioner were lying in the bottom of the tub. The toilet bowl had no water. But it was still intact.

"How…?" Ora asked.

"I don't know," Ehren said. He wasn't even sure what she was asking. His grandfather's Navy ring lay in the sink. It was too big to get past the drain plug. He grabbed it, slid it onto his finger.

"Hope we can get outside," he said. "We can climb out one of the broken windows I suppose."

He stopped. Ora was staring with dewy eyes at the American Flag candle sitting on the bathroom counter. Red, white and blue. It looked like it had hardly moved.

"I love this candle," she said softly. "It's my favorite candle in the whole world."

Ehren gave a small smile. That old candle flying Old Glory. How long had he had it? It'd become such a permanent fixture in his bathroom that he often looked right past it. But he knew what Ora meant. She picked it up.

"I've dusted this candle every time I've cleaned in here," she said. "Makes me feel proud." She would later tell Ehren it had always endeared him to her.

"Glad I never lit it," he said.

She looked at him. He nodded quickly. She stuffed the candle into her bag.

As they were walking toward the front door, Ehren found the dusty contract agreement and also his briefcase. They paused at the front door. He opened it slowly; hesitant the entire front wall of the house might collapse without its support. The door swung smoothly on its well-oiled hinges. Nothing else moved.

Outside sat damage aplenty. Trees were cracked, broken. The driveway was split—one half coming up over the top of the other. Car alarms chirped down the street. The back half of the drive was completely gone, as was Ora's Hyundai and Ehren's black Model 3. The vehicles must have found new homes at the bottom of the canyon.

Above the Verdugo Mountains sat a bright sun in a quiet sky.

Another car pulled in. A white Lexus. It was Jan. She stopped short of the chasm in the driveway and got out. Ora swallowed, taking a step back. Ehren crossed his arms.

"Holy moly," Jan said, closing the car door. She had her hair in a bun and was wearing her green Lululemon yoga pants. "M-My house!"

Jan glanced at them as she jogged around the cracked driveway and into their destroyed home.

Ehren felt little desire to move. No desire to speak.

Chop-chop-chop-chop!

In the distance, helicopter blades beat the air. Ehren put a hand over his forehead to block the rays of the sun. He watched Brad Cerdan's helicopter swing softly down out of the sky looking for a place to land. Ehren and Ora backed up. They shielded their faces from the wind-blown dust. Brad set her down on the one solid patch of asphalt.

"Here he is," Ehren said.

Just then, Jan ran back outside.

"Oh, fuck you! Is that what this is?" she asked.

Ehren regarded his future ex-wife with boredom. All Jan promised were long, sad conversations about all the things she wanted in life but wasn't getting. He turned to Ora Salazar. The honesty, the goodness, the playfulness underneath. Effortless. *Yeah, maybe I is a sucker. But for a while I'll be a happy sucker.*

He turned back to face Jan.

"*Well?*" she said her hands on her hips.

Ehren said nothing.

Instead, he opened the passenger door to the helicopter and helped Ora climb in. Jan railed behind them.

"You slutty little immigrant!" she shouted. "Hensley, I'm gonna sue your ass! We're going to court! This house and everything in it is mine! Hensley, you bastard!"

"Peace in the Middle East," Ehren said. He flashed the peace sign, set his briefcase on the floor of the copter and closed the door. After helping Ora get buckled, he sat back

"All set?" asked Brad from the cockpit.

"Hit it, sir," said Ehren. "Brad this is Ora Salazar. Ora meet Bradley Cerdan."

"How do, Miss?" Brad asked.

"Thank you," Ora said. "Thank you so much."

"My pleasure, *da nada.*"

The helicopter rose into the air. To Ora it felt like twenty floors in two seconds in an elevator. She put a hand to her stomach. Ehren brushed the damp, dirty strands of hair out of her eyes.

"It wasn't the San Andreas," Brad said. "Blind thrust fault somewhere close."

A Hensley epicenter, Ehren mused. Ora held tight next to him. He took her hand and held it.

As the helicopter made the transition to forward flight there was no turbulence in the tranquil blue sky. And when Ehren saw the house from above, he realized it was the master bedroom at the far end that had broken off and ended up at the bottom of the mountain.

THE END

'BRYCE CANYON'

⟶

THE HIKING TRAIL OPENED—SILVER-BARKED ASPENS and majestic ponderosa pines gave way to a steep cliff. Abe Jacobson stared across the chasm, wheezing. Autumn sunlight bathed the far rocks in an orange glow. Thom Rogers let loose a devilish grin.

"You've never seen anything like it," Thom said.

Just over the side, embedded in the cliffs according to Thom, were gem caves—quaint little alcoves that glittered like a million colored mirrors. Thom had called Abe to wish his friend a happy 60th birthday. He'd also persuaded Abe to get off his duff and hike into Bryce Canyon with him to search out these shiny disco crevices. Now they stood at the edge of an abyss. Abe felt swindled.

"Let's go back to the car," he said, all out of breath. "Been out here all day." Thom's red baseball cap disappeared over the side. "Hey *man! We're missing Topless Tina's!*"

Abe wasn't in shape for this nonsense. The pursuit of anything outdoors had left him long ago. He'd worked hard his entire life; much of it punching numbers in a cubicle. These days he even felt like a number. And surely Bryce Canyon was filled with subtle and intimate beauty, but all he wanted this Saturday was supple flesh tickling his lips and exotic lotion drifting up his nose. It was after all his birthday.

Thom Rogers was the only one—the only one who could have talked him into this gibberish, that sly bastard.

Abe slid his belly over the crags. His fingers groped at every nook. Glancing down, he saw Thom hanging off a tiny tree growing out of the side. *How do you have this much energy?* Abe wondered. *We're sixty, not thirty.* The valley below swayed like heat waves in a mirage.

"We're teenagers again!" Thom cried. He stuck out his tongue. Abe was trying to concentrate but Thom wouldn't stop. "Hey, Jacobson—did ya hear the one about the American, the Brit, the Canadian, and the Anteater who walked into the Glory 'Ole Saloon?"

Abe chuckled. He lost his grip and started to slide. He yelled for Thom to get clear but Thom couldn't move and they collided.

Rust-colored rocks crumbled underneath Abe. It burned his backside. He shot down the face of the cliff like a demonic rollercoaster. He whizzed past three large boulders. He passed Thom Rogers who was tumbling backward hard.

The ground below was moving quickly up to meet him. Ninety feet, fifty feet. Ten. *Ungghhh!* Abe wiped out at the bottom in a cloud of dust.

Hot pain seared his ankle. He yelled. His voice echoed off the canyon walls and carried along the desolate valley floor. He staggered over to an old tree stump, untied his boot and peeled off his sock. His ankle was swelling and turning purple.

Meanwhile, Thom landed a few feet away in a crumpled mess. Gone was his red baseball cap. Abe hobbled furiously to where his friend lay covered in dust.

"See what happens, you idiot! You see?"

Laughter was always the best medicine Thom would say. He'd bark malpractice jokes while observing open heart surgery. But Thom didn't move. His neck lay cranked to one side. Blood seeped from a hideous gash in his throat. From the back of his inverted leg dripped a bloody bone.

Abe put an ear to Thom's mouth. Felt for a pulse at his neck. Nothing. He lost his lunch.

How *did I let this happen?* Why *did I let this happen?*

Abe wiped his mouth and stared at the spires of cliffs above that stretched for miles. His backside felt barbequed. His ankle burned. He tried once to climb but toppled over immediately. Lying on his back, his mouth sticky, his lungs fighting for air Abe gave up. Even healthy and with the best gear he couldn't make a climb like this.

After gathering what wits remained, Abe ditched his boot and grabbed a gnarly tree branch for support. The terrain down here was different. Scraggly Utah junipers dotted the edge of a trail. The trail followed the winding canyon walls. Behind him stood a dark wood. It made Abe shiver. Pinnacles of pink rock formations stood in reflective glow from the setting sun. It all should have looked so beautiful. But now the beauty and the solitude only mocked him.

Abe grew resentful. He'd have a ton of police reports to fill out after this fiasco. And he probably wouldn't make it out of Bryce Canyon before midnight. *Happy birthday, sap.*

It was Thom's fault. Abe had slipped up letting his friend talk him into this stupidity, but it was all Thom's fault for bringing them out here in the middle of nowhere and then acting the fool. *Now it's my destiny to be stranded down here? Alone?*

No. Abe would not accept this. He tottered over to his dead friend.

"Thanks pal," he said. He spit on Thom's corpse. With wild abandon he yelled: "*What'd I do to deserve this? Huh?!*" His echoed voice answered. A strange feeling settled over him though he couldn't decide what it was.

Abe moved away from the dark wood. Slowly he weaved down the worn trail. The sculpted columns, arches and hoodoo of Bryce towered over him. Regal ponderosa pines. It all would have looked breathtaking if his damn ankle wasn't burning with every step.

Abe Jacobson made it a quarter of a mile. A stabbing migraine dropped him to his knees. He rose once on shaky legs and collapsed on the trail.

Blackness.

⌒⌐

Abe wasn't sure how long he'd been unconscious. A voice was calling out. He turned his head.

A bearded man was running toward him. The man wore a camping pack and had a long rifle slung over his left shoulder. He knelt at Abe's side.

"You all right, man?"

"My ankle," Abe said. The man looked to be in his early thirties with helpful eyes and a friendly smile. From his pack he pulled a camouflaged water canteen. Abe fought to a sitting position, took it and drank.

"That your partner back there?" the man asked.

Abe wiped his mouth. "Ex-partner, apparently," he said. He took another swig and returned the canteen. "Thanks. I never got your name."

The young man shook Abe's hand.

"Matt," he said. "Matt Kincaid."

"Abe Jacobson."

"Oh, baby," said Matt. He nodded at Abe's stick. "Is *that* what you're using?"

Within minutes, Matt Kincaid had constructed a solid pair of walking crutches using felled branches and some twine from his pack. In another warm gesture he also fixed a splint for Abe's ankle. Then he gave him two aspirin and a granola bar.

The two men got going. They moved quietly down the winding trail. Abe prayed they'd soon be out of this insane nature asylum. Occasionally a rock would hurtle down the side of a cliff and they'd stop to listen. The scraggly trees were becoming fuller and denser.

A short while later they decided to rest. Abe shook his traveling partner's hand again.

"You saved my life, Matt," he said. "I can't thank you enough. How'd you come to be stuck out here?"

"Well, it's kind of embarrassing," Matt said. "My girlfriend and I were backcountry camping. Having a great time. Or so I thought. When I woke this morning, Sue was gone. Just totally up and split."

"Wasn't kidnapped was she?" Abe asked. Matt shook his head. "Or an animal?"

"Not unless a cougar made off with her pillow, her purse and the park map."

"Maybe she just went into town for something," Abe said. Matt stared with sad eyes. *No*, thought Abe, *I wouldn't believe that either.*

His eyes fixed on the setting sun disturbingly close to the tops of the canyon walls. The day seemed in a sprint to the end. Especially under the oppressive canopy of trees that seemed to be coming out of nowhere.

"Thom and I had dinner plans," Abe said. "I usually don't go out— hate wasting the money—but we had a whole evening of debauchery planned for my birthday."

"Happy birthday, Abe."

"Thanks."

"Mine's in March. Two fishes. Pisces."

"Think I'm a Virgo," Abe said. "But the stars have never meant that much to me. Where are you from originally?"

"All over," Matt said. "The travel bug bit me early."

"*Ahhh*, to be young again."

Matt straightened up.

"So, you said that your friend Thom brought you out here to hunt for gems?" he asked. Abe nodded slowly. A revolting suspicion already knew Matt's reply. "There are no gem caves in Bryce Canyon."

Matt Kincaid turned out to be a knowledgeable traveling partner. He'd worked for three years on the island of Roatan, Honduras making pottery. Climbed the Cascade Mountain Range in Washington. Worked a rustic music venue in Talkeetna, Alaska. Hunted in Caribou, Maine. He was into travel and survival and possessed respectable ken in both areas.

"Did you know Bryce was formed hundreds of millions of years *after* the Paleozoic era forged the Grand Canyon 200 miles south?"

"I had no idea," Abe said.

"I'm full of useless information like that," Matt said.

"Maybe you'll win a ton of cash on a game show," said Abe. "*THIS* ... IS ... JEOPARDY!*"

"That'll be the day."

"You never know."

"More like '*This is Your Life*'," Matt said smiling. "All my trivial knowledge coming back to haunt me."

Abe's heart grew heavy joking with Matt. He'd always kept the prospect of family at arm's length. In a way, Matt Kincaid felt like a son he might have once had. Long time ago.

Just as strange, however, was the dubious feeling growing toward Kincaid. The younger man seemed exceptionally intuitive—a witty know-it-all—and the more Abe listened to Matt, the less he trusted him. *Maybe he feels the same about me?*

Evening drew on. The trees continued to grow thicker and the trail turned into an overgrown path. Matt pulled out a small, battery-powered lantern but it was little help. Deep shadows were seeping in all around them. Matt shared the last bits of food from his pack and they found a few Pinyon nuts to munch on, but it wasn't much. Both men were hungry.

When a mountain cottontail appeared on the dim path in front of them, Matt slowly shouldered his rifle. He cocked the hammer.

"Muzzleloader," he whispered. "One shot. Then we'll have to reload."

One shot did it. Right in the animal's head. Matt was pleased as the bullet hadn't wasted any edible meat.

They built a crackling fire. Soon, Abe was gnawing charred rabbit off the bone and drinking strong instant coffee. A brilliant ceiling of stars shimmered overhead. The fresh mountain air was invigorating. Abe felt young again.

"Don't think I've ever seen a night sky so bright," Matt said.

"I hear ya," said Abe. "It really is something. Don't feel bad about Sue. My wife left me ten years ago and honestly, I don't miss the conniving little bitch one bit. Her greedy little fingers were all over my money. And my nerves."

"Some people are only in it for themselves," Matt said. The two men nodded. In the twinkling eyes of Matt Kincaid, Abe recognized something. He couldn't tell what it was, only that it made him grin.

"Just be glad you weren't married," Abe said. "Twice as painful and thrice as expensive. I've heard kids take it to a whole new level. What's the quote? Happy are the parents who never had any." Abe sipped his coffee.

"How old are ya?" Matt asked. "If you don't mind."

Abe sat lost in thought. He struggled to remove his eyes from the fire.

"Forty-nine," he finally said. He didn't mind fibbing by eleven years. Matt adjusted his seat while Abe smiled bitterly. "The ironic part now is I pay *all* my women. Pay them to go away afterward. More cost-effective."

Matt chuckled softly. Abe laughed too. But his laugh was more of a reaction to his eyes being drawn toward Matt Kincaid's rifle.

⌒

After breaking down the fire and covering the hot ashes, they returned to the path. Abe felt like they'd been traveling all night. He hadn't slept. But he wasn't tired. It was hard to believe but he felt fantastic.

Overhead, the stars were fading and the sky was growing lighter.

"If I remember correctly," Matt said, "there's a trailhead close by. The slope is nice and gradual. We should be able to get you up it. From there we can flag down a park ranger, or at least hitch a ride back to our cars."

Abe was eternally grateful he had driven instead of Thom. He jingled the keys to his BMW in his pocket just to reassure himself they were there.

Something flashed on the path in front of them.

Abe stopped.

"What's that moving?"

"Where?" Matt asked. "I don't see anything."

"Something disappeared into that spruce grove," Abe said. "Better reload."

Matt poured a charge of gunpowder down the barrel of the muzzleloader, seated a bullet with the ramrod and inserted a primer. He handed the rifle to Abe.

"I have a tactical flashlight in here somewhere," Matt said, unzipping his pack.

Abe couldn't stop the cruel grin from stretching across his lips. What a huge mistake his new friend had just made! He was no fool. He knew *exactly* what was happening.

Meanwhile, the soft light of the rising sun rippled the sky pink. But, wasn't it rising in the West? *How is that possible?* Maybe Abe was turned around. No, no he wasn't. He found it even more bizarre that Matt didn't seem to notice any of this being the nature freak he was. It all smelled fishy.

A young woman in a flowing white gown stepped out of the spruce pines. She waved and pirouetted into some evergreen shrubs.

"Whoa," Matt said. "Who the hell is that?"

Abe slowly brought the rifle to his shoulder. He cocked the hammer.

"Abe, what are you doing?"

"You drugged me, you bastard," Abe said. "You and your girl in white have something planned, don't you? Some kind of trap? *Ha!* Not any more. Get marching, bub. Try anything and I'll put one through your liver."

Matt Kincaid appeared hurt and confused, but Abe wasn't buying any of it. He directed Matt to the evergreen shrubs where the young woman had disappeared. They came around the bushes. Rustled through the brush. Searched the scrub. But there was no one there.

Matt shrugged his shoulders.

"What are we looking for again?" he asked.

Abe fired. The muzzleloader flashed brightly in a plume of white smoke. Matt Kincaid jerked stiff, his hair standing on end. But he didn't go down. He barely moved.

How did I miss? Abe wondered. *It was point blank!*

Abe stepped back. He gripped the rifle with both hands, ready to swing it like a club. Matt stared at him with defeated eyes.

"I know you," he said.

"I know *you*," Abe said.

"I'll bet you do."

Something felt seriously wrong. A whistle started low. It quickly reached full shriek in Abe's head, and in a flash he *did* know. He knew the face. He knew the beard. The color of the eyes. They were *his* eyes. Abe Jacobson's eyes. He was staring at … *himself?*

Matt Kincaid was Abe Jacobson. A younger Abe from long ago.

"Remember sophomore year at Brigham Young?" Abe dropped the rifle into the dirt. "Man, we loved gloating to the pious, the atheists— *everyone.* We loved telling them that it was man—not God, not Allah, not the earth goddess, Mr. Smith, or even the Great Spirit—it was *man* who judged himself at the end. Objectively. Unsuspecting."

"This is a nightmare," Abe said shaking. "It can't be."

"It is. You were right. You can't hide from yourself."

Abe's eyes spread wide with horrible knowledge. The dirt below his feet grew spongy and hot.

"It isn't fair!" Abe screamed.

"It was your choice."

"Matt help me!"

"Who's Matt?"

Abe's younger image floated into the air, morphing once into the face of Thom Rogers before vanishing in the orange stripes of the rising sun. An echo pulsed in Abe's mind: *If you don't trust yourself, who can you trust?*

Abe felt himself burning.

His feet caught fire. He was sinking. It wasn't into quicksand, it was a lava swamp. Death flames licked higher. The blaze engulfed the anguished body of Abraham Jacobson, while an evil laugh emanated from somewhere beyond the canyon.

THE END

'QM3'

⌐⌐

OUT IN THE DARKNESS OF Panama Bay, the USS Bonnar (FFG 93) tilted her bow up and down. She nodded at the twinkling lights. Ten nautical miles in the distance food, drink, and the tantalizing women of Panama City enticed many a sailor.

The crew was excited for liberty call tomorrow morning. They'd been at sea for three weeks, conducting drills with the South American Navy, practicing their own maneuvers and keeping their sea legs limber. This would be their last port call before returning to the U.S.

Lieutenant Mark Xavier assumed the watch as the Officer of the Deck. It was 2335 (11:35 p.m.). The Bonnar turned over watch teams on the half hour before. Xavier's team had just taken the 0000 – 0400 watch. Some called it the balls to four. Most often it was referred to as: The Mid Watch.

This is LT Xavier. I assume all duties and responsibilities as Officer of the Deck. Ensign Matthews has the Conn.

This is Ensign Matthews, I have the Conn.

As Conning Officer, Matthews gave the orders to the Helmsman on what course to steer, how much rudder to use and what speed to ring up. As Officer of the Deck, Xavier was in charge of the Navigation Bridge. In the absence of the Captain, he was responsible for executing the plan of the day, and, more importantly, for the safe navigation of the ship.

The only navigation the USS Bonnar was doing tonight, however, was cutting slow circles in the ocean. Marking time. Awaiting Sea &

Anchor detail tomorrow morning for their three day visit to Panama City, Panama.

It was a calm night. Foggy haze hung in patches over the water. The Bridge was dark and quiet save for the red lights of the instrument panels and the occasional whispers of the Seamen and Petty Officers standing watch.

Xavier stepped out onto the bridge wing. Stars popped in the night sky. The air was thick with salt. It was muggy near the equator. Even in January. Like many in the United States, Xavier was used to white in the winter months, yet in this southernmost country of Central America they never got any snow, ever.

A voice came from the back of the bridge wing.

Evening, sir.

Who's that? Xavier asked.

QM3 Schwartz, sir.

Schwartz, how's it going?

Outstanding, sir.

Honestly?

A little tired, sir. If you want to know the truth.

With you on that one, Xavier said. It's pretty crazy what we get used to, isn't it?

Yes, sir.

They admired the quiet waters of Panama Bay. Shy wavelets lapped against the side of the ship. Millions of stars twinkled like a huge planetarium. Nights like these made one feel honored to serve.

Ready for liberty call tomorrow? Xavier asked.

Yes, sir. Me, STG3 Williams, and YN2 Hart are gonna grab us a good meal, and then we're hitting the streets for some serious shopping.

Not pricing any of that poon tang are ya?

No sir, not me. I'm married.

Really? I don't know why but I never would have guessed.

Yes sir, married four years with two kids, Schwartz said. Twins.

Very cool. Congratulations.

You, sir?

Nope. It's just me all by my lonesome.

Must be nice with all that Officer's pay, Schwartz said.

In the darkness of the bridge wing, Xavier felt himself shrug.

You know what they say. The more you make, the more you spend. It's usually just stupid junk, too. That said I'd still take a raise.

I believe it was Henry David Thoreau who said *Superfluous money can buy superfluous stuff only*, Schwartz replied. Something like that.

Well put.

My wife and my kids get all my pay anyway, sir. I was just joking about the serious—

Schwartz stopped. Xavier saw it too. *Green light. Green emergency light. A green glow stick from an emergency life vest floating in the sea.*

Is that...?

Yes sir, I think so, Schwartz said.

Man overboard, starboard side.

LT Xavier stepped over the water tight hatch back onto the Bridge. He nearly collided with QM1 Mariah and BM2 Weatherford gathered around the chart table.

Agh! Damn it—Boats? Boats, where are you?

Right here sir, Weatherford said behind him.

Man overboard, starboard side.

For real, sir?

Yes! Go! Matthews! Ensign Matthews!

Got it, sir. *Helm! All Engines Ahead Full!*

All Engines Ahead Full, aye, sir! Seaman Amanda Batcher rang up full speed ahead. The gas turbine engine drove the propeller through the water with massive horsepower. The USS Bonnar began to shudder.

Right Full Rudder!

Right Full Rudder, aye sir! Batcher turned the helm 30° to starboard.

Boats! Xavier yelled. Six short blasts on the ship's whistle.

Six short, aye sir!

A sudden rush of adrenaline—a shipmate over the side in the ocean coupled with the deep blast of the ship's whistle—snapped everyone to attention. The Bonnar groaned as she sliced through the water. The ship heeled countering the starboard turn. The watch standers on the bridge spread their feet and held on to whatever they could grab.

How's the radar? Xavier asked. QM1!

Radar's clear, Mariah said.

Schwartz! How we looking out there?

QM3 Schwartz stuck his head in a moment later. Clear to starboard, sir.

Boats! Send someone out to hoist Oscar.

It's night, sir. We don't need to raise the flag.

Shit, thanks. LT Xavier held onto the cable that spanned the length of the Bridge while he speeded through his pre-planned responses. He was forgetting something. He had to call the Captain, obviously, but he was sure Captain Toncray was already up and getting dressed. Xavier couldn't imagine how light a sleeper one must be to command a warship. It stressed him out plenty being a Junior Officer.

Stay sharp, Xavier said.

He picked up the bridge phone and dialed 115. Four rings, no answer. Behind him, a gruff voice said:

Mark, what the hell's going on?

Captain's on the Bridge, Weatherford announced. Xavier hung up the phone.

Man overboard, starboard side, Captain, Xavier said.

Captain Toncray rubbed his eyes as he grabbed the overhead cable. He finished buttoning his Navy coveralls with one hand. He was awake and alert, yet looked foggy and groggy. Toncray didn't have the usual white t-shirt on under his coveralls—probably from getting dressed so quickly. Strangely, Xavier was shocked noticing the amount of chest hair sticking out of Captain Toncray's coveralls.

Blast it, Toncray said. I'd just started to dream. He shuffled over to his Captain's Chair and climbed aboard. Good eyes, Mark. Do we know who it is yet? Any reports?

No sir, Xavier said. We confirmed a green glow stick in the water and we're setting up for a port-side recovery.

Very well, Toncray said. He rubbed the bridge of his nose.

Ensign Matthews! Xavier said. How we looking?

Just ... about ... there...Matthews replied. *Rudder Amidships!*

Rudder Amidships, aye sir! Seaman Batcher replied. She returned the ship's rudder to 0°. *Rudder is Amidships!*

Very well, Matthews said.

The Bonnar began to right herself. Everyone on the Bridge, indeed the entire ship, re-centered their balance. Ensign Matthews shouted:

Engine Ahead One-Third!

Engine Ahead One-Third, aye sir! Engine is Ahead One-Third.

Xavier stepped over to the helmsman, Amanda Batcher.

How you doing, Batcher?

Good, sir.

You're doing a fine job. Just stay focused, we're almost there.

The bridge phone rang, probably the first of the muster reports coming in. BM2 Weatherford picked it up.

Captain, Supply Department all present or accounted for, he said.

Very well, Toncray replied. QM1 keep tally. And see if you can get XO on the radio, please. Tell him to come up here.

Left Standard Rudder! Matthews yelled. *Steady on course 348°.*

Steady on course 348°, aye sir!

Xavier stepped onto the port bridge wing. Down below, Deck Division was getting the RHIB—the Rigid Hull Inflatable Boat—ready to lower into the water. The Search & Rescue swimmer stood at the ready. Xavier saw the green glow stick about a hundred yards out. The ship approached slowly. Ensign Matthews would drive the person down the port side. He'd try to stop the sailor below midships. Then they'd scramble to recover him. Or her. On Xavier's first ship, the USS Mandeville, he'd seen a young seaman go over the side and they'd bare-ly had time to revive him after the amount of sea water he'd sucked in.

Engine Back One-Third! Engine Back Two-Thirds!

The USS Bonnar shuddered as the propeller blades reversed. The green glow stick was passing slowly down the port side. Captain Toncray was out there with his night vision goggles. Lights were being shined upon the water. They were close. Very close. It was difficult to see. The ship was slowing … slowing…

Engine stop!

Engine stop, aye sir! Engine is stopped.

The Bonnar floated next to the green glow stick. After a long mo-ment the crew realized that that's all it was: a green glow stick floating in the ocean. It wasn't attached to an emergency light vest. No bodies were attached to it. No one.

The muster reports continued to come in: Combat Systems Department, all present or accounted for. Operations Department: all present or accounted for. Engineering Department: all present.

Captain, all departments present or accounted for, Xavier said. No one's missing. Looks like a false alarm.

Are we sure? Toncray asked.

Yes, sir.

Captain Toncray drew a long breath. Very well, he said. I'm going back down to my cabin. Don't look too hard for anymore green lights. In the dim red lights of the Bridge, Xavier saw the Captain wink. You didn't hear that from me.

Captain's off the Bridge! BM2 Weatherford announced.

Xavier walked over and put a hand on Ensign Matthews's shoulder. Spot on driving.

Thanks Mark. I appreciate it.

Really excellent job.

Thank you, sir.

Outstanding work, Xavier said to his bridge watch team. Way to get it done. Now, let's do our best to have a quiet rest of the night, shall we?

After everyone but the watch team had cleared out, LT Xavier stepped back out onto the bridge wing. Schwartz was still there standing his watch. Such a strange feeling how the entire ship—jazzed and wide awake forty-five minutes ago—was now back to sleep, save for the handfuls of people in Engineering, the Combat Information Center, and up here on the Navigation Bridge. The stars above Panama Bay were as bright and serene as ever.

Whew, Schwartz said, a hand to his chest.

That's how it is, said Xavier. Had me going, too. I don't even smoke and I was ready to take it up just now for my health.

Xavier wondered if he'd done the right thing. Did he jump the gun? Maybe he should have searched for an actual person in the water first. He'd gone with his gut. He'd rather it was a false alarm than the other way around. He knew Captain Toncray felt the same. Better safe than dead.

Made me realize how much I would miss my family, Schwartz said. Or should I say how much they might miss me.

Xavier nodded. They gazed out at the dark sea.

You ever thought about jumping?

For real?

Yeah.

Hell no, sir.

I hated my first ship so much, Xavier said, I actually contemplated it one night. I was ready to give it all up. But then I was like, nah, I'm not going to end up in the stomach of a Hammerhead. That's gotta be pretty gruesome. And you have no idea how large the ocean is until you're out here floating in it. It's almost certain death.

You got that right, Schwartz said. Not a place I'd want to find myself in.

So, where were we? Xavier asked. Before all this other stuff happened?

Were you ever married, sir?

Never, Xavier said. Couple of serious girlfriends, nothing big. No kids that I know of. Although, that one time we pulled into Curaçao—well, I *hope* not at least.

Most of those girls couldn't afford to come find you anyway, Schwartz said.

I try not to think about it, Xavier said. What can I say? They know precisely what we're looking for after a month at sea. It's not fair.

Remember Manta, Ecuador? Schwartz asked. That crazy—who was he exactly?—a Liaison?

Juan Jimenez, Xavier said, nodding.

That's the one, said Schwartz. That guy was hilarious.

Crazy old Juan, Xavier said. That guy was all about hooking you up. *You want girls? You want drinks? Gambling? Juan Jimenez YOUR man! I hook you RIGHT up!*

I thought it was pretty cool when he said: *We're ALL America! North, Central, South—not different, we all ONE!*

It never crossed my mind to think of the Americas that way, Xavier said. It was cool. I'm sure old Juan gets plenty of kickbacks recommending places for our U.S. dollars.

Kinda crazy, sir, don't you think?

What's that? Xavier asked.

Just how crazy some guys get? Schwartz said.

Guys *and* gals, Xavier said. I've been on three ships now. I'd say the infidelity rate is probably one in four. I don't know, maybe less.

I hear ya, sir. It's tough.

I don't fault anyone, Xavier said. We all get lonely. But I love my freedom.

I love being married, Schwartz said. My friend, Deyshawn, he got divorced recently. He said for the longest time he thought it was something with him. Then he said he realized it was her.

His wife?

Yes. Ex-wife.

What was "it" that was wrong?

I don't even think Deyshawn knows for sure.

Fair enough, Xavier said.

Everyone will be abandoned at some point in their lives, sir, Schwartz said. The lucky ones only at the very end. I guess that's what scares me the most. My dad was never around much.

My folks were around plenty, Xavier said. Maybe that's one of the reasons I joined the Navy.

They stood quietly. They tasted the salt tang in the air; felt the stickiness on their skin. Both men, shaken by the events two hours earlier, now breathed and ruminated on the night's events. Silence spoke the loudest.

Xavier pushed the button on his Indiglo watch. 0307.

I'm done, he said. Stick a fork in me.

Me too, sir.

What's your name? Your first name?

Uh, Dennis, sir. Dennis Schwartz.

Dennis?

Yes, sir. Yours?

Mark.

Pleasure talking with you this evening, sir.

You too, Xavier said. I'm gonna get ready to turn over the watch. That's my fun limit for one night.

The three days of liberty went quickly in Panama City. After an eight-hour transit through the Panama Canal, the USS Bonnar was once again in the Atlantic Ocean. The Atlantic side of the canal was often rougher than the peaceful Pacific. On a particularly rough night while transiting the southern Caribbean, one of the crewmembers, a Torpedoman's Mate, was thrown from his rack and broke his arm. He had to be airlifted to Roosevelt Roads, Puerto Rico for emergency surgery. Another time they stopped to send over medicine to a sick crew aboard a fishing vessel. Otherwise, it was a quiet voyage back to Mayport.

⟶

The Bonnar had a warm homecoming after spending six-months in Counter Drug Operations around Central and South America. For the 250 crewmembers, a little over 1,000 family members and visitors eagerly waited on the dock. They were waving flags and wearing FFG 93 memorabilia. Xavier's roommate, LT Jay Wesberry, said it felt like they were riding pine doing Counter Drug Ops while the real war was being fought in the Persian Gulf.

Not everyone felt that way.

Mark Xavier had all of his stuff packed. He was looking forward to his two weeks of leave that started as soon as he stepped off the Bonnar. He was craving Taco Bell. His stomach wanted five Chalupas, three soft tacos and a Nachos Bell Grande. A six-pack of Molson Ice would wash it all down.

As he walked toward the quarterdeck, he spotted QM3 Schwartz.

Lieutenant Xavier, please meet my wife, La'Keisha. And my two sons, Jamal and Rory.

Pleasure to meet you, La'Keisha. I'm Mark.

Nice to meet you, Mark. These are the twin tornadoes.

Xavier slapped Jamal and Rory high-fives as they chased each other around their parents.

You've got a beautiful family, he said.

Thank you, sir, Schwartz said. Think I'll keep 'em for a while. He and La'Keisha smiled at one another. Well, you guys ready?

Xavier watched Quartermaster Third Class Petty Officer Dennis Schwartz salute the national ensign. The Schwartz family took their leave. They strolled casually down the ramp, glancing now and then at the rippling waters of Mayport basin.

As they left, Xavier felt joy for all of the families. He felt proud to have finished another sea tour. He also felt a little sad for himself. He had no one there to meet him. Was something missing? Some*one* perhaps?

He shrugged it off.

LT Mark Xavier came to attention and saluted the stars and stripes. Grabbing his green sea bag, he hefted it to his shoulder and walked down the ship's ramp to solid ground.

THE END

'PENNY'S BLUEBERRY FARM'

SAGE AND SOMETHING PEPPERY DRIFTED into Paul Marsh's nose. His body shivered pleasantly. A truck door slammed behind him. Paul pulled his nose from the bouquet of herbs hanging on the roadside stand. A woman in faded jeans walked up out of the gold dust afternoon.

"Hey Paul," she said. "Long time."

Paul recognized her beautiful eyes immediately. Without saying a word he shook her hand. It was tough yet warm. Paul couldn't hold her eyes for more than a few seconds as it took him straight back to being a kid again. He looked at her sign at the side of the road. A sign of an overflowing bushel of fruit with the words *Penny's Blueberries* painted above it.

"I used to babysit you and Steven. Remember?"

"Of course," Paul said. *Penny Bowman.* He could never forget. "The summers before fifth and sixth grade."

"It was Junior and Senior year for me," Penny said. "After that, your Ma and Pa let you guys watch yourselves and I went off to agricultural school at Michigan State."

"You're a Spartan?" Paul asked.

Penny nodded.

"It's about the *only* time I've gotten out of the Green Mountain state," she said. She clapped a hand to Paul's shoulder. He jumped. "Great to see you. I guess with all of our farming and such I thought we'd run into each other sooner. How's little Stevie?"

Paul cracked a shy smile.

"He's doing well," he said. "He's in graduate school. Southern New Hampshire."

"Remember when we used to watch *Jaws*?" Penny asked smiling. "You'd do that scene where the old fisherman, Quint, asks you wanna see something permanent? Then he pulls out his false tooth and whistles through it?"

"I can't believe you remember that," Paul said.

"My *God*, you and your friends watching *Star Wars*, and *Krull*, and *Excalibur*, and *The Beastmaster*, over and over again. You'd come in for Kool-Aid and a PB&J, watch half an hour of a movie, and then be right back outside swimming at Garver Creek, or playing Ditch'em with your bikes."

Paul's eyelashes fluttered. They never did that. Penny Bowman plucked emotional moments out of the past so easily it made Paul feel tipsy. He felt the need to cover himself.

"I kind of thought the same thing," Paul said, crossing his arms. "That we'd run into each other at some point."

"I'm never in St. George unless I'm on my way to Burlington."

"No real reason to be 'less you live there," Paul said. Penny smiled. It was the same smile she'd tattooed onto his heart all those summers ago. "Well," he said, rubbing his palms together, "I suppose I should be going."

"Do you want some blueberries?"

"Uh, sure, how much?"

Penny placed a plump basket in his hands.

"On the house," she said. "But next time it's full price. I ain't getting no government subsidies out here."

"Thanks."

"Sure, Paul, anytime."

He walked back to his pickup truck on air. Balancing the basket of berries like it was five dozen eggs, he reached for the door handle.

"Hey," Penny said. "I'm just thinking out loud. Wanna go for a coffee sometime? Or a beer? Reminisce about the old days?"

Paul felt zapped by electrical current. An unspoken fantasy. He couldn't imagine going *anywhere* with his old babysitter. Ever since those summers before 5th and 6th grade, Penny Bowman had found ways to wander back into his memory and leave her scent to linger upon his dreams.

He set the basket on the edge of the driver's seat. His judgment was skewed. He let go too soon and the blueberries spilled all over the dusty driveway. A sudden gust of wind blew the small wicker basket down the road.

"Aww, just leave 'em," Penny said. "We'll getcha another."

⌒⟶

Tuesday evening. 9:30 p.m. Paul was usually sawing logs by this time. Maybe thumbing through a magazine, or a few pages of *Robinson Crusoe* that he'd found on an old shelf in the barn. Lately he'd been tranquilizing himself with late-night TV. It worked as well as anything. When you owned a farm you were always tired. You could always sleep.

Tonight he felt something else. He felt restless.

He wasn't a slacker—quite the opposite—he had no social life. Paul hadn't dated in three years. The last girl ended things by saying she couldn't date a farmer. Caring for animals and enduring their fragrances was way too hick. It left a sour taste in Paul's mouth. When it came right down to it, he didn't have the time or the energy to pursue a relationship anyway. With Steven away at school it took everything he had to keep the farm running.

Tonight Paul had poured himself a glass of scotch. Macallan 18. Single malt. A gift from his Uncle Will ten years ago to celebrate Paul's

21ˢᵗ. He usually only drank beer. If he drank at all. It made him feel tired. Worn down at thirty-one. How pathetic.

Paul picked up the telephone. He paused. Then he dialed the number for Wade Crabtree.

"*Ya-llo.*"

"Wade?"

"Yup."

"It's Paul Marsh, over in St. George."

"Hey Paul, what say?"

"Sorry to call so late."

"Naw, we're up."

"Good."

"What's the word?"

"Well, this is kinda outta the clear blue yonder," Paul said. "But I know you've been around this area longer than I have."

"Yup."

"Do you remember a Penny Bowman?"

"Penny Bowman … as in Penny's Blueberries out in Hinesburg?"

"Yes, sir."

"On Hill View Road?"

"Yes, sir."

"Yup," Wade said. "I remember her."

"Well, I ran into her earlier today," said Paul.

"Ya don't say. Didn't she used to babysit y'all?"

"She did," Paul said. "Long time ago. Anyway, we talked for a spell and I ended up buying some blueberries from her. Actually, she gave me a basket. And I was just wondering—"

On the other end of the line, Wade laughed heartily. He cleared his throat.

"*Ahhh,*" he said. "Now I get the gist."

That Friday, Penny and Paul met at Lentini's Italian restaurant. All week they'd had unseasonably rainy weather. It poured for the better part of three days. Then it drizzled. Then it came down in steady showers that seemed destined to never end. Many farmers felt frazzled at the amount of sitting water threatening to drown their fields.

Penny walked into Lentini's wearing dark blue jeans, a checkered flannel shirt and a silver rodeo buckle. She brushed the rain from her clothes. Her face may have weathered a bit, her hair no longer stylish, but her full-moon eyes and dimpled smile still captivated him with their strange magic.

Paul had arrived fifteen minutes early to get a table. And to fortify himself with liquid courage in the form of an Old-Fashioned. Penny continued to shake off the rain as she approached the table. Paul stood. She got seated.

"How have your folks been?" Penny asked.

Paul raised his eyebrows as he sat back down.

"Still resting peacefully," he said.

Penny slapped a hand to her forehead.

"This time I had my entire *leg* in my mouth," she said. "Right up to the hip." Paul chuckled. She reached across the table and put a hand on his arm. "I'm sorry."

"It was a long time ago."

"So, now that we've got *that* behind us," Penny said, "order whatever you want. It's on me."

"No, I got it," said Paul.

"I asked you," Penny said. "So hush up and order."

They had a fine time chatting, catching up and enjoying each others' company. Time flew. Before Paul knew it, he was standing on Penny Bowman's front porch staring into her eyes. He still couldn't believe it. Answered prayers from grade school years.

The rain had again slowed to a drizzle. Nonetheless, they huddled close as if to keep dry. Paul's heart was beating like a rabbit.

"Thank you again for dinner," Penny said. "Next time, seriously, my treat." She unlocked her front door. Paul looked around nervously.

"Think it'll ever stop raining?" he asked.

"It always has," Penny said. "Would you like to come in for a nightie-cap?"

"Well, I can't just stand here getting wet I suppose."

Inside Penny's old farmhouse it was warm and comfortable. He'd never been there before. Penny had inherited the farm from her folks much the same way Paul had inherited his own family's farm. Old knick-knacks adorned the shelves. Little figurines of an oxen team pulling a plow through cornfield stalks held Paul's attention for several seconds. He assumed they were mostly Penny's late mother's things. Many of his own mother's things were still up in his farmhouse.

"How about some tequila?" Penny asked. "El Toro? It has a sombrero cap."

Paul stared at the ceiling in ecstasy. His entire being felt afloat. He couldn't move, he couldn't speak. He only wanted to *be*.

"Just toss that cummy towel in the corner," Penny said. "I'm doing laundry tomorrow." She kissed him and stepped into the bathroom.

"Is there any water?" he asked.

"There's a glass on the nightstand."

Paul drank. He lay down and pulled the comforter up to his chin. He listened to Penny flush the toilet and wash her hands. *We made love. We made love.* Now Paul felt *in* love. Safe to say he'd always been. If he could stop time right here, sell his family farm and move in with Penny for the rest of their lives, he would. Never had he felt so content.

Penny rejoined him under the covers. Her eyes glowed. She buried her face in his chest and Paul wrapped his arms around her warm body. He pulled her close. Breathed her in. Like heaven.

"What time do you need to get up?" she asked.

"5:00 works for me."

"Me too," Penny said. They kissed. "Good night, Paul."

"Good night, Penny."

Penny Bowman.

⟞⟝

They hung out again two days later. Between spending time with Penny and driving the ½ hour back and forth to work his own farm, Paul was busier than ever. But he'd never been this happy. It gave him a new-found energy. Nothing felt like work anymore.

They helped each other with chores. They discussed planting and harvesting strategies. They made love out on the hills amidst Penny's blueberries.

It was such a pleasant change having female company. Much more exciting than hanging out with the same old handful of guys at *The Golden Omelet* every morning. Paul felt focused. He had something else—some*one* else—to live for. And damn if it didn't feel good.

⟞⟝

The following Friday, Paul picked up Penny and they went to see a band at MacGregor's Scottish Pub in Burlington. The pub was already busy when they arrived. Paul hadn't been in a packed house in a long time. The busiest place he frequented these days was the feeding trough with his cows.

He and Penny ordered pints of Piper Down Scottish Ale. They toasted.

"I'm really having a lot of fun with you," Penny said. "Cheers honey."

"I've been having a great time, too," said Paul.

"Our age difference doesn't bother you?"

"Age isn't anything but a number, right?"

"True," Penny said. "I just don't want it to be an issue."

Paul dropped his head. He didn't speak for several moments. Penny also stayed quiet. Finally he said, "I've enjoyed every moment, Penny. I don't want this to end."

"What was the last girl like that you dated?" she asked.

Paul chuckled.

"She was totally obsessed with her Blackberry phone," he said. "And with Japanese anime."

"I don't even know what those are," Penny said.

"Me either," said Paul. "I already felt a generation removed when I was born, and now I feel two gaps. I have no idea what's awesome anymore."

"Paul, even *I* know kids don't say awesome anymore."

"I rest my case."

Paul sipped his ale. Near the stage up front, a band was setting up their equipment. The sign behind them read: ***PICTURE PERFECT CROSSROAD—LIVE TONIGHT!***

"Can't remember the last time I saw a band," Paul said. "I think it was *Astro Return* on my 21st birthday."

"I have one of their CDs!" Penny said.

They laughed. Someone tapped Penny on the shoulder. They both turned.

"Hey Penny," a man said. "How's it hanging?" He was a big guy in a sleeveless flannel shirt wearing an Eagle Claw cap with a fishing hook attached to the brim. Paul felt Penny bristle at his side.

"Hey Bubba," she said.

"Who's your friend?"

"Paul," Paul said. He offered his hand. Bubba didn't shake. Only nodded.

"'Sup, man?" Bubba said. He moved closer to Penny. Penny inched away. Paul felt his blood starting to surge. "You replacin' me? You know I can't leave it at that."

"We were never each other's to replace," Penny said. She rolled her eyes. "I've already told you that. We saw one movie together. That was it. It's obvious we didn't have much in common."

"Don't start no shit, Bubba," said a bouncer nearby.

Bubba didn't even regard the man.

"What'cha up to tonight?" he asked.

"I've got plans, obviously," Penny replied.

Bubba slid a sleeveless arm around Penny's shoulders and she removed it instantly.

"Hey," Paul said. He stood up. "She *said*—"

⌒

"Just stay down," Penny said.

Paul had no idea where he was. It slowly started coming back to him. Out for drinks with Penny Bowman. Scottish Pub. The Picture Perfect band.

He was lying on the sticky floor of the Pub with a bunch of people gathered around. In the distance, Paul heard ambulance sirens.

His chin was throbbing. He had the beginnings of a terrible headache. Something was wrong.

"Is that ambulance for me?" he asked.

"Shhh," Penny said. "Just lay there for a minute. I'll drive us home."

⌒

The Farmhouse was quiet that night. Paul sat on a hard-backed chair in the corner of the living room. He rested his head in his hands. The quiet was disconcerting.

I got knocked out.

In the silence of the living room he felt himself shaking. He felt powerless. Pitiful. He heard someone sobbing and realized it was himself.

I got knocked out. A man enforced his will over mine. He punched me unconscious. He could have done anything he wanted to Penny and I couldn't have stopped him.

Paul wiped his eyes. He looked around at the Farmhouse his great-grandfather had built—the creaky wooden staircase; the nooks and crannies; the wooden porch out front that was still standing. It had always been the home of his family. The Farmhouse even smelled like home. It had its own scent. Some family members might be gone but they would never die. He thought of his animals—the chickens, the cows, the goats, the ducks, the pigs, especially the little piglets that he no longer would have been able to feed if things had turned out worse tonight. He thought of all the things around the farm that required his care. All the work he'd done as a boy. All the memories he now bore alone. When he and Steven were gone it would only be a house. Tonight it had almost been….

Paul went to his gun rack and pulled down his .30-06 deer rifle. For a moment….

No. For God's sake, Paul, don't be stupid.

He put his rifle back. It was only embarrassment. In the end, embarrassment, like pride, was no real emotion. He was mature enough to realize that things happen. He wasn't dead. He was *alive*. His chin may be black and blue but his jaw wasn't broken and the only thing that had really been injured was his feelings.

Maybe it was best to move on. Without Penny Bowman. He didn't blame her. He had enough on his plate without wallowing in pity that he wasn't good enough.

He didn't have time to wallow in anything.

Let the dead bury the dead. Living men have work to do.

He had only spoken with Penny Bowman once after the incident with Bubba three weeks ago. He told her he needed space. He wasn't sure he trusted her. In a sense it seemed like a dream. Who knows what trouble might have brewed had the bouncer not smashed Bubba in the head with a beer bottle and knocked *him* out. He actually felt bad for the guy. After the ambulance took Bubba to the hospital he was having trouble speaking. A few weeks ago he could have shot the man. Now he felt empathy? He couldn't deal with these powerful emotions that Penny Bowman stirred up.

How could Penny have ever been interested in him? He was inexperienced in the sack. He couldn't protect her in a fight. Why?

All moot questions. He'd press on with stoicism like he always had. It was the only thing to do. But he'd re-discovered a new feeling in life. *Passion.* Passion rules the universe, Wade Crabtree had told him. That's love. Gotta fight for love. You don't always win.

Maybe he'd find another woman who gave him that same charge of excitement.

Paul laughed.

No. No woman was like Penny Bowman. And no woman was worth the sacrifice, the devotion, and the inevitable heartbreak. He knew that now. Like Wade said if he kept on repeating it to himself, one day, when he was an old hermit living alone in the woods he might believe it.

Everything happened for a reason. Right? *Right.*

Paul finished brushing his teeth. As he was putting his toothbrush back into the brass holder, the phone rang. *Don't answer it.* It rang again. *Don't.* A third time.

He walked into the bedroom and picked up the receiver after the fourth ring.

"Hello?"

"Hey."

It was Penny.

"Hey," he said.

"I'm in your neighborhood," she said. "Mind if I stop by?"

Paul closed his eyes.

"Don't mind at all," he said.

THE END

'MASTER PROCRASTINATOR'

AWAKE. YOUR HEAD THROBS. YOU grunt to a sitting position off the cold concrete floor. Your vision's blurry. *Where ... am I?*

With grim determination you push to your feet. Your balance returns. You wrap your arms around yourself as your eyes begin to adjust. *What is this? A basement?*

Your black dress pants are chilled and wet. You must have been lying in a puddle. There's a damp spot on the concrete floor. Lengths of cut rope lay scattered about. Your burgundy satin shirt has three buttons missing. Right down the middle. You only wear this shirt while you're out socializing.

Right? Wait. My name? What? What's my name? I can't think of my name! Who am I?

I live in the city. This much you know. Tommy. *Tommy.* The name is stuck in your head, lodged in permanently like fact. The only name.

Tommy. That must be me.

A dim bulb dangles from the basement ceiling. It's quiet. Damp. Dirty. Feels like you're alone. *Daytime? Night?* No clue. No windows down here.

On opposite sides of the walls stand two heavy steel doors. You walk to the far door and try the cold knob. It won't even jiggle. Your legs are tingling. It feels like they're starting to wake up. You walk quickly across the room for the other door but stop halfway when you spot the two bodies.

How did I not see them?

You stoop down.

Both white men.

Both dead.

The man on his back is in a black hoodie with an intricately-carved goatee. The other man lies face down on the cold floor. Dark red blood has seeped out of his corpse. Neither man looks familiar.

I don't even know what I look like.

Fear rises in your chest. You decide not to search their bodies. *I've gotta get outta here. Gotta get home.*

Home. *Home is west of the city. I remember that.*

You try the second door. The knob turns. The steel door opens revealing a stone staircase. A naked bulb hangs from the stairwell ceiling. Dim stone steps lead upward.

Cautiously you climb one step at a time, staying on your toes, straining your ears to pick up sound of any kind. *Tommy. Tommy.* You can't remember your last name or where you where before this, but you have deep feelings about yourself. You're humanitarian. You stand up for your family and friends. You have morals, principles. Hard work has gotten you far. Other feelings and memories are dawning as if you're just coming back to life.

As you climb you check your pockets. Your arms feel sore and bruised. No wallet. No ID. Just a crumpled ten dollar bill.

Faint voices drift down from above.

You backpedal quickly down the stairs and duck around a wall partition of stone. There's nowhere else to go. *Sit tight.* You can do this. You're a survivor.

The voices are growing louder. Footfalls echo down the stairwell. Laughter.

"Windy City's full of dogs," says a man's deep voice. Two figures step past you in the darkness. "Sooner or later you're bound to step in—"

"He's gone," says a raspy female voice.

Your blood comes up. Adrenaline spikes your body. You watch the large backside of a man with shaggy hair, and a thin, scraggly woman in tight jeans walk into the room you just slipped out of.

"Jesus," says the woman. "They're dead."

You tiptoe out of the corner shadows.

"Hey!"

You sprint up the stairs, but the big man is right on you. Out of instinct, you kick backward and drill the man in the chest knocking him back into the woman. His arm hits your leg as he falls, tripping you. You drop hard on the edge of a stone step.

A bright pain shoots down your leg. You wince as tears drip, but you don't yell. You're too disciplined for that.

Gritting your teeth, you hobble up the remaining steps. The man and the woman lie motionless at the bottom. No other sounds can be heard.

You shuffle down a long corridor. There are windows up high but they're not letting in much light. Your senses are skewered from a massive headache. But at least your throbbing hip doesn't feel broken.

A set of double glass doors lies ahead. You push through them and stumble out into the cold night. Snow falls softly. You pull your shirt tight and see yellow streetlights and people dressed in coats, scarves and hats. Checkered cabs. A few SUVs rolling across the snow-covered streets.

It must be late. You're in the brownstone area of the city and most of it seems to be asleep.

The wind bites and rips at your flimsy satin shirt. *Cold.* You're shivering. In the distance you see the John Hancock building and Water Tower Place. It's not your turf but you know Lake Michigan is to the east and it gives you a reference point. Chills well deep inside. You give a violent jolt as cold continues to invade your body.

Find a place. Get warm.

Down the street, you see signs for Kirby's Underground Bar. You stumble toward it, your hip throbbing, your mouth watering at the idea of warm air. You amble down the steps.

The smell of stale beer, sweat and leather rises into your face. You close the door behind you. Around the corner, loud Indie music jams from a stage unseen. *Yeah. I've been here before. Not often. But I've been here.*

You move into a corner under the buzzing warmth of a heater. The place is pretty crowded. Not crazy. But busy. The crowd seems mostly Goth and Emo misunderstood youth. You keep your head down. You don't want to make eye contact with anyone. Not yet.

Once you're thawed, you approach the corner edge of the dingy bar. The bartender, a girl with black make-up and two silver hoops through her eyebrow asks what your venom is. It takes a few moments to think of something.

"Ginger ale."

"Are you all right?" she asks.

You feel yourself swallow as you say, "Yeah, why, don't I look all right?" She points to your head. You slowly finger a painful knot, more like a hill, on the left side of your forehead. You shrug. "You should see the other hombres."

The bartender sets your Ginger ale in front of you. You scrounge out your ten dollar bill and lay it on the counter. Grabbing your chilled glass you immediately wish you would have ordered something warm, a coffee or a hot chocolate. *Not that this place even serves hot chocolate.* The bartender brings back six dollars. You pocket the cash. She rolls her eyes and walks off. You sip the Ginger ale. It calms you. *Just like it always has?*

You ask some dude next to you where the bathroom is. He thumbs toward the far end of the bar. You spot a neon blue sign: *Restrooms.*

Need to look at my face in the mirror. Need to see my eyes.

One of the bouncers, a large man in black leather, moves up behind you. You feel his presence before you catch him out of your peripheral. From down the bar, a voice says *"Hey yo, Tommy!"*

"Hey!" you yell. *Tommy. That is my name!*

The man who said it moves cautiously down to your end of the bar. Meanwhile, the large bouncer is right behind you. He grunts. You step to the side. He moves forward and you breathe easier when you realize he was waiting to get the bartender's attention.

"Yo man, what you doing here?" the guy says. He's Hispanic, dressed in a tight black shirt, dress pants, bracelets and gold rings. He smiles. But there's a warning behind his smile. He puts his hand on your arm and you both lean forward like you're looking at something on the bar. "Are you crazy, man?"

"I'm not supposed to be here?" you ask.

The guy stares at you.

"Not here, amigo," he says. "What happened to your head? You get jumped?"

You don't know this guy, but he seems genuine. You can usually spot a liar.

"I don't remember," you say.

"They tipped off the motherfucking cops, man."

"Who did?"

"Ryder and the Olde Town boyz."

"What'd I do?" you ask. The man looks at you, stunned.

"You didn't pay off that Mustang did you?" he asks. You have no idea what he's talking about. "Why didn't you just pay it off, Tommy? You waited until the last minute. Now they sold your ass out, man. You *had* the bread."

You wonder if you still have the money and where it might be.

"How much time do I got?" you ask.

"Not much," the guy breathes. "Not around here, especially not this neighborhood. You know this ain't your territory. You might still could square things—"

"Got a question for you," you say. Your friend leans forward. "What's my last name?" The guy shakes his head, bewildered.

"Martinez," he says. "Why you ask me that, Tommy?"

"Keeping you on your toes, Mano," you say.

He nods.

"I unnerstan. Hey, how's your grandma?"

Grandma. I'm staying with her. We're helping each other out. I need to get home and check on her. We've only got each other.

"She's fine," you say, swallowing back tears.

"Don't worry, man. I'll make some calls tomorrow. Get you more protection."

"Look, man, I gotta split."

"I unnerstan," says your friend. He looks around, then grabs your hand and shakes it. He slips you a knife. You pocket it. "Que vaya con Dios."

"Dios ayuda a quienes se ayudan a sí mismos," you reply. *God helps those who help themselves.*

Stepping back out into the cold, you immediately wish you would have asked your friend if you could borrow his coat. At this point you're ready to steal one. But you don't want to go back into the bar. You were starting to get some bad vibes from a few faces looking in your direction. Things are coming back to you.

Who the hell was my friend, anyway?

You didn't get his name.

⌒

After wandering westward for ten minutes, you're freezing again. *Was my coat stolen? Did I even have one?*

You're stumbling down street after street, looking for someplace warm but nothing is open. Store after store is closed. Door after door is locked. It's hard to think with your chattering teeth.

You spot a clock above a Panera Bread store. 2:59 a.m. You shiver and watch it turn to 3:00. The Soul's Hour. The Witching Hour. The Devil's Hour. You've heard it called all three.

Things are looking more familiar. You're getting close. You feel it in your bones. You keep moving. Dropping your head against the blast of the wind, you wrap your arms tight around yourself. *Soldier on, amigo.*

When you turn left onto Hudson Avenue that's when you see them. Five or six dark figures coming out of the shadows and from behind trees in a nearby park. You stop. But they've already seen you.

"Hey Martinez!" one of them shouts. "Where's your car?"

You bolt. Your hip aches but the rush of adrenaline tranquilizes it.

Behind you they shout: "Go get him!"

You're not quite sure where you're going, you're relying on instinct. You're quick on your feet. But the guys behind you are catching up and they seem well-prepared for a fight.

Ducking down a side street, you sprint into the Mary Magdalene church parking lot. Three of the thugs come around the corner. You pivot, slip on the ice and go down. Your hip burns. You jump to your feet. As quickly as you're up, three other gang members come up behind you, trapping you. One's got a blade.

"Carve you up, mijo," he says.

You whip out the knife your friend slipped you. Your blood pulses to the nth degree.

"Come on!" you yell. "Let's do this!"

You keep both groups out of the corners of your eyes. You'll strike whoever's closest first. Strike hard, strike fast. You'll keep slashing until every one of them is bloody pulp. *'Less they get me first.*

A light comes up behind you.

"Scatter!" someone yells.

Breathing a sigh of relief, you quickly realize it's the last time you'll breathe free for a long time.

"Freeze!" a voice commands.

⟝⟞

The two cops handcuff you and stuff you into the back of a police cruiser. Red and blue strobes are flashing. It's warm inside the cruiser but not that warm. The cops leave the door open. Snow swirls in.

"Who is he?" asks the older cop. "I feel so out of touch working the desk these past months."

"Tom Martingale," says the second cop. He's baby-faced with a starchy-pressed uniform and veins up both his biceps. He's not even wearing a coat. "Sometimes goes by the name of Tommy Martinez."

"Who?"

"Just another white wigger trying to be Antonio Montana," says the baby-faced cop pulling his radio from his belt. "Trying to take the easy way out." He keys the radio. "Hey Chief?"

"Go ahead, Roberts," a husky voice replies.

"We got him."

"You got him? You guys nabbed Marco Cameron? Outstanding! Good on ya!"

"No, Chief," the baby-faced cop says. "Tom Martingale."

"*Tom Martingale?*"

"Yes, sir."

"Who the hell is that?" the Chief asks. "*Tom ... Mart ... Standby.*" You hear clicking sounds over the radio like someone typing on a keyboard before the signal disconnects. A pause. "Oh, okay," comes the Chief's voice again. "Bring him in. Bring in Hazel Martingale, too. His grandmother. 1100 North Larrabee, just south of Division. Apartment #364. That old pill-pusher is behind most of this. She's been putting her grandson up for the rest."

"10-4, Chief."

"Hazel Martingale," the older cop says, bringing a finger to his mouth. "Wasn't she a mid-wife at Northwestern? I think my daughter requested her specifically. In fact, I'm sure she did. It might have been a few years ago, but—"

"Maybe," says the younger cop. "We've had tips she's been dealing opiates for a while now. Where you been? Filing folders? Pushing papers behind a desk?"

The older cop smirks and closes the door to the cruiser. The dome light goes off. It starts to warm. In the darkness, you sit quietly pondering the sound of your real name.

THE END

'HALFWAY HEAVEN'

PILLOWY CLOUDS LOOKED THE SAME as they ever had to Teddy Niemar. They swirled like heaven incarnate—angelic harps strummed gracefully by the Prime Song. From them came the most delightful melodies.

Lately all the grace was wearing thin.

Who cares where I go?

Teddy put his hands over his eyes and stared through them at the Earth below. He'd been in this frenzy for a while now. *So much to discover. So much I'll never know.* It was bad enough to feel this way. But to say anything could be devastating.

A fellow sublime materialized. It was Simon Aubrey.

"You didn't hear the news."

"Must have missed it," Teddy said. He felt minutely intrigued. Simon smoothed out his silk robe and combed his hair to perfection with a swipe of his hand, and then raised an eyebrow in the air like he always did.

"Travel is so discombobulating."

Teddy smiled dryly.

"What's the grand news, Aubrey?" he asked. "Don't keep me waiting in limbo."

"*Well*," Simon said, "Tina Rathburn decided to take a fantasy trip."

"Did she?" Teddy perked up. "She must have gotten over her vertigo." Simon put a hand on his hip.

"Swinging through the clouds and twirling loop-de-loops was never Tina's bag," Simon admitted. He grew serious. "She had foolish courage elsewhere. Remember how everyone felt it was a fluke her being up here?"

Teddy stayed silent.

"You wanna stay here for another decade?" Simon asked. "A century? A millennia?"

"Excellent question," Teddy said. "One I'm trying to find an answer to."

"I've felt your questions," Simon said.

"I've felt Tina's conundrums," Teddy replied. *"Anyplace else is always someplace better? Is it jealousy?"* Teddy stared at the dreamy clouds floating behind Simon Aubrey. It was so glorious it was laughable to ever think of leaving.

But lately, Teddy was having a crisis of conscience. He was losing faith. No longer could he convince himself that this all wasn't just a silly dream.

"I've got a lot going through me," he said.

"You may think you know my friend," said Simon, "but you don't know. Tina fell."

Teddy drew a hand to his mouth.

"You're *kidding* me!"

"Can I lie?" Simon asked. The two sublimes faced one another. Their eyes connected, then their souls. In an instant they shared many thoughts, dreams and personal fears.

"You CAN'T be serious!" Simon said.

Teddy brought a finger to his mouth.

"Shhh!"

"Do you understand the ramifications?" asked Simon. "Do you understand it's too late for Tina? Teddy, you could come up the other way. Your roots might reach to the sky while the sun bakes you into the ground. It's happened before. Many times."

"Is that for sure what happened to Tina?"

"She jumped. I'm not sure. You know we're not privy to—"

"See? Tina didn't have a plan either."

"Tina had been thinking about it for a long time."

"And I haven't?" Teddy asked.

"Human life is different these days," Simon said. "They're well into the 21st Century. It's been a while since you've been hustling down there to survive."

"Is that an excuse not to try? To not be curious?" Teddy asked. He knelt and ran his hand through the white vapor carpet. He knew this. He knew all of this. Life on Cloud Eight gave you nearly every insight. It was wondrous, exalted limbo. The best of everything. *Before.*

But it wasn't everything. Far from it. Although time turned differently up here, year after year it was all still the same. No longer did he wish to be entertained.

He wanted to create.

And he was willing to risk.

"I'm only running at 78% into the next plateau," Teddy said. "Lately it's been a real drag."

"78% *is* heaven!" Simon said. "You know this. Anything above seventy-three percent is golden money in the bank you'll never have to spend."

Teddy shook his head.

"I might do better with another chance." He cupped a hand to his mouth and pulled Simon close. "I want to fly on my own."

Simon Aubrey closed his eyes. It made his soul ache when another spoke of this. They'd already lost Tina. How was her *new* old life progressing? Or regressing? Talk was dangerous. Talk made things real. Talk made things happen. Daydream all you like, when you started speaking things had a tendency to manifest.

What was to gain?

With another life as a human Teddy might make it a few rungs higher. Soar a little closer to Prime. Always a chance, right?

On the other wing, there was the unending torture of screwing things up royally, not to mention another ride on the merry-go-round as a living breathing flesh. It meant clean memories. No recollection of anything that had come before in previous lives. You could find yourself at the mercy of your antithesis never realizing you were once on the doormat to true enlightenment. Trials and tribulations always.

"I'm merely thinking out loud," Teddy said.

"Banish it," Simon pleaded. "It's the path of eternal regret."

The two sublimes were turning somersaults amidst solar flares when they were summoned back to Cloud Eight for a Talk. For the first time Teddy felt saddened. He never thought it possible up here. It wasn't horrendous loathing sadness. Nothing like he'd experienced on Earth. Just a vague depression. It added weight.

Teddy Niemar and Simon Aubrey gathered with the other sublimes on Cloud Eight.

The Song resonated: *"Teddy's joining Tina?"*

The lyrics of the Song snapped everyone to rigid attention. Teddy felt exuberance like nothing he'd ever experienced before. The Song was serenading him.

"Yes," Teddy said. "I'm considering it."

"Before your decision is spoken; like to hear how Rathburn has woken?"

"No," Teddy said.

A light gasp went through the league of sublimes. Thunder cracked in the distance.

"Interesting … Interesting … Plenty more than interesting…." Purred the Song. *"Theodore Niemar, I listen anew, ponder the moment, yes, take it with you."*

"I will," Teddy said.

"I adore and I implore."

The Song was already drifting.

"Use perception and wisdom … Amateur philosopher."

In the clouds, there was such a thing as fame. Maybe it was *infame*. Or even disgrace. Many labels were indistinguishable because they were earthen terms that didn't fully translate up here. Teddy had known others in passing who'd also contemplated leaving the symphony in the sky.

Yet nearly everyone was still here.

Sometimes there were ironic celebrations held in honor of prodigal sons and daughters who threatened to leave but never did. A handful of them *had* moved onwards and upwards afterward. Others, like Tina, fell.

Teddy Niemar entertained plenty of second thoughts. Judith Vitolo found him and shared her dreams with him. He fell instantly in love with her. They shared lifetimes of unending happiness. Harps strummed softly. Every note was unbridled ecstasy. Pure love. Pure fun.

Nonetheless, after lifetimes had passed not a second had gone by and the twirling question mark was back in Teddy's mind.

He was forgetting circumstance.

He was forgetting the time, the work, and the sacrifices that had *gotten* him to Cloud Eight. Unconditional unrequited love. The first half of Teddy's human life hadn't been easy, but the second part had been drudgery trying to make it all right again. He'd made the cut. He'd made the 73% line in the clouds.

73% of what?

Was this some kind of masochistic challenge to himself? What can you do when you've done it all? Roam among silent obelisks? Bask in faded memories? Chase subtle levels?

Was he scared? Sure. But the intrigue wouldn't leave. He felt confused. Considering leaving gave him that iron taste of fear in his mouth.

Simon Aubrey appeared.

"Well?" he asked.

Teddy smiled. The clouds around them swirled faster.

"Think I'm gonna go for it," he said.

Simon shuddered. He placed a hand on his fellow sublime's shoulder. "I suppose," he said. "I can understand."

⌒

Teddy Niemar flew most everywhere. He indulged in most everything. He felt amazing, appeared absolutely splendid and reminded himself how truly wonderful absolute wonder can be. These final moments on Cloud Eight reminded him of great holiday celebrations with family and friends back on Earth. He'd make certain to leave this exalted limbo with no regrets. If he could remember it all.

On Teddy's day of rest he sat in peace amidst the gardens in the sky.

"An instant of decision?" the Song crooned.

"Is it?" Teddy replied. "You tell me."

The Song answered by humming elevator music. Teddy realized it was his choice alone.

"Whatever way I want?" Teddy asked.

"That is the way … The way only…."

"One moment," Teddy said.

"A moment of eternity … at your sole and solemn command…."

Silence.

⌒

Teddy paused. Jessica Mansfield appeared. A bemused look covered her face. Jessica was the granddaughter of Harold Mansfield, one of Teddy's good friends from Dixie High School. On the day Teddy had died, he'd met baby Jessica after having reconnected with the Mansfield's at their home.

"I hear you might be taking a trip," Jessica said. Teddy stared with sentimental eyes. He respected her like his own daughter.

"Good news travels fast," he said.

"How could you leave?" Jessica asked. "This is more wonderful than I could have ever imagined." She was a newbie. "You wanna explore with me?" she asked.

They toured the atmosphere, painting themselves in many fantastic colors. They shared a joy without end. But end it did. They always came back down.

"Amazing," Teddy said, yawning.

"Most truly," Jessica said. She felt his doubt.

"Now what?"

"I know everything about you," Jessica said. "I still don't know whether or not you'll do it."

Teddy shrugged.

"I believe I will," he said.

"Saying it and doing it are two different things."

"I know, Jess."

"I hope you decide what you truly feel is best for you."

"Thank you," Teddy said. "That's the best advice I've received yet." They smiled at one another. "I hope we recognize each other again."

Teddy Niemar had died coming home from Harold Mansfield's house by the train tracks near his home. Divorced from his wife, Brie, for five years, Teddy finally discovered new eyes to look upon life. He was enjoying himself. Seeing old friends. Having fun. He could awaken and flow with the day. He was a father first. But that was easy. He loved his little girl more than anything and it was never work to him. He could laugh. He could love. He could smile. He could wait for this train to pass while singing along with Annie Lennox to a new rendition of The Lover Speaks' song in the freedom of his car.

His little girl sat next to him. She was four.

"Lydia, look at that choo-choo," he said. The train was whizzing by carrying huge freight containers.

"Look how tall those are," Lydia remarked. Teddy felt a moment of inspiration. His little girl was noticing something real in the world, noticing something that maybe a lot of other kids her age might not.

"Yes, honey, they certainly are."

He stopped.

The track snapped. Before the train completely derailed, it bucked a large red container into the air.

Teddy watched in slow, surreal motion—time literally bending before his eyes—his life coming to an end. He marveled at the red box car. It was the length of three vehicles and massive enough to smash any living thing. He watched it bounce up off the train and come down at such an angle to crush the hood of his car as Annie Lennox crooned in his final moments: *No More I Love You's ... the Language is Leaving Me in Silence....*

Lydia Niemar lived. She sustained a broken femur that healed quite well attributed to her young age and the craft of a good surgeon. Her father, Teddy, passed on that day.

"I wasn't really thinking of much when it happened," Teddy said. Simon Aubrey nodded. He was receiving zero distortion. "My biggest regret is the truth. I wasn't thinking about my daughter at all. I was only sitting there in amazement at the tenderness of life." He remembered watching the box car. Unable to move. "I felt selfish. I didn't even try to save my own daughter. Those were my final emotions. Sadness and regret."

"Your daughter knows you love her," Simon said. "She's always known."

"Sure," said Teddy.

"Why go? Why tempt this fate?"

"Because I never told her," Teddy said. "My daughter never heard it from me. Even at sixty-eight years old, she still needs to hear her daddy say: "I love you, sweetheart.""

"Teddy."

"What?"

"She passed today."

Simon Aubrey said nothing more.

"Out of reach again," Teddy finally said, his face dropping. "Maybe I'll have another daughter. Or a son. I have an opportunity, Simon, an opportunity to not make the same mistake. It's a gift."

"It shouldn't be viewed as a mistake," Simon told him. "I died holding my son's hand. I never told you. He never made it up here."

Teddy swallowed.

"We were crossing Ashland Avenue," Simon said. "Coming home from a Cubs game. Right in the middle of the walkway my heart attacks me. I grab my chest and crumple. My last vision is of my son's face staring helpless as he watches his Daddy die. It was terrible. It affected him his entire life."

"I'm sorry," said Teddy. "I thought I knew everything about you."

"I keep that one close," Simon said. "Do what you will. It's your choice and it's always been your choice."

⌢

The league of sublimes gathered quietly. Teddy Niemar positioned himself at the edge of Cloud Eight. He looked around for Simon Aubrey, but his closest friend was nowhere to be found.

Choices. We all make choices.

Please guide me.

Teddy gazed over the side. He readied himself to feel gravity take hold, to feel the wind whistling through his hair as he gave up his soul for the density of human flesh. He tried to recall how his feet felt on Mother Earth.

"Daddy."

The voice stopped him. The words sank deep. He turned back.

"Theodore Niemar has chosen ... Chosen majestic transcendence!"

Chords of music swirled delightfully. The Song became visible. It morphed into his good friend, Simon Aubrey.

"Excellent choice," Simon said. "I'm going with you. Let's go up and say hello to Lydia."

In less than an instant, Teddy Niemar knew he was golden.

All he could say was "Oh, *wow.*"

THE END

'MRS. SAKUMAN'

⌒

THE BARE KNUCKLES OF STEPHANIE Rachel Aldean stung as she rapped them against the cold aluminum screen door. A second time. A third.

Ow.

"I'm starting," Stevie said aloud. "She'll only ask why I didn't."

She re-gloved her seventeen-year-old hands. She'd been stuck with the nickname Stevie since kindergarten soccer. She grabbed the snow shovel leaning against Mrs. Sakuman's house. In no way did she wish to be the recipient of Gladys Sakuman's faultfinding stare against the mollycoddles of her generation and their degenerative work ethic.

As Stevie shoveled the steps, she continued reminiscing on the past. It came easily today being New Year's Eve. Like many in her Senior class, she was apprehensive about her future. She'd made the Honor Roll. She was the natural selection for volleyball MVP. Her parents made above average money. She was dating Mike Jones, one of the coolest boys—er, young *men*—on the wrestling team at Ryker High.

Why did she let Mrs. Sakuman get to her? Why did she feel the need to help her out?

Why?

Because she was a *good* girl. That's why.

If she could help and she didn't she felt guilty. It gave her parents something to gloat about. And yes, most days it made her feel good.

Most days.

But tonight she had plans. Plans for an evening of fun. *Fun*, remember? Something so difficult to come by these days, so focused was she on all of her projects, ambitions and dreams. Laughter felt buried beneath preparation.

Mrs. Sakuman liked her porch shoveled first. After that, she liked it swept off with the old iced-over broom that sat outside her screen door. Then she liked the salt spread to melt the ice. In that order. In that *exact* order, *Little Missy!*

Figures, thought Stevie. *She calls me yesterday absolutely adamant that I get her shoveled out before the New Year because she's going to visit her daughter and her granddaughter, and now she doesn't have the courtesy to wait for me? Really?*

When she had arrived, Stevie *had* noticed the day-old tire tracks leading out of the garage through the snow but she didn't think much of them. Now, before sweeping the steps, she peered through the garage window. Mrs. Sakuman's beige Chevy Citation was gone.

Thanks, Gladys. Ya old Beech. This is your world; I'm only living in it. I wish I had time to be a shut-in all day ... to sit around ... have people wait on me, then take off whenever I like. Sounds like the good life. And you're not even supposed to be driving!

Now she wouldn't get paid today either.

Awesome.

As Stevie salted the sidewalk, she thought back to how her mother had once described Mrs. Sakuman. According to Mom, Gladys Sakuman had been adorable. Most photogenic at Ryker High – 1963. A sweet, natural beauty. In the years after, she worked as a nurse at Pine River hospital and all in all was considered a most pleasant lady. She was a member of their church but Stevie hadn't seen her there in years. Father William delivered communion to Mrs. Sakuman at home these days. She was no longer fit to drive.

Rumor had it she was becoming a menace. Twice last summer she'd gone through stoplights. An open cornfield and an open subdivision had been the only things on the other side. She'd been lucky. Very lucky, her daughter had said before taking the keys away.

Maybe that's what is making her bitter, Stevie pondered. *Her family and the state taking away her driving privileges. Deteriorating looks. The loss of other freedoms.*

But still, wasn't life about how you reacted? All the manuals for living Stevie had ever thumbed through said that the only thing you can change in your life is your own attitude.

Hear that Gladys?

And *why*, for that matter, was she still called *Mrs.* Sakuman? Gladys Sakuman had been widowed for twenty-two years. Shouldn't she be a *Ms.?*

Why do I even care?

Stevie still needed to shower. She needed to press her shirt and get her hair ready. She had to pick up Mike. She'd have to drive them to Barnaby's. She needed gas. If she was to stay on schedule, she'd have to hustle.

She dug into the snow at the top of the driveway. It was thick and heavy. Her back ached. The overcast sky was turning darker. *How the heck did Mrs. Sakuman even make it down the drive?* She might have blown some red lights, but at eighty-five Gladys Sakuman certainly wasn't a hot-rodder. *She must have really gunned it to get out of here. Maybe her daughter had an emergency?*

Well whatever it was, it was.

By the time Stevie was done it was 4:45 p.m. Night fell quickly in the northern latitudes. The sky had turned into an umbrella of midnight blue.

She leaned the shovel against Mrs. Sakuman's house. The cold air burned her lungs. She was tired. She banged on the door one last time venting the last of her frustration, but of course there was no answer.

Stevie trudged down the driveway. She slogged back down the snowy street toward home. Once again she knew her greatest obstacle in life would be standing up for herself. Putting her feelings first. Not letting others' wants and needs eclipse hers.

She'd have to borrow money from her folks tonight. Mom would lecture her. Dad would frown. Mom wouldn't accept Stevie's excuse that she had, in the spirit of giving, overextended herself this holiday season. Anything extraneous (cars, boys, make-up, dinner, fancy clothes) Stevie already understood was hers alone to buy. And she did. She worked hard to be able to do so. This was the way the world worked. She understood and felt fortunate.

Still, doesn't one good deed deserve some company once in a while?

It was what it was.

Stevie picked up Mike Jones at his Dad's house and they arrived just in time for their dinner reservation at Barnaby's. They were double-dating with Abby Johnson and Pete Yeager. Along with her sweetie, Mike, Pete was co-captain of the wrestling team. Abby was an old friend. A dear friend. Probably her best friend back in second grade. She'd recently ended a nasty relationship with a redneck Theta Chi at Ballman State. She'd been taking night classes at the high school and not many people had seen her this year. Abby's hair was longer. It looked like a large curly mane. Stevie had recently gotten hers trimmed.

They got seated.

"I love your hair," Abby said.

"Thanks," Stevie said. "I cut it for volleyball."

"How is volleyball?" Abby asked. "I thought of trying out this year but I had too much on my plate."

Stevie felt her face give way to a big smile. Abby's cheeks dimpled. They'd missed each other.

"We practice so much it doesn't even feel like winter break," Stevie said.

"I hear that," said Abby. "Cheerleading was really becoming a drag. No more spirit sprinkles for me. I'm done with after-school sports."

The boys were chatting about the possibility of ordering a beer. They were nervous about being carded. Pete had grown some serious stubble over the holidays and could probably pull it off. Mike, on the other hand, lacked the look.

It worked for Pete. He ordered a tall Busch Light draft. Mike was carded by the waitress and obviously couldn't prove his age.

"Fucking bitch," he said as she was leaving.

"Classy, Mike, real nice," Stevie said.

"No worries," said Pete. "I'll split mine with you and I'll keep ordering tall boys. We're solid, brother." The two boys shared a soul brother handshake.

Stevie turned to Abby.

"So, you're glad to be done with what's his name?"

Abby nodded. Her curly brown mane bounced up and down.

"What a pretentious jerk," she said. "College boys are worse than high school boys. And frat boys are the worst. They're little purple dickheads running around."

Stevie snorted.

"Sorry to hear that, Ab," she said. "Maybe it's a good thing. I haven't seen you this happy in a long time. Who am I kidding; I haven't *seen* you in forever."

"I missed you too, sweetie," Abby said. She held her old friend's hand. "It was a sad situation. He really turned out to be a hot mess."

Dinner was over. The four teens on the verge of adulthood sat around the table feeling fairly bored and wondering what to do next. Barnaby's was clearing out. Mike had just gotten a text about an impromptu New Year's Eve gathering at Youn Kim's house. His parents took a last minute trip to Koreatown. Youn always threw the coolest parties.

Mike and Pete were each working on their third tall one. They were becoming obnoxious. Stevie was becoming annoyed. She could see it grating on Abby as well.

Stevie excused herself to the bathroom. When she returned and was getting seated, Mike spilled his beer. The beer ran across the table and splashed all over Stevie's black purse, the nice one she'd saved for earlier in the year.

"Dang it, Mike," she said. She grabbed a handful of paper towels and mopped up the mess. "You're drunk. And you just sit there laughing."

"You're doing a fine job," Mike said. "You wouldn't want me to interfere." Stevie wiped her purse and glared at him. "It really shows your years when you make faces like that you know."

"Screw you, Mike."

"Absolutely," said Mike. "But do you have to be such a sweat about everything? It gives you premature wrinkles. Damn, Pete, check those bags under her eyes."

Stevie's phone buzzed in her purse. She wiped off the remaining Busch Light and unzipped it.

"Late night booty call?" Mike joked

Stevie had had it up to here with her little wrestling-singlet boyfriend. She tapped the pass code on her phone and opened up the text. It was a message from Mom. Good grief, *now what?*

As she read the text, she felt her hair standing on end.

Hey, it's Mom. Gladys Sakuman was found murdered in her home an hour ago. Heather Ulrich stopped by to tell us. It must have happened late last night. Her jewelry was stolen. Her car was stolen. The police caught some speed freaks joyriding it down Elkhart Road. Not trying to ruin your evening just thought you should know. Happy New Year, Stevie. Be safe.

Stevie stared at her phone until Abby asked:

"What? Is it bad?"

Mike and Pete were laughing uncontrollably at some stupid joke they'd overheard at wrestling practice.

"Something really sad happened," Stevie said. "Scary."

"Really?"

"Yeah."

"Oh *what*, did they cancel your tanning appointment?" Mike joked. Stevie amazed herself controlling her emotions. *Who is Mike Jones anyway? Another jackass jock with zero care for anything except sports and his fragile little ego. Laughs at anyone's expense. Look at him. He's the washed-up high school football player drinking every night at the Downtown Tavern. Where are you taking your life? Really, Stevie? Really?*

Stevie stood and grabbed her purse. Mike grabbed her arm. She jerked it away.

"Sorry, Ab. Have a Happy New Year. I'll call you later."

"Stevie, wait."

"Leave me alone, Mike. Don't ever talk to me again."

Stevie was making a beeline for the door as Mike turned to Pete and started giggling. Pete tapped Mike's arm. He pointed.

"No worries," Mike said. "She's not going anywhere. She's just playing."

"I don't know man, she looks pretty pissed."

Mike called out: "Hey Stevie! If that's what you want I'll leave you alone forever!"

The door had already closed.

"I can't believe it," Mike said. "I made that dork look cool. I even paid for her dinner. She can't leave me. I'm the best thing in her life."

"Not no more," Abby said.

"Well good riddance," he said. "Come on, let's go to Youn's party. And you know what? Know who I'm hooking up with tonight?"

"Who?" Pete asked.

"Lucy Ellis."

"Capricorn Chick?"

"Damn straight," Mike said. He squeezed Pete's shoulder. "She's been giving me the eye all year. Serious eye. Time to capitalize."

Pete shook his head in astonished disbelief.

"Wow," said Abby.

"Shit, can I get a ride?" Mike asked.

"Sorry, man, all we got is my mom's Miata," Pete said. "I could maybe squeeze you into the trunk. Wanna ride on the hood?"

"Thanks a lot, Stevie," Mike said. "We'll see how you like Lucy wining and dining your man tonight. This is ridiculous. No one breaks up with me!" His fist pounded the table. Glasses jumped. He turned away.

"Let it alone, man," Pete said. "It is what it is."

THE END

'Never Always'

⌒

Alt Moss opened the garage door. His grandson Tyler stepped in.

"Grandpa, what is *that*?" he gasped.

Sparkling blue paint. White racing stripes up the hood, over the roof, down the trunk. **SS** on the grille. *Dang*, Ty thought, *it looks like a vintage heavy metal rocket ship, from the past* and *the future*. It was the kind of car you'd see in those really old movies. But Ty had never seen any of those old movies. He was only eleven.

The car was a 1969 Chevrolet Camaro Super Sport. It had a Turbojet 396 engine. Black leather interior. Hurst four-speed shifter. Fuzzy dice. The old leather smelled delicious.

"Grandpa! Hey, *Grandpa!*" Grandma Moss was calling out the window. As Ty continued to be mesmerized by the antique car, Alt walked out of the garage to check with his wife. "You guys haven't left yet?" she asked.

"Hold your horses, we're getting ready to," Alt said.

"Would you mind grabbing the mail, sweetheart?"

"You get that junk mail, Granny."

"*Pretty pretty please peach plum pie?*"

"All right," Alt said. "My little tulip bug." He grabbed the mail and rejoined his grandson in the garage.

"You and Grandma talk funny sometimes," Ty said. Alt raised an eyebrow.

"When you've been married to a woman for forty-three years, you can do that," he said. "She says her bit. Then I disagree." Forty-three years. *Forty-three years.* In many respects, it felt like he and Priscilla were just getting started.

"This car was built in 1969?" Ty asked. He ran his hand over the smooth, sparkly paint. Admired the contours of the hood. Mom's Solectra was nothing like this.

"1969," Alt said. "Lotta dipsticks like the '67 because they're sheep. But this '69 is a badass. It was *my* grandpa's car. He bought it when I was nine years old."

"Sixty-nine, Grandpa," Ty said. "Just like you."

"I'm only sixty-eight you little whippersnapper."

"No you're not, Grandpa."

Alt did the math in his head. He chuckled.

"Well, there's another thing that slips your mind."

"I can't wait till I'm your age, Grandpa," Ty said. "You and Grandma always have time to sit and watch the sun set. I'd love to do that when I get older."

Alt laughed and said, "Might've looked that way to you because you didn't do any of the work beforehand. Lotta times when you and Mom come to visit, we've been working out here all day. That's why Grandma and I get so tired."

"I know," said Tyler.

"And because we're old."

"I know," said Tyler.

"You're not supposed to agree with that last part."

Tyler smiled. Alt Moss felt pity for the first time in a long time. He *was* getting older. He could feel it all through his body. Tyler was a smart kid. But Alt had secrets his kids and grandkids would never know.

"I pick up sticks every day," he said to Tyler. "And wait till you're old enough to mow this baby. It'll kick your butt." Alt swept his hand through the air trying to demonstrate the amount of grass that must be passed over with the mower to make it look so nice and tidy. He'd mowed these three acres for the last thirty-five or forty years. *Forty years?* What's a man come to after forty big ones go down the drain in a snap?

"Why don't you and Grandma move?" Ty asked.

"Can't just *move* if something gets hard," Alt said. "Life's tough, man. You gotta bite, kick and claw for what you want. Grandma and I love this property. This land's been good to us over the years."

"Why don't you pay someone else to cut the lawn, and pick up all the sticks and branches and rake up all the leaves?"

"Don't need to pay someone else," Alt said. "That's good money down the drain. Besides, no matter what you pay a person, they'll never do a better job than you could have done yourself. Remember that."

"I know."

"Do ya?" Alt asked. "Learn it now before you get older. It'll help you know what you're worth."

"What if I don't get older," Ty asked. "What if one day I get, like, accidentally run over by a space ship?"

"Suppose it won't matter at that point," Alt said. "Don't dwell on them things. Life's short enough. You gotta plan for your future in case there is one. Come on; let's finish this conversation in the car. Our ladies are going to turn into werewolves if'n we ain't back soon with their macaroni salad."

〜

The '69 Camaro rumbled up to the Interstate on-ramp. They waited at the red light. Tyler was amazed at how deep and powerful the car sounded. The smell of the carburetor. Gasoline engine. All cars these days were electric autopilots. You could still drive a car with an internal combustion engine on the weekend if you had antique plates.

The 1969 Camaro had antique plates. Alt waited for the light to turn green. Tyler sat beside him, buckled in.

"You ready?" Alt asked.

"For what Grandpa?"

The light turned green. Alt popped the clutch and floored it. The engine opened up. The front end started to lift off the ground and

Ty shrieked and held on. The Holley carburetor and Edelbrock intake sucked down air, while the Flowmaster exhaust roared it through the dual tailpipes.

Alt went quickly through the four gears and they were doing eighty in a few seconds. As they entered the Interstate, a car full of college girls whistled as the Camaro barreled up beside them. *Woo! Hoo! Hot Stuff!* They cheered.

"Look at that," Alt said. "I think they like us."

"Just a little," Ty said, keeping his shy grin to himself.

The girl in the passenger seat dropped her window. Alt rolled his down.

"Get on it!" she yelled. "Peel those wheels!"

"How 'bout you show us them things first," Alt yelled.

"What'd you say?"

"Show us them titties!"

The two girls in the back seat giggled. The girl in the passenger's seat pulled up her shirt and bra and flashed them. Ty blushed. He looked down. Even Alt felt his cheeks turn pink.

He nodded, dropped the Camaro back and then put it to the floor roaring past the girls who were screaming with delight.

⌒‿⌒

They pulled in to *Dream Cones Ice Cream Shop*. Alt wanted to treat his grandson to a waffle cone of Blue Moon. *Dream Cones* also had a small market and deli. He could pick up the macaroni salad after they were done.

"So, you have a girlfriend?" Alt asked. Ty licked his cone. He stayed silent.

"Is that a yes?"

"Yes."

"Who?"

"Kitty Mulvaney," Ty said.

"Kitty?"

"Yep."

"That's her name?"

Ty licked more Blue Moon ice cream.

"Yep," he said. "Kitty Kat Mulvaney."

"Man, I thought we had some unique names," Alt said.

"We hardly ever see each other at school," Ty said. "We usually just pass notes in the hallways."

"You're young," Alt said. "Shouldn't be seeing each other every day at your age anyway. A piece of advice? Don't do what we just did out there on the highway. Yeah it was funny, but it wasn't very respectful. A lot of girls would slap you for saying something like I said. And they'd have every right. I didn't set a very good example there."

They finished their desserts. Alt ordered a large container of macaroni salad and two roses, one for his daughter, Ty's mother, and one for Grandma Moss. They walked out to the Camaro.

"Those girlies were fiery weren't they?" Alt asked. Ty blushed again. "Hey, you ever drive a real car before?"

Alt drove them to a secluded country road. He hadn't been out here in years. It was out of the way, but Alt wanted as much solitude and as little traffic as he could get.

He put the car in neutral and set the parking brake. The car idled. Ty looked over.

"You ready?" Alt asked.

"I don't know, Grandpa," Ty said.

"You can do it."

"Okay."

They switched seats. Alt ran through the steps of how to drive a stick shift. After a few more minutes of training Alt said, "I think you're ready. Don't pussy-foot it now. Hit it!"

Ty released the parking brake. He clutched, revved the gas, put the Camaro in first gear and let her rip.

The Camaro peeled out. Ty tried to keep the steering wheel steady, but the power was too much and he shrieked as they fishtailed sideways and went flying off the road.

"Lookout!" Alt shouted. "Brakes! Brakes! Brakes!"

Tyler shoved in the brake pedal and the Camaro skidded backward through someone's yard and hit an old Cypress tree. The stop jolted them. The Camaro stalled.

Alt reached over and turned off the ignition. He and Ty got out.

"I'm sorry, Grandpa, I'm so sorry."

"It's okay, it's okay," Alt said breathing heavy. He was just as scared. "We're all right, that's what's important," Alt said. He checked the car. The rear bumper was cock-eyed and had a nice dent in it. But otherwise the car was fine.

Just then, an older man jogged out. He was tall, all white hair and was breathing hard as well. Alt turned as the man approached.

"You hit my tree!" he exclaimed. "I saw that kid there driving. What the hell! He's not sixteen!"

The man was pointing at Ty. Ty slid behind Grandpa.

"It was an accident, sir," Alt said.

The older man ran his hand along the gash in the Cypress tree. The tree was starting to weep sap.

"My Grandfather planted that tree," the old man said. "This Cypress is sixty years old. You killed it!"

"We didn't do it on purpose," Alt said. "That tree will be fine."

"Like hell! You had that under-aged kid driving like a hot rod!"

Alt stayed silent. His nerves were becoming agitated.

"What the hell?"

"You wanna do something about it?" Alt asked.

The old man puffed up his chest and said, "Well hell, if you're so tough, why don't you bring it on over here?"

"You're not even worth it, old timer."

"Old? Who you calling old, senior citizen? Bring it on over here!"

Tyler felt butterflies multiplying in his stomach. They were going to fight? He wasn't sure *what* to do.

Alt and the old man squared off. It almost looked funny, but Tyler couldn't laugh. He felt terrified. He'd never seen a live fist fight before, especially not one involving his Grandpa.

The two men assumed boxer stances. Tyler hid behind the Camaro. Alt cocked his fist. The old man stepped up. They swung at the same time, both missing. The old man's swing carried him off balance and he crashed to the ground. Alt's punch also missed. He grabbed his chest, breathing heavily. It felt like he pulled a muscle.

The old man lay on the ground. He struggled and groaned as he pulled himself to his feet. Alt rubbed his chest. The old man looked at him, then at the car and brought a hand to his chin.

"I ain't seen one of them old cars in years," he said. The man seemed calmer. Both men were over the hill for a throw-down. They knew it. "This feller Alton Moss had one just like it back in the day."

"Well, hell, that's me," Alt said. *"I'm Alton Moss."*

"You don't say," the older man said. "I'm Jerry Sizemore."

"Jerry Sizemore?"

"Yes, sir."

"Well, I'll be," said Alt smiling. "I remember hanging out with your brother, Ross. I thought y'all had moved to Texas?"

"We moved back a few years later and re-purchased our old house. Hey, I remember you coming over here," Jerry said. "Remember you driving this Camaro when you first got it. Well how the hell are ya?"

"Still alive," Alt said, rubbing his pectorals. Even he had trouble remembering that far back. The two shook hands. Ty crept out from behind the Camaro.

By the time they got home with the macaroni salad, the two women were fuming. Grandma came out the front door with a big spoon. She waved it at both the boys.

"Took ya long enough!" Grandma said. Tyler's mother joined her. "You boys must not want to eat."

"Let's not mention to Mom or Grandma any of the stuff that happened," Alt whispered to Ty as they got out of the Camaro. Ty nodded. He stood by his Grandpa. "We were having fun," Alt said, handing Grandma the macaroni salad and the rose. Tyler handed his rose to his mother.

Grandma Moss smirked.

"Thank you," she said. "Did you get the mail?"

Alt opened the passenger door to the Camaro. He grabbed the mail that had slid onto the floor. He handed it to Grandma and rubbed his sore chest.

"Got a letter from your sister," she said smiling. Alt nodded. Grandma's smile dropped. She handed Alt a letter that he hadn't seen. It was from Life-House Health. He swallowed.

"I'll be inside," Grandma said. Ty's mother followed her in.

Ty was checking out the Camaro again. Alt figured no time was better than the present. He ripped the letter open and started to read.

Wow. *I beat it.* His lung cancer was gone. From Stage III to cancer free. A 50/50 chance. He couldn't believe it. They hadn't cured cancer yet, but they had cured him.

A couple of tears slid out of Alt's eyes. He wiped at them quickly. Tyler still noticed.

"What's wrong, Grandpa?"

Alt smiled. He almost let loose as he looked at his grandson, but he contained himself.

"Nothing is wrong," Alt said. "I feel so good I could howl at the moon. Ow ow owwwww! I've got one last lesson for you today."

Ty swallowed. He looked nervous.

"Dance, buddy," Alt said. "You never know when it's your last tango. Dance in the sunlight. Especially in the moonlight. And always dance in the rain."

Alt Moss clapped his hands, stomped his feet and yodeled an old prospector's jig while his grandson Tyler doubled over in high-pitched laughter.

THE END

ABOUT THE AUTHOR

COLIN KNAPP RECEIVED HIS DEGREE in English from the US Naval Academy in Annapolis. He spent ten years as an officer in the Navy and served in the Persian Gulf War.

After his time in the military, Knapp lived in Chicago, Illinois, and Los Angeles, California, where he pursued screenwriting and acting. Now, he is turning his creative talents toward fiction. He and his family live in Michigan.

www.ingramcontent.com/pod-product-compliance
Lightning Source LLC
Chambersburg PA
CBHW051455170626
46811CB00002B/489